She Raced into the Blackness of the Field . . .

and flung herself, face down, on the short grass. Frantically, she began clawing her way through it . . . She stopped, exhausted, gasping in fire.

Then, suddenly, she thought of Matt, her son. Alone in there. Gagged. Tied. Maybe suffocating.

She should have stayed with him, no matter what!

"Keller!"

She froze. Then, slowly, very slowly, raised her head.

"Keller!"

Oh, God have mercy!

Near the barn, someone was holding up Matt, a light on his anguished face. They'd taken off the gag.

"Mommy! Mommy!" He was twisting, writhing.

"Keller! Two minutes! You're not here, he's dead!"

"MOM-MEE . . .!"

HOLY SECRETS

SEYMOUR SHUBIN

PUBLISHED BY POCKET BOOKS NEW YORK

This novel is a work of fiction. Names, characters, places and
incidents are either the product of the author's imagination or are
used fictitiously. Any resemblance to actual events or locales or
persons, living or dead, is entirely coincidental.

Another *Original* publication of POCKET BOOKS

POCKET BOOKS, a division of Simon & Schuster, Inc.
1230 Avenue of the Americas, New York, N.Y. 10020

ISBN: 0-671-47575-4

First Pocket Books printing July, 1984

10 9 8 7 6 5 4 3 2 1

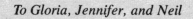

To Gloria, Jennifer, and Neil

And whatsoever I shall see or hear in the course of my profession in my intercourse with men, if it be what should not be published abroad, I will never divulge, holding such things to be holy secrets.

—Hippocratic Oath

HOLY SECRETS

Prologue

She made her way slowly down the stairs, no longer afraid of the night or of strange creatures emerging from the walls or of accusing voices, but only of being seen by a nurse, which was a perfectly normal fear and showed she wasn't goofy anymore (she *hated* that word, but that's what the patients, laughing, called each other). It showed she wasn't goofy because if a nurse saw her it might mean back into the locked section. But this was a risk she was willing to take because the most important thing was to get to a phone and tell Nora she was thinking of golf again and all good things; that it was days since she'd had a hallucination—or was it *an* hallucination? They used to be so fussy back in that fancy school, the memories of which were still so vivid after all these years, especially of Miss Gallipo and her "Let's hear the vowel sounds, girls" in a voice which would go shrill now and then as if she were being goosed. This morning, for instance, she'd been real good and pointed out who had started the fire in the bathroom. And later at Ruby Klein's birthday party—Ruby Klein always spoke of herself as Rubyklein as if it were a first name—she had felt good enough to clap with all the others when the nurses marched in with the cake, and then she had sung happy birthday with them, too; and not once did any of them become wavy, like in one of those funhouse mirrors, nor did any creature show up.

She paused now, near the bottom step, the fear that she knew was normal becoming sharper, making it a little hard to breathe. But she knew there was a pay phone here on the first floor, and that Nora would want to hear. They'd probably let her call tomorrow, she knew, but she was very worried about her number nine iron, her favorite nine iron, which, Nora had happened to mention on one of her visits, that Glenda Coleman, that piece of shit, had borrowed. Why, she'd almost scratched Nora's face, and Nora swore never to let it happen again. But she had to tell Nora again, *tonight,* not tomorrow—it might be too late tomorrow. She had to tell her she wanted all those irons just where she'd left them, *untouched,* hear?

Slowly Helene opened the door to the first floor and peered out. No one was in the corridor; it gave off a feeling of everyone being asleep, though somewhere a radio or TV was playing. She wondered where the phone was. She'd seen it several times in passing, when they took her out on the grounds, a regular, enclosed pay phone against one of the walls, but she wasn't sure where. Maybe, just maybe, around that corner over there. Clutching her coins (big deal, they gave her back some of her very own money for "good behavior") she stepped out and walked quickly past a couple of rooms. All at once she froze, then ducked in panic into the gaping blackness of a room, closing the door slowly, her forehead pressed against it, heart galloping. A nurse had come from a room far down the hall. But she could have been heading the other way.

2

Helene kept trying to think what she'd say if she were seen, if the door flew open.

Nurse, I want to call my friend Nora.

But it's after nine, dear. You know it's a no-no.

She counted to twenty-five. Then she counted to fifty, moving her lips silently. Gradually, now, her body loosened; she straightened up. She reached out with one arm, took a few hesitant steps, then her fingers touched something. It felt like the back of a chair. She started inching closer when suddenly the room went bright, and the first thing she saw was the clowns.

They were staring at her, smiling. Then a man hurried in. He looked scared, kept turning in one direction and then another, to the clowns, to her. He looked like one of the doctor-men, only he didn't have on a white coat, he was wearing a jacket. Then there were two other men, and one had a gun. They grabbed hold of him and were dragging him out; he kept struggling, looking at her as though for help. Then the room went black and she slumped onto the floor, on her knees, crying and biting at the skin on her hands.

A nurse found her later, walking dazedly to her room.

"I saw clowns. I saw a man. I saw two men." She was sobbing uncontrollably.

"Shh, shh, everything's all right. You're all right."

"I saw a man. I saw two men."

"Everything's all right now." The nurse had an arm around her waist, guiding her somewhere. "Everything's all right."

Had she just . . . thought it?

But it was all so real!

Yet hadn't all the others always seemed real too? And if they were real, why hadn't those men done anything to her? Why had they left her alone?

3

Chapter 1

At first Carla thought she was dreaming that some-one—a child—was crying out, but now she was sitting up in bed, her heart hammering away. She slid out of bed quickly and went into her son's room. She could see in the light from the hall that he was asleep; though he didn't cry out anymore, he kept moving his lips as if he were thirsty or, more likely, trying to talk to some-one in a nightmare. She sat next to him on the bed. Her big, beautiful second-grader! She touched his hair, the back of his neck; they were damp. She tried drying them with a corner of his sheet, but he began to stir and she smoothed the sheet over him, wanting only to touch him, to let him know in his sleep that she was touching him, that she was there.

Please, let him be dreaming of playing soccer. Or something he saw on TV.

No more coffins. No more of those nightmares about coffins.

She sat there, stroking his shoulder. After about a minute he took a deep breath, a really deep breath, and then let it out; his body went limp in its sleep and his lips stopped moving.

She stood up slowly.

God, what a burden he had to carry all his life. That he had a father who didn't want to live to see him grow up. That maybe he himself had been responsible in some way, had been "bad," hadn't "listened" all the time. All that shit, that terrible shit!

But this, though worry enough, wasn't her biggest one for him.

She knew that the children of suicides stood a greater chance of one day ending up suicides themselves.

Carla wasn't consumed as much by the memory of the actual sight itself: of the garage door sliding open in the white glare of her headlights, lifting to reveal first his dangling feet, then the full length of his legs, then all of him, face contorted and tilted to one side as though seeking comfort from the rope itself. A lifetime, let alone two and a half months, could never blunt the horror; but it was more the loss now, the ache of him gone, and all the unanswered questions: Why? What could have gone so wrong in his life?

At times—something that always amazed her later—she was even able to put the whole thing out of her mind for hours. Today, for instance, she was so busy she didn't have time to think of herself. It seemed that every two minutes she was being called to a different part of the hospital. A patient breaking down and going catatonic after hearing he had multiple sclerosis. A pretty young thing in a panic that her husband wouldn't want to touch her now that she had to wear a colostomy bag. The mastectomy patients and all their fears. The cardiac patient who'd been foul-mouthing and grabbing every nurse before finally admitting in tears he was afraid he wasn't a "man" anymore. The rounds with the psychiatric residents

6

rotating through liaison psychiatry. Jesus, she'd even had a laugh or two.

And then, of course, there was the tremendous relief when she'd called home a few moments ago to tell Matt she'd be a little late for dinner, that she was going over to the other hospital for a while. He had told her, yes, he'd stayed after school for the peewees' soccer tryout and thought he did okay; and yes, he'd be going out again tomorrow.

She'd been so afraid that he wouldn't, that he would keep staying locked within himself.

Oh, it was so good to hear.

Before leaving now, she looked again for the earring she lost somewhere in the physicians' lounge. She checked under the cushions as before, pushed aside the same chairs, stared around the floor. Nowhere, damn it. She made a stop in the john, washed her face hard and pushed a little at her short black hair. In her office, she hung up her lab coat and put on her suit jacket. She spoke for a few minutes to the psychiatrist in the next office about a patient she'd covered for him, then swung her handbag to her shoulder and walked to the elevators. Waiting, she cleared her throat a few times, wondering if her voice was going a little: she'd been born with this crazy voice, sort of raspy and as though every word needed a push from her lungs, but never once did it go until Mark died. Then she'd lost it for two whole weeks; that and her period, which she finally had three weeks ago.

In her car now, leaving McCallum General and driving to the Cartwell Institute, she could feel the ache coming back. And the anger, sometimes she just couldn't help the anger.

Yet how many times had she told families of suicides not to be angry, to look on them as having been sick, to try to understand? But at times it was so hard, so

7

goddam hard. Mark had had the proverbial "every-thing." At thirty-four, assistant director of Cartwell. More than twenty published papers. A growing national reputation. A beautiful home. Two cars.

But fuck the cars, the homes, the papers.

Forget even Matt for a second.

Her. He had her, they had each other.

Mark and Carla, Carla and Mark. If ever there was a couple to envy. Young. Same profession. World at their feet.

But he'd said screw you to it, to her. To her love for him.

Her eyes started to fill up; but it was still the anger that did it, and she didn't like that, knew it was really a way of helping her cope with his suicide. Soon she was able to think only of him again, and how tormented he had to have been.

But over what? Yes, a patient had committed suicide. And the son had called a few times to blame him. And Mark had been down, had even talked about leaving Philly to work in rural Vermont where they could have a "nice easy life." But Mark, as far as she knew, had never been that fragile, and certainly had not been a fool. He knew, as every psychiatrist should, that you can lose a patient to suicide the way any other physician loses a patient to organic disease. You can't watch over people every minute of the day; you really can't stop the person who's made up his mind to die.

Knowing Mark, his suicide made no sense. Even the way he'd done it. She had heard him say on at least two occasions that he couldn't understand how anyone could ever hang himself. Pills maybe, he'd said, but hanging?

But that wasn't all.

With an ache around her heart she thought of how

8

the two of them, only a week before his death, had talked so animatedly about having another child this year.

The silver-haired man stood in the doorway to his room, looking up and down the hall. During the past month a vise had been gradually loosening on his brain; he could smile occasionally, he'd even stopped wearing pajamas all day and would put on a nice sport shirt, like this one, and slacks. He'd even given back a lot of the little things he used to steal from other patients and staff—pencils, pennies, shoes.

Klepto. It was hard to believe that in his old age he'd become a klepto.

No, in his sickness—whatever it was that had happened to his head. But he was getting better, and soon he would give back the last of the stuff, and then they would let him out of here.

He felt particularly bad about Dr. Mark, though, about lifting that stuff from his jacket as it hung over a chair in his office.

Could never give it back to poor Dr. Mark anymore. But once in a blue moon his wife would come by, and there was always the temptation to call out, "Hey." He could never get up the nerve, though, as if Dr. Mark being dead made it worse and then they'd never let him go.

No. If he was ever to be all better, he had to give it back.

He stood there waiting, wondering what he'd do this time if he saw her.

There was remarkably little traffic for this time of day, enabling her to make particularly good time getting from South Philadelphia, where McCallum General was located, to the Chestnut Hill section of the

9

city. She slowed to just a few miles an hour as she drove under the iron grille archway at the entrance to the institute. There were occasional yellow-painted humps across the tree-lined drive that led to the main hospital and then splintered off toward a dozen other buildings, including adolescent and pediatric facilities, an alcoholism center, and a barn complete with farm animals. She parked in a section of the parking lot reserved for courtesy staff physicians, which was next to the section for staff people, each of whom had a name plate indicating his or her space.

She still dreaded coming here.

Just inside the huge, domed lobby she stopped briefly at the office to check for messages and to say she would be in room 203 for about the next half hour.

She had just one patient to see, a manic-depressive young woman who was being stabilized on lithium.

Actually she had very few private patients, maybe three or four at most at any one time. She preferred liaison psychiatry, treating the psychiatric problems of medical and surgical patients, and serving as a consultant to other physicians.

"Hey."

She turned to see Mr. Devereaux. One of Mark's patients—perhaps, from the little he'd spoken of him, one of his favorites. President or vice-president of some large corporation. Mental deterioration but, apparently, mostly depression.

He was waving her to him from the doorway. But, as she approached him, he went back into the room. Then he came out again, holding out a handful of things to her.

She lifted up a little ringed cluster of keys, a ballpoint pen, an envelope.

There was a sudden flaring around her heart.

The envelope was addressed to Mark. It had been

sent to him at a post-office box number. The name on the return address was Darby Houses, Inc.

She ripped it open, read the letter quickly, dazedly. It welcomed Mark "into the Darby Houses family"— and confirmed an agreement that for two hundred and eighty thousand dollars Mark had bought an interest in a Darby House restaurant in Los Angeles.

It was signed "Jim Darby" and was dated six days before Mark's death.

She stood there weakly, the letter dangling by her side, sound rushing in her head.

Mark?

Where in God's name could he have gotten that kind of money? Why hadn't he told her?

Chapter 2

Howard Tompkins fit the stereotype of a distinguished attorney, just as his office fit the stereotype of a distinguished attorney's office. He was a tall lean man of fifty-four, quite patrician looking but with a warmth about him when he smiled. His office was richly paneled and had the appropriate massive desk, thick burgundy leather chairs, and ranks of books on the shelves. He had been recommended to them when she and Mark had bought their first home and had run into a serious problem involving the title. He not only had remained their attorney but had become quite friendly as well.

She had called him from Cartwell, and he had told her to come right over.

He was leaning back in his chair now, reading the letter. When he looked up he seemed puzzled. "What do you mean do I know anything about this?"

"Howard, come *on!* I'm going crazy. Mark"—she gestured helplessly—"bought a *restaurant?*"

"Carla, are you telling me you didn't know anything about it?"

"I absolutely did not!"

"Oh, this is crazy. He never told you anything about it?"

"No. I'm telling you no."

"I can't believe this," he said with a slow shake of his head. He sank back in his chair as though everything had gone limp in him.

"Howard, did you represent him on this?"

"Of course I did."

"Just bear with me, please just bear with me." Her heart was threatening to drum itself out of her body. "Did he pay this money? Is it all paid?"

"Yes. Actually it was in the works for about three months. He had a bit of a problem raising the money."

"A *bit* of a problem! Howard, you're talking about three hundred thousand dollars!"

"He told me he was negotiating a loan."

"A loan! From whom?"

"I—don't know."

"You didn't handle it?"

"No."

"Didn't you—ask?"

"Carla, all I know is that he didn't ask me to handle it. And I wasn't about to ask questions."

"Well, who would give him a loan like that?"

"I don't know if it was for the whole thing or not. He said he had securities, that they were doing well."

"Jesus Christ in heaven, am I on 'Candid Camera'? Howard, we had maybe ten thousand in the market. I know what we had! We always filed a joint return!"

"Then maybe he borrowed the whole thing."

"What would he have to give as collateral? And goddam it, wouldn't they be coming after me for payment?"

Howard didn't seem to know how to answer. She said, "At the time he died we had ten thousand in the market, another ten thousand-something in certifi-

13

cates, a house we still owe fifteen on, a paid-up car, one car with payments—and that's it."

"Do you know of anything else he might have had?"

"I don't know anything, Howard," she said weakly. "I thought I knew everything, but I don't know anything." She was trying not to sound frantic. "Who was I married to, Howard? Who was Mark Keller? For all I know, there's another wife somewhere."

"Come on. He loved you very much."

Tears burned her eyes. "Bullshit. Two hours ago I wouldn't have doubted that for a second. But now it's bullshit, double bullshit, and triple bullshit." She made herself sit up firmly, determined to be strong. "Tell me about the restaurant. Who else is in on it? What kind of place is it, and why California?"

"Well, it simply happens to be a good investment. You probably never heard of Darby Houses—I know I didn't until Mark came to me with it—but it's a successful franchise operation in the West and Midwest. They're going to start opening here soon, I think New York first. Now, there are two other owners. One's a fellow named Leonard Eastwick, who's had years of restaurant experience. He's the one running it. He's got the majority interest. The other fellow is in it strictly for an investment, just as Mark was; they had equal shares. He's also a psychiatrist by the way. In Cleveland. Let me get you his name and address."

He produced it from his files. She didn't know him personally but had read several of his articles and had once heard him give a paper. "What happens to Mark's interest now?"

"I've been in touch with their attorneys but nothing's been finalized, which is why you haven't heard from me on it. Part of the agreement was that if one partner died the others had the first option to buy. And they're exercising it. The problem is that the place has

14

only been open a month, so there have been no profits yet, just expenses. We have to work it out in dollars and cents."

"Do you know of any other investments he made?"

"No. None that I handled."

She took a long deep breath and then made herself stand up. Howard Tompkins got up slowly. He said, "Carla, let me just say this. I can't begin to understand this, but you're in the business of understanding hang-ups. Mark was a fine psychiatrist, I understand, but the point is he obviously had his hang-ups, his problems. Like the rest of us."

"I'm almost afraid to find out if there's anything else in his post-office box."

He wanted to say: then don't. But he knew it wouldn't do any good, that she would never be satisfied until she dug as deeply as she could. He walked her to the door to the suite, then looked at her as she walked down the hall, trim and well tailored in her gray suit and black pumps, handbag over her shoulder. She wasn't a classic beauty, far from it, but those large black eyes, the freshly scrubbed look, and that voice made her tremendously sensual to him. But he wasn't thinking of that now. He was worried about her. Once she started digging, he had no way of saving her life.

It probably was too late even now.

Chapter 3

After lunch—and quite a decent lunch, she thought—
Helene Tysdal put on a sweater and went out to sit on
one of the park benches that dotted the grounds and
lanes of the Cartwell Institute. She sat back and closed
her eyes to the pleasantly warm spring sun.

She felt relaxed, good. She was thirty-three years
old and tan from winters in Palm Springs and summers
on the club golf course—when she wasn't *here* of
course. But she was convinced now that this would be
her last trip here. She had been in Cartwell three times
in the past ten years, and twice in two other places
before that. Daddy had always seen to it that she went
to the best places for rest; but Daddy, of course, was
long gone, as was Chase, her husband of seven years,
who had always been oh so patient about these little
fits, as he called them, and who would have the
martinis cold and waiting on the little foyer table when
she came home.

But that, gawdammit, was part of the problem. She
was schizophrenic as hell; she accepted that and was
always pretty well controlled as long as she took the
pills and just didn't keep them between her gum and

cheek when she swallowed with Nora looking on. But the thing was, she must absolutely not drink. Drinking and being schizo did things to your brain, my dear; at least to *her* brain. She told that to everyone at the club when she was being good and would say no, no, no at the bar; she was not ashamed of people knowing she was crazy now and then. Everyone was crazy in a way. It was just that her craziness occasionally *interfered*. Still, they would send back her dues as fast as you could sneeze, she knew, if she wasn't women's "champeen," as that dear boy, the assistant pro who had an eye for her, would say.

Well, she was getting out of here. They didn't say *when*. They never said *when*. But they were starting to say *soon*. And soon was always better than we'll see.

The one thing she regretted, though, was telling a couple of nurses what she'd seen. But it had just come out. And then afterward, once she *had* said it, she had to convince them she wasn't, well, goofy. But it only worked in reverse. The more she tried, the worse she sounded. So, finally she had simply backed off. Never said another word. It *never* happened. You can torture me until I die, it never happened.

Vicious cycle, as Nora said. You was trapped in a vicious cycle.

You're perfectly sane as anyone in this world, Nora also said. But that, my dear, was *bull*. Or bullshit to use the naughty word. She was sane *most* of the time. The psychiatrists gave all kinds of reasons. One said it was because of her grandfather, who was an absolute certified crazy—but with one bit of his brain a marvel when it came to the stock market. Someone else said it was *part* Grandfather and *part* Daddy, which was really stretching it, for Daddy wasn't crazy, he just had, as he put it, a *flaw*. He had, it turned out late in life, a *fondness* for marines. A special fondness, ap-

17

parently, which she seemed to have inherited: she had been with, as the saying went, three marines when she was just fourteen, which is what another psychiatrist thought was at the heart of her problem. She was a nymphomaniac, was what he was driving at, with a guilty conscience. Well, whatever.

She wondered if Nora was coming today.

"I know when you're going into one of 'em fits," Nora once said when she was angry. "It ain't Nora this, Nora that anymore, it's suddenly nigger."

Nora, Nora, I wouldn't hurt you for the world.

She got up soon and wandered through the hothouse, where a group of patients were planting and potting and watering things under supervision. She'd never liked horticulture therapy, as they called it. She didn't like the name—it sounded like whorey-culture—and she didn't like getting her hands dirty. But she touched at a plant here and there as she walked through. Outside, she headed toward the house.

Dr. Mackey had moved her from the hospital to one of the residential houses yesterday; it was his way of showing his confidence. He had been a friend of Daddy's. And whenever she was here, and he wasn't off somewhere in Europe or Asia, he would cut through all the flunkies and handle her himself.

She sat on one of the rocking chairs on the porch of the Rose House, which was shielded from the hospital by huge bushes and many trees. She wondered when it would be tea time; they had the most delicious little cookies. Idly she picked up a copy of the *Hello*, the institute's dreadful little newspaper, just a foldover really, and glanced through it. Moments later she was staring at it aghast.

A headline on the front page said: NEW WING NAMED IN MEMORY OF MARK KELLER, M.D.

Below it was a photograph of the man she'd seen dragged from the room.

All that day and all that night she kept it to herself, afraid they would think she was hallucinating again. And she never did intend to tell, though Daddy always said that certain kinds of secrets, the kind that hurt someone, were bad, because when you hurt someone you hurt God. She didn't eat breakfast, and had just had a few sips of soup for lunch, but she could hardly even swallow that.

She didn't believe in God anymore, she really didn't. But if there *was* a God, if there just happened to be, then this was the kind of secret that offended Him and hurt Him. And if there *was* a God, then she would pay.

Still, she wasn't going to tell.

But later that afternoon, when she saw Dr. Mackey walking slowly, with a group of doctors, along the grounds toward the hospital, she ran to him, then stopped, facing him.

"What is it, Helene?"

She began to cry.

"Helene, why are you crying?" He was holding one of her hands.

She stared at him. Her chest was heaving. Then she said, "If—if I tell, you won't lock me up?"

The other doctors were impressed by the way Mackey handled it. It would have been easy for him to have simply told her that she was mistaken, that it couldn't have happened if for no other reason than that the two men wouldn't have just left her there. Or he could have taken the other easy route so many doctors took, because it involved little thought or effort, and gone along with her story, then ordered some medication. Instead he spoke to her quite seriously about it, now and then asking certain questions that were aimed at helping her see for herself, with a sense of accomplishment, that it couldn't really have happened.

"Helene, why do you think these men you say you saw didn't take you with them?"

"I don't know. I wondered."

"They knew you would tell on them, didn't they?"

She didn't answer. But she seemed to be puzzling over it.

"And why do you think the clowns you say you saw were smiling? Why wouldn't they have been as frightened as you were?"

"I don't—know." She was beginning to doubt herself.

"I'll tell you what. I've got a meeting with these doctors, but I'll be over to see you in about an hour. Okay?"

She nodded at him gratefully.

Mackey came into the office toward noon the next day, his left jaw still numb from the dentist's needle. He'd hated going through a root canal, but at least he'd been able to save the tooth.

He sat down at his large desk and started sifting through the mail and telephone messages.

William Mackey, president and medical director of Cartwell Institute, was one of those physicians who inspire confidence just by walking through a hospital corridor in a long white lab coat. A balding, compactly built man of fifty-three, he rarely did psychotherapy anymore, which he rather missed. But with all the headaches of running this place—the last remaining Cartwell was a doddering figurehead—he still managed to do a few papers a year, was frequently called on for quotes by the media, was a popular speaker at psychiatric meetings, and was extremely active in the American Psychiatric Association. Indeed, he probably could be president one day if he wanted it. And he wanted it.

He was almost finished reading the last letter when Mrs. Lewis buzzed him from the outer office.

"Dr. Greenberg would like to see you. He says it's very important."

Greenberg's face was flushed as he walked in. He was one of the psychiatrists who had been with Mackey when Helene had walked up to him.

"I hate to break in on you like this. I may be wrong, but I think I've found the clowns."

Chapter 4

After milling around in conversation, the members of the board of directors of the Cartwell Institute took their places around the long conference table. More than the usual number had shown up—nine out of fourteen. Dr. Leo Cartwell stood up to start the meeting but became involved in conversation with two of the members he hadn't said hello to yet. He and his father had started the Institute thirty-five years ago as an alcoholism treatment center. In the past twenty-five years it had mushroomed in size and scope and reputation. Cartwell, white-haired and slightly stooped, was, at seventy-six, one of the grand old men of psychiatry: a past president of the American Psychiatric Association and member of several presidential commissions.

He started off the meeting with, as usual, a vague little joke which got the usual laugh, and then in his thin phlegmy voice spoke in a rambling way about some possible research projects. Mackey spoke next, on the international seminar to be held at the institute in the fall, then of the effort the outpatient department was making to develop new geriatric programs. Then the president of the executive committee, a man named Penta who was head of a shipping company, reported on the status of the corporation's recent investments, which won applause, and then on general income from longstanding investments, patient fees, grants, and endowments. Afterward he asked Edwin Haywood, president of the Decton Corporation, an international engineering firm, if he would head up a committee to get things moving on enlarging the youth center. Haywood accepted with a slight nod.

After the meeting broke up they gathered in little groups. As usual, Haywood, who had graduated from Wharton, found himself engaged in some banter with Penta about Wharton versus Harvard, Penta's school. Then he excused himself and took the elevator to the second floor. He stopped at the doorway of one of the rooms, walked in and closed the door. "Sam?"

The man in the chair, who'd been sitting staring at the floor, looked up slowly. A smile flickered on his lips. Though it was one of Samuel Devereaux's bad days, and his thoughts kept drifting, he tried to talk about business.

Chapter 5

When Carla came home Matt was reading in his room, and her housekeeper, a widow in her early sixties, was just finishing up at the stove. Although Mrs. LeVine had worked for her for several years, she had started living in only after Mark's death.

"How's my guy today?" Carla leaned over behind him and kissed him on the cheek. He nodded, barely looking up. "How was soccer?"

"Okay."

"Just okay?"

"Good."

She knew she mustn't press him, just as she knew she mustn't keep examining him all the time for signs that he was becoming seriously depressed again. She would drive him crazy and herself crazy.

The way he'd taken the news of Mark's death had been frightening. After breaking into tears and running to his room, he had never once cried again, had never said he missed him, was mad at him, hated him, loved him, anything. It was so dangerous, a seven-year-old bottling everything up—and not only keeping every-

24

thing in him, but not wanting to see his friends, wanting only to stay close to home as though this were his only security or, as Bill Mackey seemed to think, to make sure he wouldn't lose her too.

Thank God for Bill Mackey. He'd seen Matt two and three times a week for two months, helping him to release his feelings, to talk, to grieve. And Matt was so much better. He'd been seeing Joey and the other kids a lot more and, of course, there was soccer.

She went into her room, and there it was as though everything that was holding her body together collapsed. Oh, Mark, what was it? Who the hell were you?

God, how do you take this, how do you handle it, what do you do?

She shook her head violently, to try to clear it, and then went into the bathroom and cupped handfuls of water on her face, rubbing hard into her eyes, pushing up at her cheeks, her temples, as though to get clear, cool blood into her head. Then she dried herself vigorously.

All she knew was that she had to keep a face on for Matt, had to keep this her secret.

Mrs. LeVine had the table set, and after two calls, Matt came out. Carla felt herself smile. All As, but chances were he'd still put on his T-shirt backward.

Still, it was like looking at Mark. The same eyes, mouth; only much lighter hair, blond and curly.

"Let me tell you something," Mrs. LeVine said as she settled into her chair. "Matt was a big help today. I had to run out at three—you'd think my daughter was the only person who ever had a baby—and he waited for the groceries and he put them away."

Carla felt her heart lunge. But she fought not to show anything.

So, he hadn't been to soccer.

He had his secrets, too.

She woke about five-thirty in the morning, heart leaping as if from a bad dream she couldn't remember. She lay there, knowing it would be hopeless to try to fall back to sleep.

She'd slept maybe an hour all night. Jerri and Don, their closest friends—the four of them had met as newlyweds living in the same brownstone—had been over until two and said all the right things. She did manage to fall asleep but after an hour, maybe two, that was it.

So staggering, so unreal.

She thought again of what Howard Tompkins had said about hang-ups. One that Mark definitely did have was a tremendous defensiveness about psychiatry. He didn't like jokes about shrinks, didn't like skits or cartoons of men with beards, couches, and Viennese accents; was supersensitive to anything he considered a slight on the profession. That time, for instance, at the Goldstein's party when they, along with three other doctors, had been introduced to a group of people. Marge Goldstein had introduced Mark and her as psychiatrists, the others as physicians.

It hadn't bothered her in the slightest, she hadn't even *noticed,* but he'd muttered later, "What the hell does she think a psychiatrist is, a podiatrist?" and he'd hardly said a word all night.

But what he had been most sensitive about was that so many physicians themselves didn't think much of psychiatry. Well, let's face it, that bothered her too. The guy who never questioned his own inability to cure rheumatoid arthritis, but who was satisfied if he helped the patient get as much out of life as possible,

26

was usually the first to say, "You people apply Band-Aids; you serve as a crutch."

But she couldn't think of any other hang-ups. Mark apparently had never had to worry about money. His parents, who had died before she met him in medical school, had been well off: his father a stockbroker, and his mother in the Oriental studies department at NYU. But Mark had always been a go-getter, never wanting to take anything from them. He had always worked at some job from the time he was in grade school, had even taken two years off after college to work on tankers so he could pay his own way through med school.

Sandy-haired. Good-looking. With a marvelous mind. And what had seemed to be so much self-confidence. If ever there were two people from completely different backgrounds, they were it. He'd gone to private schools and lived in Manhattan, in apartment buildings with doormen, while she was from a little row house in Trenton, where every Italian family including hers seemed to have women in black. Her father, who'd died when she was nine, had been a bartender—and for a few years before that, a boxer. Her mother was a hairdresser; only one of her brothers—they were partners in a wholesale plumbing supply business—had finished high school. She often remembered how her brothers used to warn her she wasn't to hang out on street corners. But then they seemed just as worried because she used to spend so much time reading.

She went through her mail first, then looked at her schedule. Not only did she have the usual load of patients to see, but the usual scattering of conferences with doctors as well.

27

The psychiatry consultation/liaison section of Mc-Callum General—a four hundred and ninety-one bed hospital—was made up of four psychiatrists, three residents, and a liaison nurse. Liaison psychiatry usually didn't pay as well as a good private psychiatric practice; it also often required different techniques since you were usually after fast results. So, for instance, you rarely had the time, or the need, to find out if an amputee who was suicidal was unconsciously grieving over his penis. Furthermore, though the medical and surgical staffs were glad to call you in when it came to certain patients—the outright suicidals, the alcoholics, other pains in the ass to them—other times many of them looked upon you as a nuisance or a threat. Why should one of their patients need a shrink after being told she had diabetes when most of the others accepted it fairly well? Still, things had improved since her residency. And—one of the things that had drawn her into this—she enjoyed being in a branch of psychiatry where you had to keep up to date on medicine.

"Good morning." It was Dr. Raphael, director of the section. He was a gaunt little man, just a few months away from retirement, whom she'd already been told she would be replacing. They discussed a lecture program she was preparing for third-year medical students, and after he left she tried to gather herself together to start the day. Instead, she quickly called the main post office. She wanted to know how a wife could get the contents of her deceased husband's box—and the three people she spoke to gave her three different answers. One said she couldn't if her husband hadn't given permission for mail to be forwarded to her. Another said she needed a power of attorney. And the third said that was a very interesting question, she had better come in because he didn't know.

She called her attorney, Howard Tompkins, but he wasn't in. The instant she hung up, her phone rang as though in protest. It was Mackey's secretary. Dr. Mackey wanted to see her; could she come over?

"I can make it in about three hours."

"Dr. Mackey told me to say it's very important. Could you possibly make it now?"

Mackey's secretary said he was waiting for her in the family-therapy room. She walked there quickly, the secretary following a little way and then looking on. Mackey and two men were standing in the corridor. Mackey, with a look on his face that constricted her throat, said to her, "I don't know if you know Dr. Greenberg."

"Of course." She took his extended hand.

"And this is Detective Harris. Dr. Keller." Harris, a husky black man, also held out his hand. Mackey said, "Dr. Greenberg brought something to my attention that I thought the police should know about. And Detective Harris asked me to call you."

"Bill, please, just tell me. What is it?"

"Let me show you."

He led her into a small conference room. He turned and faced the two-way mirror that was used to observe what was going on in the family-therapy room.

Why, she wondered with a deep frown, was he pointing to that painting on the wall facing the mirror, the painting of the two clowns?

Chapter 6

She was too stunned to do anything but stare at Mackey as he went through the story of Helene Tysdal and explained that the nurses she'd originally told it to had assumed she had been hallucinating. He looked rattled, as though he hated to be the one to inflict further pain on her; not only had he taken a personal interest in Mark from the time he was a resident here, but he and Jeanne, his wife, had become their close friends.

His words sounded distant, unreal. ". . . and Dr. Greenberg's the one who figured out she might have really been in this room while it happened in there. But she's a very sick woman, Carla, though she's under control now, so who the hell knows what she really did see? And don't forget, the nurses said Mark left here about six, and this would have had to have been sometime after nine. But, of course, there's no question the police should look into it. If nothing else, I don't want any suspicion of a cover-up."

Greenberg said, "Of course, as we discussed, he could have come back without anyone seeing him."

Though her brain felt glazed, Carla knew what he

meant: there was a small office on the other side of the family-therapy room, with a door to the parking lot. But as Mackey was saying, "That would have been quite unlike him. As far as I know he always let someone know when he was here. And why would he go into that office? Why not his own?"

Detective Harris, middle-aged, sort of tired-looking, said, "Maybe they were chasing him and he ran in there."

Carla, her voice tremulous but hardly believing it sounded so controlled, asked if Helene Tysdal had recognized either of the men. Harris answered that he'd only been able to speak to her briefly—she was quite upset—but she apparently hadn't. He said, "Would you have any idea who they might be?"

"No." She began to tremble. She sat down and leaned forward and held her face in her hands until she regained control . . . Murder? Now, *murder?*

Greenberg, looking sorrowful, excused himself from the room. After waiting until she achieved further composure, Detective Harris said, "I really hate to make you go through this again, but Dr. Mackey tells me you found your husband's body. Could you tell me how you happened to find him?"

"I—was in New York all day, at a meeting. I came home about one and—when I opened the garage door—I mean—there he was . . ."

"Did he leave a note?"

"No."

"Was anyone else home at the time?"

"My son. He's only seven. He was asleep."

"Do you know if he heard or saw anything that might help us?"

"I don't know. I had no reason to ask."

"Would you?"

She nodded quickly, eyes closed.

"When did you see your husband last?"

"That morning. At breakfast."

"How did he seem?"

"He—seemed all right."

"Did he seem worried at all? Upset? Nervous?"

"No. No, not really."

"What do you mean by not really?"

"Well, he seemed all right, he read the newspaper, he said he'd try to wait up for me. But he had been quite upset most of the week. But I felt he was getting over it."

"What was he upset about?"

"One of"—it was so hard to think, let alone talk—"one of his patients committed suicide. And the patient's son was giving him a lot of aggravation. He would call my husband, he—" She stopped all at once, suddenly jolted by the implication of what she was saying.

"Do you know if he threatened him?"

"I don't know about that, but I know he blamed him for it."

"What's his name?"

Mackey answered for her. "Wayne Delman. His father—his stepfather, actually—was John Delman. You know, of Delman and Sharples." Delman & Sharples Pharmaceuticals was a large drug-manufacturing firm in the city.

"Oh, that suicide," Harris said, nodding. John Delman, one of the principal owners, had made headlines when he had leaped from a bridge in full view of a crowd of people.

"I don't know if you remember reading this or not," Mackey said, "but he'd been in a car accident in which his wife was killed—he'd been driving. He went into a depression. He was referred to me and I treated him for a few weeks as an outpatient. He didn't want to be hospitalized, I guess nobody does, and I tried not to. But it became obvious there was no other way. Mark—Dr. Keller—took over his day-to-day care, though of course I also saw him. A few weeks later he simply slipped out and—did it. But there was no way to have predicted it. He had improved quite a bit and didn't seem dangerous to himself or anyone else. We took the normal precautions, but we don't make a practice of locking people up simply to lock them up. It's a hospital, not a prison."

"Did he ever call you?"

"Who? Wayne Delman? Yes, I got the same kind of calls Dr. Keller got."

"Did he threaten you?"

"I wouldn't call them actual threats, no. Just a lot of blaming. After I think the third call I told him he had to stop it. I told him I could understand his feelings, but it had to stop."

"Did it?"

"I don't know if there was one other call or not. But it did, yes."

"What do you know about him?"

"Nothing, really. Except that he's in his thirties and is with the firm."

"Do you know anything about him, Dr. Keller?"

"No."

"Now, is there anything else you think I should know?"

She hated mentioning anything about the restaurant in front of Bill Mackey. It was hard enough letting a stranger, let alone Bill, know there was such an important part of Mark's life she had known nothing about. But she had to; it could be tied in in some way.

Harris wrote it down matter-of-factly, as if he had

heard too much in his time to be surprised by anything. Mackey, ever the psychiatrist, showed nothing of how he felt—except for a gentle squeeze on her shoulder.

Mackey called her at home that evening.

"How're you holding up?"

"Just great."

"Yeah. Matt?"

"Well, okay." She lowered her voice because he was in the next room. "I'd really appreciate it if you'd see him again."

"What is it?"

"I—I don't think it's as bad, but I'd like you to talk to him. And maybe you can also find out what Harris asked for—if Matt saw or heard anything."

"Sure. Carla, dear, look—I don't know if this affects anything but I spoke to Helene Tysdal about an hour ago and she told me she remembered something else. She said the day she saw Mark dragged out was the same day one of the patients had a little birthday party on the floor. Ruby Klein. I checked the date of the party. It was March second."

Carla felt everything within her sag. Mark had died the night of the fourth.

So Helene Tysdal must have been hallucinating.

But, as she sat by the phone now, she didn't know whether to feel relieved or not.

Chapter 7

She and Mark had looked for almost a year until they had found this center-city townhouse. It had been so right in every way for them, even to the small garden which opened up from the living room through a sliding glass door. Some of her friends had suggested she and Matt move out of here, but she knew there was no running away.

Still, it was always hard to drive into that little garage under the house.

This evening, though, it had been a total horror again.

For this time she'd been thinking of him struggling, *not wanting to die.*

"Mom?"

"Yes, dear."

"Could you help me with spelling?"

"Of course."

She sat on Matt's bed, next to his desk. He gave her a list of words to ask him. He struggled with most of them, and she found herself wondering if it was normal struggling or difficulty concentrating. But he finally got them right.

"Would you like me to read to you in bed?"

"I can *read*."

"Oh, Mr. Wiseguy. I know you can *read*. I didn't ask *that*. I asked would you like me to read to you."

He nodded.

"Good. You call me when you're ready."

In the living room, sitting with head thrown back, staring at the mounted African masks that Mark had collected, she wondered if Bill's discovery meant that the police wouldn't follow up on Mrs. Tysdal's story.

Couldn't Mrs. Tysdal simply have been confused about the birthday party? It certainly didn't have to mean she didn't see what she said she saw!

But even if they did follow up on it, how seriously would they do it? How seriously would they take what a schizophrenic said—especially now?

Jerri called shortly after Matt fell asleep. As she usually did since Mark's death, Jerri talked mostly of lighthearted things—this time about what one of her students did in chem lab, and how there was such a pervasive odor that even the cat ran away from her when she got home. But after a few minutes Carla made some excuse to hang up. She hadn't told Jerri anything about Helene Tysdal, didn't want to burden her with it just yet, but wasn't up to talking about anything else. For an instant she wondered if she might have been too abrupt, but realized that was silly; it would take an awful lot for them to offend each other. They'd been friends ever since the first evening she and Mark, two first-year med students, had moved into that brownstone near the university and Jerri and Don, who were in PhD programs, had come to their door with a cold six-pack. And they'd shared so much through the years. Why, they'd even had their babies—Jerri and Don also had a boy—within six weeks of each other.

Oh, those were good days. Such good, good days.

Strange, though, she hadn't particularly liked Mark at first. She used to see him in class, of course, but they'd really met for the first time at a party. And her first impression was that this was someone who had a little too much not to be "spoiled"—not only good looks but an easy charm and, if his sport jacket and slacks meant anything, money. She remembered thinking: a real preppy, who probably eats sliced white bread three times a day. So she'd been a little surprised when a group of them went to an Italian restaurant afterward and he joined her with calamari while the others exclaimed *squid?* It was, the two of them used to joke later, probably the only romance that sprang from food.

On their second date, kissing her in the vestibule of her dorm, he asked if he could come up to her room.

"No, please."

"Why 'please'?"

"Don't make fun of me."

He kissed her again. "Then mine."

"No."

He looked at her. "No, please?"

She returned the look. Then slowly said, "No. Please."

He took her by the hand. She held back for just a few moments. Then she followed. In his room he kissed her again, then held his face against hers. He started to lift off her sweater, but she kept her arms around him. Then slowly, her heart in tumult, she lifted them.

She watched from the bed as he undressed. He slid next to her and held her. He kissed her lips, all around her face, then her breasts; she pressed hard against him. Suddenly she could feel him struggling to find her, and all at once he was in her and she pushed up against him. And almost instantly she felt his release.

"Oh, Jesus!" he said.

"Don't."

"Oh, Jesus."

His fingers reached for her.

"No. Not right now."

"I want to."

"Just hold me."

That was all she wanted. She suddenly felt close to tears but she wasn't sure why. Then it struck her: was this Roger all over again? She a goddam nymph?

She hadn't thought of Roger in a long time. And she was thinking of him now without feeling—all feeling for him had died long ago. Still, she was tempted to tell Mark about him, how there was this grad instructor in college she'd still taken five months to break off with after she'd learned he was married.

She wouldn't—but why did she want to tell him? To prove what?

He was kissing her again. Soon she could feel him pressing his softness against her.

She said, "Just hold me. Please."

His arms came around her. Then he began to try again. She wanted to say don't. But he seemed desperate. She kissed him on the mouth, rubbed at his back, his shoulders. His tongue found hers, his hands were molding her breasts again. She could feel herself starting to writhe again, against his leg. She kissed him on his throat, then around his chest, his belly. She took him in her mouth. She drew on him until she was full of him, and now he was lifting her back and he was sliding into her and she was meeting his thrusts, meeting them, meeting them, and then fading with him.

38

Five months later they were driving to her home to announce to her mother that they were getting married. Sitting close to him as they drove, she found herself wondering for the dozenth time if she was letting it happen too fast. She loved him; no question about that. He had just about every quality she could want in a man: he was kind, wanted to work to help people, had a nice sense of humor, loved her deeply. Oh, he could drive her up a wall the way he waited until the last moment to do things—school assignments, keep an appointment, get to a train, a movie. She was so much the opposite, so compulsive. But he always came through, so she guessed she could learn from him.

He seemed to sense what she was feeling and he reached down and took her hand. They squeezed at each other.

"I love you," he said.

And it was then she sensed that something else was bothering her. That she was embarrassed because her mother weighed two hundred and sixty pounds. She didn't like herself for that, but it had always embarrassed her from the time she was a kid, even though most of that weight was heart.

But she should have known better. Mark was at his charming best, soon was even calling her Mom. One of her first questions, of course, was how they were going to support themselves when they were going to school. She nodded somberly—though Carla could see a slight brightening in her eyes—when Mark told her how much he'd saved working on the tankers, and about his parents leaving him money. But her eyes didn't really brighten until he had satisfied her about the wedding. Mark, a Unitarian, had no objections to being married by a priest, to their children being raised Catholic. It hadn't really mattered to Carla.

That night Mark met her brothers and their wives, and again Carla couldn't help admiring how he fit himself right in, as though they'd known each other for years. Joe, her eldest brother, tried to impress him by saying that when Carla was a kid you'd never see her without a book, honest to God.

"Really?" Mark looked at her severely. "I didn't know that. You never told me you read a book."

Joe seemed startled, as though he'd said something wrong. But when he saw Mark smile, he grinned at the others and kept jerking an approving thumb toward him.

"But I want to warn you," Frank spoke up. "Watch out for her left. She takes after Pop. Did she tell you he won twenty-three out of twenty-six?"

"All of them over his weight," Joe said.

She hadn't told him that, but she had showed him the picture hanging in her mother's room near the crucifix—the framed glossy of a skinny kid in boxing trunks, posed in a crouch, black hair slicked back, fists cocked. All of that was before her time. Sometimes she had trouble remembering anything at all about him, other than the day all the police and reporters came. He'd jumped over the bar where he worked to take on two gunmen, and died for his boss's money.

A month later, the wedding. She in a bridal gown, he handsome in a cutaway. Afterward, people tossing Jordan almonds at them as they came out of the church. Then the big reception, and her uncle playing the squeeze box. And her feeling of sadness for Mark that none of his relatives had been able to come.

In fact—something that had troubled her all along, but never the way it did now—he had never taken her to meet any of his family, the few cousins he said were living in Los Angeles.

* * *

She woke with a start, then lay in the brightly lit room, a little surprised that she'd slipped off to sleep. She got out of bed and looked at her watch: it was a little before midnight. She looked down at herself groggily, hoping she wasn't still fully clothed. She got undressed and put on a robe, trying to decide whether to shower tonight or in the morning. Instead she sat down on the bed, her heart beating fast again: she had simply erased, for a few waking moments, all that had happened today. But it was back, it was all back.

She soon found herself staring at the bureau, at the set of keys Mr. Devereaux had lifted from Mark.

She stood up and walked over to them.

Mark had always carried spares, she knew, and she had immediately recognized two of them—one the house key, the other the key to his car. But she had never given a thought to what the other three keys were for.

It struck her for the first time that one could be the key to the post-office box.

She examined them quickly.

One of them was stamped USPO.

The following morning she called the post office, gave the box number on the letter to Mark, and asked if they could tell her where it was located. The woman she spoke to either would not or could not. She tried again, about ten minutes later, and another woman answered.

"Do you know what the zip code is?"

"Hold on."

Carla got hold of the envelope and read off the numbers. The woman gave her the name of the branch.

The small building was crowded with people waiting

in a cordoned line to be summoned to the one open window. She walked over to the wall lined with boxes, searched quickly for 478. There. She turned the lock and opened the door.

She reached in and drew out three letters.

Out in her car she set them on her lap and opened the first one. It contained a pamphlet from Darby Houses, Inc.—on courses the company gave for new owners and managers of their franchises. The second contained a printed prospectus for potential investors in a projected shopping mall; a business card was stapled to it—on it was printed the name of a local investment house, Pauley & Staub—and scrawled in ink across the card was SAUL. The third envelope didn't have the name of the sender or a return address. It held a single small newspaper clipping, enclosed in a sheet of paper.

LOCAL M.D. DIES IN FALL

Dr. Stephen Cohen, 46, was found dead last night in the basement of his home at 3991 E. Lorn St. Dr. Cohen, an internist, had been living alone since the death of his wife last year. His body was found by his brother, who entered the house after Dr. Cohen failed to keep an appointment with him.

Police theorize that Dr. Cohen, who was on crutches as a result of a recent skiing accident, lost his footing at the top of the stairs . . .

On the paper was typed a date—three days before Mark died.

And underneath, unsigned, was typed: THOUGHT YOU OR YOUR FAMILY MIGHT KNOW HIM.

42

Carla's body went icy. A warning Mark had never lived to see? A warning for all of them?

William Mackey sat in his office, clutching his clenched hands to his chin. He couldn't keep his body from trembling.

Fortunately, Ruby Klein's birthday party *had* been on March second and not on the fourth, when Mark died. So Helene was mixed up about that. And, just as fortunately, so far he was the only one she'd told about the fire that same day in one of the bathrooms.

According to their daybook, that was on the fourth.

Chapter 8

Helene clapped her hands in delight. Nora, who had just left, had walked in tall and strong with the good news that she had marched right into Dr. Mackey's office and told him they were driving her baby crazy with their did you see this and did you see that and no you didn't. She wanted her home, she said, or she was going to see her lawyers; her baby wasn't *committed,* she just got *sick* now and then. And, after checking around, Dr. Mackey came back and said yes they would be letting her go home in a few days on her first overnight.

Helene knew the procedure. If you did all right, then they gave you another, then *another,* and then you were *all* right.

Ross stepped out of the shower and dried himself vigorously. He'd just come back from a five-mile run—he tried to jog or get in a few games of handball each day as a noontime break—and his body, even to the roots of his hair, tingled as he rubbed himself hard. There were times when he came back from a run feeling that he'd simply accomplished a chore; but most times, like now, he felt charged up, totally alive. He gave his hair one more rough rub with the towel, then walked naked into his small kitchen and looked through the refrigerator. He decided, finally, that all he really wanted for lunch was a large glass of orange juice. He drank from the carton, staring out to the living room, to the picture window that overlooked the center-city buildings and the long arcs of the bridges into New Jersey.

He went into the bedroom, flung aside the cover and lay on his back on the cool sheet. After a catnap, he got dressed—dungarees, sport shirt, sneakers—and went into a book-lined room he used as an office. He sat in front of his word processor but spent a few more minutes looking out at the city. He was working on what he hoped was the last draft of an article for the *New York Times Magazine* on the latest research into hemophilia. It should take him another day or two. Afterward he would go back to his book on hypertension.

The phone rang as he was about to begin. His hand reached out for the receiver. "Ross Robbins."

"Ross, this is Carla Keller. Do you have a moment?"

"Of course. How are you?"

"Oh—okay. You?"

"Good."

"Ross, I was wondering something. Do you happen to know Wayne Delman? Delman and Sharples?"

"Yes, I know him. Not all that well, but fairly well."

"Ross, I'd appreciate it if I could see you. Would you be free sometime today?"

"Whenever you'd like."

"I won't be finished at the hospital until—I don't know, I'd say about five-thirty. Would you be free then?"

"Sure. Whenever."

"I'll be there sometime around then. If I'm going to be late I'll call you."

He hung up slowly. He had known Carla and Mark for three years, ever since he'd interviewed them for an article he'd written on husband-wife physicians. He had seen her just once since the funeral, just by chance on the street—she lived only about eight blocks from his apartment. But he often thought of how he'd sat in church that day, looking at her in the front row and telling himself, as you usually do in those situations, never to envy anyone anymore. For he had envied them slightly, particularly that one evening—the "anniversary" of his divorce—when he'd been to a party at their home and they were so obviously happy as they mingled with their friends.

And that, it was so hard to believe, was less than a month before Mark killed himself.

Carla had to buzz from downstairs for Ross to release the door to the lobby. He was waiting outside his door as she stepped off the elevator on the twelfth floor. As she approached, he smiled and said, "Would you excuse me for about five minutes? I'm on a call to California. So just make yourself comfortable."

"Please. Forget I'm here."

She walked into the living room while he went into his office. She stood by the picture window, then looked around the room. She and Mark had had him to the house for dinner parties two or three times, and he'd invited them here once. She remembered the young woman who'd been his date. Stunning. Long glossy black hair. But he'd been with different women the other times she'd seen him.

She didn't recall seeing these two paintings before.

She walked over and looked at them carefully—semi-abstract beach scenes by the same artist. She looked around. Everything here was in such—right taste. She even remembered having used that expression when she and Mark had left that evening.

He'd said, "Right taste? You mean your taste."

"No, I don't mean that at all. I mean—you know you're in a man's apartment who has good taste."

"Hey, were you in his office?"

"I looked in but I didn't go in."

And that was when Mark had come out with something that had made her wonder if he hadn't deliberately "collected" Ross, after he'd interviewed them that time. You should have seen, Mark said, all the medical and science-writing awards he's won. Then he said, "I've been wondering. If he'd do a book with me."

"On what?"

"Something in psychiatry, of course."

"I would guess that. But on what?"

"I don't mean a text, anything like that. I mean one of those popular things where you can make a million. You know—*How to Make Love on the Roof.* I don't know."

No, he didn't have any ideas yet; lots of fragmentary things were going through his mind, but no real ideas. But he thought Ross might come up with something, or they'd brainstorm it together; then while he would supply the case histories, things like that, Ross would do the actual writing. "I'm sure, in those books, they make a lot of the case histories up."

"Mark, do what you want. But if you're asking me—I don't think he bothers with crap like that."

"Who's talking about crap?"

"Well, aren't you?"

47

"I'm"—he was backing down "talking about a book that could help a lot of people—and, well, make us a lot of money. What's wrong with that?"

"Nothing. But then come up with a good solid idea. He must get a hundred get-rich-quick ideas from would-be best-selling doctors."

"Sorry I mentioned it." He held up his hands. "It was just a thought."

She remembered putting her arm through his, smiling and squeezing his arm to her; remembered how badly she felt for having jumped on him. But from the time she was a resident, she must have met fifty psychiatrists who talked about coming up with a way-out how-to book that would make them rich and famous. And she couldn't help it; it had bothered her that he'd sounded like them.

Carla was back at the window now, sitting on one of the soft, curved chairs. Ross called out to her, "Give me just a couple more minutes."

"Please, forget about me. Go about your business."

"A very appropriate word."

She had no idea what he meant until she heard a door close—apparently the one to the bathroom. She smiled slightly. From what she knew of him—not only from what he'd told her, but from his bio on book jackets and from a couple of newspaper interviews—he was thirty-eight, had a master's in biochemistry from Yale and had taught for several years at Columbia. But instead of going on for his doctorate and remaining in academia, he'd become a science writer for *Newsweek*. He'd married during the time he worked there, then left *Newsweek* after a year and a half and traveled with his wife through Europe; there he did free-lance medical and science writing. When they'd come back to this country, he'd worked as a medical and science writer on a couple of newspapers, first in Chicago and then in Philadelphia. He'd resigned four years ago to finish a book he was writing on genetics, *The Body Remembers,* which was very well received. And he had followed that up with another popular book, a layman's guide to the neurologic system and its evolution. Meanwhile, he and his wife—who had gone to law school while they'd lived in Chicago—had gotten divorced. He had a daughter, who was probably fifteen or sixteen now.

Carla had thought of him in connection with Wayne Delman because last year Ross had hosted a popular series of shows on public television—he'd interviewed renowned scientists and physicians. The program had been sponsored by a grant from Delman & Sharples.

"I'm so sorry to keep you waiting," he said, coming into the room.

"Don't be. Please."

He leaned over and kissed her lightly on the cheek. She felt so diminutive looking up at him. But it was true even when she was standing. He was six-three, a lean, rugged six-three. Even Mark, at six feet, had seemed slight next to him.

"Can I get you a drink?"

"No. No, thanks."

He drew up a chair. He had a good, craggy face, with a strong nose and a long sweep of black hair that was starting to show some flecks of gray on the sideburns. For some reason she thought of the time she'd tried to fix him up with her best girl friend from medical school who'd been visiting her from Boston. She'd had Mark call his apartment, but he'd been away.

"I don't know how you're feeling," he was saying, "but you look very well. How do you feel?"

"Oh—okay."

"Which means not so okay."

49

"Well . . . " She was trying to figure out where to begin. "You look very well. Nice and tan. Were you away?"

"In Martinique. Just five days. Tell me about Matt. How is he?"

"I'm really not sure. Better than he was, much better than he was, but— When did I see you last?"

"A couple months ago. You were coming out of the market."

"I remember where, but I wasn't sure how long ago. Did I tell you he was seeing a psychiatrist?"

"Yes. You said he was having a rough time of it."

"Yes. Oh, God. Well, as I say, he's much better. There's no comparison. But there's still something I don't like and I want to nip whatever it is, so I'm having him see the psychiatrist again."

"I think you said he's a friend of yours."

"Yes. Bill Mackey. You know of him, don't you?"

"Oh, sure. I interviewed him a few times. In fact— don't you remember?—he's the one who referred me to you and Mark for the interview."

"Yes, that's right."

"But I didn't know he was still doing therapy."

"Well, he has a few patients. And he used to be in child psychiatry. Since Matt had met him, and Bill knew Mark, I felt things might go faster and easier. He agreed. And he's been just wonderful."

"Good. Oh, I'm sure it will work out fine."

She was aware, suddenly, that she felt relaxed. Almost, anyway. And that Ross had done it. The way he spoke. His manner.

"Ross, I want to talk to you about Wayne Delman. But—I want you to know that I don't want you to break any confidences of any kind. It's just that I want to get a kind of picture of him in my mind." She

50

paused. "Ross, there's a possibility Mark was murdered. I think a good possibility."

A look of shock exploded on his face.

"I really don't know, but— Let me go back a bit. I know what I'm going to say will seem to be only my emotions talking, but I never understood Mark killing himself. It never made any sense. We were making plans. Even—the way—hanging. He actually told me he could never see how anyone could ever hang himself. But as I say, that may be my emotions talking. But several things have happened."

Although she hadn't expected to tell him everything, it all just flowed out: Mark's investment in a Darby House restaurant, the news clipping of Dr. Stephen Cohen's accident, the secret post-office box, the words typed on the clipping—THOUGHT YOU OR YOUR FAMILY MIGHT KNOW HIM.

Ross said, "Did you know him?"

"No, I never heard of him."

"This restaurant—Darby House?—how did you learn about the investment?"

"Our lawyer handled it for him."

"And he didn't realize you knew nothing about it?"

"He assumed I knew."

"Who is he?"

"Howard Tompkins. Did you ever hear of him?"

"No. But fortunately I don't know too many lawyers."

"A very large, distinguished firm. And he's been a good friend of ours."

"What happened to Mark's investment? Do you have the interest in the restaurant now?"

"No. The other partners have the first option to buy it and they've—what's the word?—exercised it. But I don't care about that. I just don't see where the hell

Mark got all that money and why he never told me!"
She had to stop, feeling the anger, the frustration,
choking off her voice. She cleared her throat. "Anyway, a few days ago, one of the patients at the institute
came forward after all this time and said that one night
she saw two men drag Mark out of a room in the
hospital. The problem is, she's a chronic schizophrenic with a history of hallucinations. And Bill
Mackey found out that she really couldn't have seen it
on the night she said she did. She said there was a
party on the floor that day. But actually that party took
place a couple of days before Mark died."

"Mark couldn't have been held somewhere all that
time, could he?"

"No. He was never missing. What I'm getting at is
this: just because she was wrong about the day, that
doesn't mean she didn't see it."

"That's possible." He nodded slowly, staring at her.
"Now what about Wayne Delman?"

"I can't think of a single enemy Mark had. Except
him."

"An enemy? In what way?"

She told him about all the calls. "He's the only
person I can think of who thought he had a reason to
do it. I thought maybe you could tell me something
about him."

"Well, let's see." He paused, thinking. Then, obviously aware, without her having said it, that she
wanted a good description in case Wayne would be
someone the patient could identify, he said, "I would
say he's about thirty-two, thirty-three. A good-looking
fellow, dark hair, mustache. In fact, one of those Fu
Manchu things. Curves down. About six, six-one.
Wears his hair pretty long. I think he's single. I mean, I
don't think he was ever married. He was adopted, you
know—the Delmans never had children of their own. I

got to know him fairly well through the TV show. He's a pretty talented guy, involved mostly in promotion when he's there. He's been trying to get me to write some of their drug promotion pieces."

"What do you mean when he's there?"

"Well, it's no secret that he's got a drinking problem. He takes off now and then—weeks, one time I know about was over a month. I've got to say I'm surprised at what you say about him carrying on about his father. I know for a fact they didn't get along. At least they didn't used to. It's common knowledge that his father cut him out of inheriting his share of the business."

"His calls were 'You killed him, you people are the crazy ones, you drive people crazy.' "

"I don't know. I have a hunch he's seen a psychiatrist or two in his time. Maybe he just has a thing about psychiatry. What do the police say?"

"They say they'll check on him, but, Ross, I really don't know what they're going to do, how much they'll check. Look, the patient's suffering from schizophrenia, and we do know she's wrong about that birthday. But all I know is what I've told you. I could never see Mark killing himself, certainly not that way. And then that clipping, those words about 'your family.' "

"This may be way off, but maybe the person who sent the clipping *thought* you knew this Dr. Cohen."

"But why not sign a name?"

"The police say anything about that?"

"They said it's unusual. The exact word. What else was it they said?" She tried to think. "Oh, maybe whoever sent it talked to Mark about the accident and then simply sent him the clipping. I don't believe it for a second."

"When did Cohen die?"

"The clipping was dated three days before Mark

53

died. And Cohen was found dead the night before that."

Ross frowned as he thought. "Can you think of any reason Mark would have a post-office box?"

"I certainly can now. If he was in Darby Houses, and God knows what else, he had plenty of reason to. He didn't want certain mail going to the institute, and he sure didn't want it coming to the house." She had to draw a breath. Several of them. "The truth is, Ross, I'm just—you know—floundering, trying to do something, to make some sense out of things. I don't know what I came here expecting to hear. But I did want your impression of him."

She was about to say something else, then decided against it. She stood up. But Ross apparently knew what it was, knew that she didn't want to put him so directly on the spot. He said, "If you were to ask me is he capable of killing someone, I'd say the obvious two things. One is no, he isn't. The other is, who knows?"

"Thank you. You made that very easy for me."

He walked her to the door, where she absently looked in her handbag to make sure she had tissues, and then to the elevator. He said, "I'm afraid I haven't been of any help to you. I wish I could have been."

"Well, you have. You've been very kind."

"Look—I don't know how, but I'll try to find out whatever else I can about Wayne."

"Thanks."

"And if there's any way I can be of help in anything, let me know."

"I will. Thanks again."

He took her hand, kissed her on the cheek and watched as she stepped into the elevator. She looked at him standing there, his tanned arms folded on his chest. The elevator door was taking forever to close.

She opened her handbag again, this time just to avert her eyes.

Returning from dinner, she and Matt entered the basement through the door in the garage and walked up the stairs to the kitchen. As she walked into the dining room her legs almost buckled. The china closet doors hung open. She started to race upstairs, then drew back, afraid someone was there. She grabbed Matt and hurried next door.

Soon the police were there and she was trying desperately to determine what was stolen, going from room to room, opening closets, looking through drawers, her brain half paralyzed and unable to remember half the things that might be missing. Some things were obvious: a little brooch, a cheap necklace of all things, a sterling silver tray. But they were the craziest burglars—the tray was the only expensive thing they took.

But they had looked everywhere.

Apparently they had even looked through the envelopes from the post office.

But she didn't give that more than a passing thought as she kept looking for what else they might have taken.

Chapter 9

Nora had felt sorry for that lady doctor this morning, that Kelly or Kellman or whatever her name, but her poor baby had started crying at what the questions were doing to her, making her think, making her remember; and oh no Nora wasn't about to let that happen to her baby. So she told the lady doctor, very polite, very soft, I'm all the family this lady's got and I got to nurture her mind, her mind's got enough troubles. She understood, the lady doctor; she was really nice and sweet, though you could see she had her troubles.

Nora was excited now; in fact, she had been ever since she'd heard the news. Helene was coming home tomorrow for her first overnight, and she wanted to get everything smelling sweet and nice, and make sure the golf clubs were in place and there were muffins because her baby liked muffins.

Sometimes people at church would say, "Ain't you got no family of your own?" Well, truth was she had an aunt somewhere, and a couple cousins maybe, but this was like her child, not that she ever fooled herself into thinking this was an *everlovin'* child. When that mind went, out came all the dirty words, including did you steal this and did you steal that, and niggers is all alike. But that was the sickness, which came maybe every two years, maybe more, maybe less.

What hurt most of all though, was when people at church, the nasty ones, would roll their eyes and say, "O-ho, you must be makin' a pile," as though she would do all this for money. Not that she would do it for *no* money, and it was a good feeling hearing from the lawyer that time that if she did a good job she would never have to worry in her life. You put in twenty years, at fifty you shouldn't have to worry. But she wouldn't do it just for that. In fact, the thing that worried her was what would happen to her baby when she was gone. Oh, then the lawyers would see to it that the child stayed there forever while they did tricks with her money.

Nora turned on the TV in the living room and sat back to enjoy her favorite soap. Afterward she went out for groceries, but had to go to two places before she found muffins with the little blueberries. When she came back and put things away, she peered through the refrigerator to see what she'd like. She took out an orange, rubbed it, then got a knife and began peeling it at the sink.

She heard a sound behind her.

She started to turn, but something looped sharp and hard around her throat and lifted her up to her toes, her head way back. Then she was struggling to breathe, thrashing from side to side, the knife flung away. Then when she started to go limp, still twitching with life, and then sagged heavily, urine gushing from her.

She probably never had a clear last thought. If she did, it might have been: who'll watch over my poor baby now?

57

Chapter 10

A big part of her didn't want to go any further, to find out anything more. But the following day, between patients, she made the call. Then, at noon, she hurried outside. The cab her secretary had ordered was waiting.

The offices of Pauley & Staub, the investment firm, were on the seventh floor of a marble-façaded building that overlooked Independence Hall and its scattering of tourists taking pictures and office workers on lunch breaks. Saul was Saul Osterman, a short dark-complexioned man whose thin face wore a sort of studied solemnity as he came out of a rear office to meet Carla by the reception desk. He took her hand in both of his and smiled for the first time, but even the smile was solemn; and as he led her back to his office she had the feeling from something he said that he had been in that long line of people who had come up to her and Matt in the church to offer condolences. In a way, it was as though he were still there, bending toward her in her seat.

But now, in his office, the smile brightened. "Here, sit here." He started to draw up a chair to his desk but then, as though it weren't comfortable enough, drew up another.

She sat down, putting her handbag on her lap. Though her face was burning, her hands were cold; the handbag gave them something to hold on to. "I appreciate your finding time for me on such short notice."

"Are you kidding? I was so glad to hear from you. I can't tell you how often I think of Mark. We were old friends, you know."

No, she thought, nothing. She knew nothing.

"So any way I can help you," he was saying, "just let me know."

"There's—maybe with a few things." Oh, Christ, her goddam voice was starting to go again. "I've finally gotten around to sorting through all Mark's things. I found a prospectus you sent him about a shopping mall and I wanted to find out, well, if Mark ever invested in anything I haven't caught up with yet."

"No. At least not with me. He'd asked me to send things along if I thought they might be interesting, which I did. But that's as far as it went."

"Did he ever say anything to you about Darby Houses?"

"Darby Houses? No." He seemed puzzled by the name, but he didn't press her about it.

She was hesitant about asking the next question—somehow, far more for Mark than herself. "Did he ever say why he wanted you to send it to a box number?"

"No." But she sensed that he had thought about it.

"How long did you know Mark?"

"Oh—since college." He smiled then, as if to lighten

things a little. Funny, he said, how they'd caught up with each other after all these years. "We hadn't seen each other since graduation. So about—what?—six months ago I was walking along Chestnut Street and he was coming down Twelfth. And we went right by each other, and then it just hit us, we both turned at the same time. When he told me he was a doctor, I was so damn happy for him. I don't know anyone who wanted it more.

"You're a doctor, aren't you?" he asked.

"Yes."

He nodded. That was what he thought Mark had said.

Two doctors. Really something.

"I was in premed also," he said, "but I knew by the time I was a sophomore I was never going to make medical school. Too much competition, and my marks weren't all that hot. So I switched to business. But Mark, his marks were always pretty good. But to never even get an *interview!* He was really crushed. So I was really happy when I found out he eventually got in. The last I'd heard he was thinking of going with Bessinger's."

"Bessinger's?" She stared at him bewilderedly.

"You know," he said, "the mail-order house over in Cherry Hill. He'd gotten an offer to go into management training. But I forgot to ask him if he ever did it. Did he ever do it?"

"I—don't know."

"Really?" He looked puzzled. Then he gave a slight shrug. "Well, if he didn't tell you, he probably never did."

Closing the door to her office, she walked quickly to her desk, dialed New Jersey information for Bessinger's number. Now she had someone in personnel.

No, they couldn't give out any information on the phone.

"But all I want to know is if my husband worked there, and what years."

"I'm sorry, doctor, but if you'll write us and tell us why you want it, we'll see what we can do."

The receiver back on the hook, she held her hand on it for several moments; held on to it through a rushing of blood in her head.

Mark had told her he'd been accepted right away by three medical schools, that he'd had to decide on which one. But he hadn't wanted to be dependent on his folks anymore. So the tankers. Two years on the tankers.

She dreaded making this next call as much as the first. Again, didn't want to find out, didn't want to know.

But she had to know, *she had to know*.

"May I speak with Mr. Osterman, please?"

He came on. "This is Saul Osterman."

"Saul, this is Carla again. I really hate to bother you."

"Please, you're no bother. Don't ever think that."

"Saul, Mark never kept in touch with any of his relatives. And Matt's been asking me. Would you happen to know where any of them live?"

"No, I really don't, I'm sorry. The only one I ever met was his mother. This was a year before she died, a few years after the old man died. She was really struggling to keep their little place in Brooklyn—you know, Bay Ridge—going. It was more of a hangout than a luncheonette by then, but she was trying to keep it alive. She was a wonderful woman."

Oh, God in heaven.

She sat back, hands to her temples.

She could almost see and hear him on their second date, two people wanting to know more about each other.

"My Dad? He was a stockbroker. Mother was a professor at NYU. In Oriental studies."

Oh, Mark, Mark.

Five days later, Mrs. LeVine was coming back from the grocery store as Carla pulled up to the house, Carla took one of the two small bags that were in the cart.

"How's Matt?" She'd called Mrs. LeVine earlier from the hospital; he'd been doing homework.

"He was watching TV when I left."

"Did he ever go outside?"

"Just for about five minutes. Joey came over and he went out with him, but he came right back."

With a slow shake of her head, Carla followed her up the stairs. Matt looked over as they walked in.

"How's my big fellow?" Carla called from the kitchen, setting down the bag.

"Okay."

She walked over and kissed him on the cheek. She stood watching the cartoon with him for a few moments. Then she went to look at the mail on the dining-room table.

She sifted through the envelopes. Suddenly, a constriction in her chest, she put down all of them but one. From Bessinger's.

She started to rip at it, but was afraid she would tear the letter. She took it quickly to the kitchen, slit it open with a knife. She drew out the letter.

Dear Dr. Keller,

In response to your request, this is to inform you that . . .

The letter by her side, she stared at the floor. Mark had worked at Bessinger's the two years he'd said he'd been at sea.

Chapter 11

The following day, all within a few hours, she was summoned to the bedside of a teenager with bone cancer who'd grabbed his clothes to run out of the hospital, was called in for consultation on the handling of a depressed premastectomy patient and her husband, held a session with nurses on the prevention of burnout, and rushed to be with a woman whose husband had died unexpectedly on the operating table. But being busy didn't help anymore; thoughts kept slipping through. And now, sitting at her desk trying to gather the strength to drive home, she let it all rush in.

The whirling maze of it. Darby Houses. Bay Ridge luncheonette. Bessinger's. The lies, the lies. The message on the clipping about Stephen Cohen—

"Good night, Dr. Keller." Her secretary waved to her from the doorway.

"Good night, Mary."

Couldn't anyone tell? Couldn't they see it in her eyes, her face; hear it in her voice? That she was fighting to hold herself together?

And that she was scared? No, terrified.

"Doc, you're worrying yourself over nothing," Detective Harris had said to her that morning.

She had called to find out if he'd learned anything more about Stephen Cohen; he'd spoken to several of Cohen's former associates and relatives, and not one of them had ever heard him mention her husband's name.

"So then how can you say I'm worried over nothing? I mean, if my husband knew him, was friendly with him—I mean, maybe the clipping would make some sense then."

"Look, just because you and I don't know if they knew each other, doesn't mean they didn't. Or maybe they didn't know each other, but had a mutual friend who wanted your husband to know about the accident. I really don't know. All I know is that the police, and the medical examiner have no reason at all to think Dr. Cohen's death wasn't an accident. Not only wasn't there any evidence of a crime, but there's no motive for one. He was highly thought of, he was supposedly a very nice guy, a very good doctor—"

"But what about the reference to 'you and your family'?"

"The what?"

She closed her eyes. "On the clipping. The note."

"I don't know. But I don't think it's anything to worry about."

But *why*, she wanted to scream, *why?*

"Look, Doctor," he was saying, "these things generally have a simple answer that will turn up one of these days. Meanwhile, take it easy, I'll keep my eyes open, feel free to call whenever."

He'd treated her, she was thinking now, exactly like a patient.

*　　*　　*

William Mackey glanced, in passing, into the security office and instantly regretted it. DeTurk, sitting at his desk, a massive burr-haired man in his usual polyester sport jacket and open white sport shirt, glanced up at the same time. Mackey looked away first. He felt his body tighten as he walked on.

After all this time, that man could still weaken him with a look.

If he could only get rid of him!

But that thing, dear God, that thing in there was protecting him. Could you imagine—his protector?

In his office he read the letters his secretary had typed and placed on his desk, then signed them and put them in the Out tray. He glanced at his watch; Carla would be here with the boy in about ten minutes. He took out a yellow legal pad from his drawer and read the few pages of the article he'd started yesterday. But his mind couldn't stay on it.

He put his palm to his lips and breathed into it. Not sure if he still smelled a trace of scotch, he opened another drawer and, bending over, squished some spray into his mouth. He tried the palm again. He was sure it was all right now, but still he gave another squish.

Once more he set down the pad. He was tempted to cross out the last few paragraphs but decided he ought to wait, that it was just his nerves.

Scared, he was so damn scared. For her. For the boy. For himself.

If he could only tell her: Carla, stop, let things alone! For God's sake, let it alone!

She arrived with Matt right on time.

"Well, how are you?" he said, putting out his hand. Matt, after some hesitation, took it. "I think you can do a *little* better than that. That's better. Well, Mother, Matt and I are going to have a man-to-man talk. Will you excuse us?"

He closed the door behind her and tousled Matt's hair and had him sit next to his desk. He looked at him, knowing the direction in which he had to lead him.

"You look so sad, Matt. You're a very sad little boy, aren't you?"

Matt stared at him.

"I don't blame you for being sad. After all, your daddy died and you're never, ever going to see him again. Ever, ever. I wouldn't want my daddy to die and never, ever be able to see him again."

Matt's lips were beginning to tremble. Bubbles of tears appeared on his eyelids.

"No, nobody wants his daddy to die. And nobody wants his mommy to die either. Nobody wants his daddy to die and then his mommy to die, because then he'll be all alone—all, all alone. There will be nobody to take care of him."

The tears were streaming down now. He was gasping.

"You don't want your mommy to die, do you, Matt?"

"No!" He screamed out the word. His fists were clenched, he was shaking his head wildly.

"Of course you don't . . . Poor Matt. Poor, poor Matt."

And as he watched the boy crying convulsively, he kept telling himself that it had to be done—for everyone's sake. That he wasn't evil.

Carla walked, while waiting, to Helene Tysdal's room. She started to go in, then stopped as though punched.

The last time she'd seen Helene she had seemed fine, but now she was lying in bed on her side, knees bent, hugging herself, eyes fixed. She didn't move. Her eyes didn't flicker.

Carla was aware that a nurse was standing next to her now. She followed the woman to the nursing station.

"How long's she been this way?"

"Oh, several days. Ever since she heard about the murder."

"Murder? What murder?" Carla asked with a frown.

Matt kept staring at his lap as she drove. It had been obvious that he'd been crying bitterly in the office, though he'd stopped by the time he came out; and although she absolutely ached for him, she took comfort in her confidence in Bill—that he was getting at feelings that were still plugged up in Matt.

She wished Matt would talk about the session, but he hadn't said a word and she felt she mustn't ask, that he should feel it was private, confidential. Bill would tell her what she had to know.

"Are you hungry?"

He didn't answer.

"How about if we stop for a hamburger? Would you like a hamburger? I'd love one."

She heard him draw a breath through his nostrils. Then softly, "Okay."

It wasn't much, but enough to open a gush of relief in her. And that feeling grew as he carried their tray of hamburgers and french fries and sodas to the table. He settled himself in the chair with a kind of vigor, took a small bite, then slowly began eating with appetite.

It was only then that she let herself really think of what the nurse had told her about the murder.

The victim, the only person Helene had to look after her.

Murdered the day before Helene was to go home overnight to test out if she could make it.

This was paranoid—and Carla let the thought cross her mind only for an instant—but it was almost as if she'd been killed so that Helene could never leave.

Chapter 12

Ross sat for several moments with his hand on the cradled phone, thinking over what he'd just learned from a friend at Delman & Sharples; then he put through a call to Carla at McCallum General.

No, Dr. Keller wasn't in the office at the moment, her secretary said; should she have her paged?

"No, just tell her to call me when she can."

He made another call, this one to his travel agent to make a change in the reservations he had for San Francisco. He'd just gotten an assignment from the *New York Times Magazine* to do a profile of a physician-scientist who was giving the keynote address at a medical convention in a couple of weeks. Ross had been going anyway, to cover some of the sessions for a medical news magazine, but this would require his being there a day earlier than he'd intended.

Carla called shortly before noon. "I just got your message. How are you?"

"Good. You?"

"Oh, I don't know where to begin. I had Matt to Bill Mackey's yesterday. It's— All I can say is it's hard, it's stirring things up again. He cried out his heart in there. But I guess that's good."

"Did Mackey say anything to you?"

"No, I haven't had a chance to speak to him yet. I called him but he's away and won't be back till this evening."

"Look, why I called. I just spoke with a friend of mine at Delman-Sharples. I don't know if this means anything or not, but Wayne's taken off again. As I told you, he occasionally goes off on a long, long spree. More than a spree—weeks, a month. Well, no one's seen him for about two months."

Startled: "No one's even heard from him?"

"Apparently not."

"*Two* months? That's no spree."

"Well, I don't know."

"They've had the police on it, haven't they?"

"I would imagine. But apparently nobody's all that concerned. They're sure he'll show up just like before. Did you speak to the police after you told them about Wayne's calls to Mark?"

"Yes."

"And they never told you he's missing?"

"No."

"That's strange."

"It's not strange at all. They're not taking it seriously."

"Or maybe they're just not saying. You don't know."

"I'm so goddam confused, frustrated. Even that woman—you know—the patient who said she saw two men drag off Mark? Even her. The only possible witness. She's become a vegetable."

"I don't understand."

"She was doing so well, she was ready to go home for an overnight, and then the woman who takes care of her—the only person she has in this world—was murdered. And Mrs. Tysdal—the patient—she just fell apart at the news. She's a vegetable. . . . God, why am I laying this on you?"

"I want you to."

She said nothing for a few moments. Then, "I even find myself thinking—this is really crazy—but you want to know what this is doing to my head? I even find myself thinking now and then that maybe that woman was murdered so Mrs. Tysdal will never get out, will always be a patient, will never be believed. I mean, that *is* crazy. I know it is, but my goddam head—"

"Listen, so many things have happened to you that would have seemed crazy, who could blame you for whatever you think? You're being awfully goddam hard on yourself for someone who's been through so much."

Again she fell silent for a little while. "Thanks. I mean that."

"So—we're agreed? There's nothing wrong with your head? It's not a goddam head?"

"Well, I wouldn't go that far." But there was something a touch lighter about her voice.

"You try to take it easy, all right?"

"Thanks so much."

"I'll keep in touch."

"Please."

He lowered the receiver. He looked at the phone, then went back to work.

She almost cried with relief when she came home and Matt, apparently hearing her drive into the garage, met her at the door with a big smile.

"The teacher liked how I read today."

"Oh, I'm so happy. But I'm not one bit surprised."

72

She kissed him, then wanted to kiss him again, this time hard and with a long, long hug; but that would reveal more than love, she sensed, it would expose her dreadful fears for him. So she kissed him again, lightly, with a quick one-two hug, and spoke to Mrs. LeVine in the kitchen before going into her room to change clothes.

Things stayed fine, through dinner and afterward. He did some homework, colored some things, and went to bed without a problem.

About ten o'clock the phone rang.

"Carla, Bill Mackey. Sorry I couldn't get back to you, but I had to be in Princeton. I just got home. Can you talk?"

Those last words, so foreboding, sent flames through her. "I'm listening."

"You mean Matt might be able to hear you."

Her silence said he might; she was in her bedroom and his was next to it.

"Call me on another phone," he said.

"I want to hear."

"Well—he regressed. He was doing fine, as you know, but something's happened."

She whispered: "It was so great tonight."

"I only know what's come out. He's very depressed. Very. I know this may be unfair of me, Carla, but he needs a lot more of *you*."

"Let me call you back."

She called from the small room she used as a study. Tears were clinging to the edges of her eyes. "Tell me what you mean. Please. More of *me*."

"You know, it's not always physical attention. There's a big part of him that seems to feel you're somewhere else in a way."

"Jesus."

"Carla, listen to me. We've talked about this before.

73

I still see a few children, but it's not like I do it all the time. If you'd like him to see someone else—"

"No, he trusts you. And I trust you."

"Well, look; we'll work on this together, and it'll come out fine. I don't mean to scare you, but you've got to know. But I'm sure it'll be fine."

Meanwhile, he suggested, Matt should see him twice a week. And he suggested that she start seeing him at least once a week.

She sat for a long while on the edge of a chair, thinking of Matt smiling, of the pleasant day. But how well she knew the way depression worked; it could be as black behind a smile as behind a frown. She didn't know about small children—she'd have to read up on this, ask—but it was a fact that many depressed, suicidal people finally became serene because they'd made up their minds to die.

She sank back in the soft, rust-colored leather chair.

She wished someone would hold her, would clamp in the jumping and quivering within her.

Though she didn't let herself think of him long, she wished Ross were there to hold her.

Chapter 13

What, Detective Harris wondered, could be so important that the shrink—it was so hard to think of a young good-looking chick as a shrink—that the shrink couldn't tell him about it on the phone? His first impulse was to call over to the few guys at the other desks that a good-looking lady was coming up; and he would have if she was an el-cheapo or, of course, was black. Except for a few so-called jokes now and then, they acted like they couldn't care less that he'd married a white woman; but he'd never forget those looks and little digs when he showed them Marie's picture before the wedding, when they saw the soft gold hair, and then when they learned she had three kids coming to live with them just as blond.

In all the three years he'd been married, only one of 'em had ever accepted an invite to dinner, though of course he'd stopped inviting after the first year.

The thing was, even Loretta, just a week before she passed away, said from her bed you ain't never meant to be alone, Ray, so get yourself a good woman when I'm gone. She can be white, a Chinee, anything, as long as she's good to my man.

He wondered again what the shrink could want.

This was the kind of case a lot of the guys wouldn't give much effort to, since it meant sticking out your neck; the kind that's considered open and shut, a suicide, and you're out to prove all of them were wrong—the medical examiner, the guys.

Maybe that was why he was working his ass off on it.

To show the guys.

Carla parked her car and walked a half block to the station house. She had called Harris to talk about Wayne Delman being missing, to find out what they were doing, but then had decided to ask to see him in person. It was too easy to fluff someone off on the phone.

Just inside the station house she followed an arrow and DETECTIVES on the wall to the second floor. From the counter, she saw Harris typing at a desk toward the back of the room. A detective came over to her.

"I've got an appointment with Detective Harris."

He turned. "Harris, front and center."

Harris stood up and motioned her in. He shook her hand, with a nice smile, brought up a chair next to his desk and sat down with her. She hadn't noticed how speckled with gray he was.

"I hope I'm not being a nuisance. But I'm very concerned."

"You're not being a nuisance, Doctor. Now what can I do for you?"

"I just learned that Wayne Delman has been missing for two months."

"Yes, but that's not all that unusual for him."

"From what I hear, it's never been this long. Not two months."

"Well, it was about five weeks once. So, a few weeks more. Anyway, let me tell you what we've done. We've gone through his apartment, we've spoken with friends, relatives. His car's gone, some of his luggage is gone, and some of his clothes. So everything points to his just taking off. It's true he didn't withdraw any large sums of money we know about, but he's always been known to carry a lot on him. Let's see what else. Yes. His friends, just about everyone we spoke to, said he was very disturbed at the time he disappeared, was still upset about his father, and was doing quite a bit of drinking. So, except for the business about his father, that's pretty much the way he's always acted before he took off."

"But there's another difference, Mr. Harris. He threatened my husband."

"Threatened? You never said he threatened him."

"I mean the calls, of course, the blaming. It's almost the same thing. You don't have to use the actual words."

"You're right," he conceded. "But let me say something else. First off, as I've told you, we're looking for him. So don't think for a moment we're not. Now, what I consider to be one of the most important things, Wayne Delman has never been known to be a violent man. Yes, I know, I know. A lot of people who seem to love dogs and cats and all their neighbors suddenly pick up a gun and shoot up the whole neighborhood. But there's something that doesn't seem to fit in this case. Let's say someone did kill your husband. That means—and I don't know any way to put this gently— someone hung your husband. Now we know from the examiner's report that your husband did die by hanging; it wasn't as if he was killed first and then someone— Do you know what it takes to commit that kind of crime? I don't mean just the physical strength. I

77

mean, the kind of mentality, the kind of thinking? The profile we have of Wayne Delman just doesn't seem to fit in with that. Not that it means he didn't do it, but my hunch is that he didn't." He paused. "Now I know you're worried about yourself and your child, so let me just say this. Even if he did kill your husband, I'm absolutely convinced he's not going to come around and hurt you."

"But the clipping—"

"Doctor, if anyone wanted to hurt you I'm sure they would have done it by now."

"But what about the clipping? I can't see it as anything but a warning to my husband."

"Truthfully, I don't know what the devil it is. But we've been through this. There's absolutely nothing about Dr. Cohen's death, or his life, that even suggests he might have been murdered. I can't find a single reason for it to be a warning. Look, you've said it yourself. From what you've told me, there's an awful lot about your husband you never knew. In many cases, a so-called secret life does end up in murder. But it can also end up in suicide—where things just pile up on the person and he feels there's no other way out. But, look, why am I telling you this? You're the psychiatrist, you know better than me."

"I—do know. But I also know that we'd just spoken about a baby. And I know, I really know, how he felt about hanging. I just know he wouldn't."

Although Harris didn't say anything, the way he looked at her made her words sound—silly; like she was just a hurting widow talking. Then, after a long pause, he said, "Dr. Keller, I assure you, you don't have to talk me into following up on this case. I am— more than you know—and I will."

"That's really all I wanted to hear. But just one

other thing. Please, please don't dismiss Helene Tysdal, the woman who—"

"Yes, I know her. I haven't forgotten her."

"Please don't dismiss her as just a schizophrenic. Remember, we know for certain that there was one thing she really did see. And if there was one, there could be two."

"Which is?" He didn't seem to like the fact that he couldn't remember this.

"The clowns."

"Oh. Yes. No, I'm taking that very seriously."

"And the fact that her companion was murdered the day before she was to have her first overnight. If that had gone well, she'd probably have been discharged soon. She can't be now, there's no one for her to live with. And it's—the shock, everything—it's turned her into a vegetable."

Harris was looking at her in a deeply puzzled way. "I'm afraid I'm not following you here. What companion was murdered?"

"Her companion. A black woman she lived with, who took care of her. Her name was Nora. Nora—I don't remember her last name. I understand she was strangled in her kitchen."

Harris was frowning as he thought. "I don't know the case. Excuse me for a second, let me check."

He went into one of the offices. She could see him talking with someone, then simply standing around as the other person made a call or was going through things.

He came out and sat down, leaning back in the swivel chair. "Doctor, that was out-and-out robbery. You think not?"

She was afraid, not just from his tone but from the way he was looking at her, that no matter what she said, no matter how she tried to explain that it had been just a thought, she had lost him for good.

That same night, Saturday, the glow from many lanterns brightened the grounds of an estate in a suburb of Philadelphia. Uniformed attendants were parking the cars of late arrivals.

Edwin Haywood had made all the arrangements for the party himself. There were almost two hundred guests, and to accommodate them all he'd had a mammoth tent set up against the rear of the house. There were four bars, two in the house and two in different sections of the tent; a strolling guitarist strummed for those who wanted to linger in the house, while a band played at the far end of the tent. Balloons hung above the crowded dance floor and an array of flowered tables. Corinne was beaming as people came up to congratulate her, while Edwin Haywood, his eyes happy behind his wire-framed glasses, a smile on his broad face, his high forehead with its curve of thin blond hair dappled with just a few little drops of sweat, wandered from table to table, guest to guest.

Their first grandson. Three granddaughters but finally a grandson.

Corinne had said they should hold off on the party until Sandra came out of the hospital. But he didn't want to wait—she could see the movies.

"Governor?" Haywood leaned over him at the table, a hand on his shoulder; the governor looked back up at him with a big smile. They'd already had a long chat, but he wanted to make sure the governor was still having a good time. The governor picked up a half-filled glass of champagne. "Another toast to the grandfather, grandmother, mother, father, baby. Ed!"

"Hey, I need a glass." He took one from a passing

waiter. Then, after extending it, he joined those at the governor's table in a drink.

"Ed, remember," the governor said afterward. "I'm counting on you for the task force." The perpetual hunt for new industry for the state.

"You just said the words, Joseph. 'Counting on you.' You can count on me."

He slid his hand along the governor's back as he walked on. The French consul next, two newspaper publishers and their wives, a banker and his wife, then to another table and several of his top executives, then another table and the Spanish ambassador, two judges, and their wives—

Ah. He waved at a couple who had just arrived and were walking toward him. Then he was shaking Howard Tompkins's hand, and then he gave the attorney's wife a hug.

Chapter 14

She arrived home from the station house a few minutes after seven. The instant she walked into the living room, Matt jumped from his chair and ran upstairs to his room. She whirled toward Mrs. LeVine. Mrs. LeVine's lips formed slow, silent words: He's been watching the door.

She closed her eyes for a moment, as though fighting for strength. She took off her topcoat, hung it up and walked upstairs. He was sitting down with a large picture book.

"Matt?"

But he wouldn't look up. He pawed once at his eyes, gripping the book harder. She kneeled next to him. "Honey, why are you mad at me?" Still nothing. She said, "You're mad at me because I'm late? Honey, I couldn't help it, I came home as fast as I could."

He seemed to be struggling against looking at her. Then he did look up, and, with a little quiver in his voice: "My stomach hurts."

Oh, God, not back to this again. Not back to those first couple of weeks. "You show me where it hurts."

"Here. Here." He jabbed with his forefinger.

"*All* over?"

"My stomach hurts!" he screamed, hitting the air as though it were her. Then he began to cry. She drew him to her. He resisted a little, then came.

"Shh. Shh. Don't cry, sweetheart, there's nothing to cry about. You're going to be all better. I won't let anything hurt you. Shh. Shh." And she kept holding him, stroking his back, his hair. She could feel his body gradually relax. Then she said, looking at him, "Did you have any dinner?"

He shook his head.

"Let me wash up and we'll have dinner."

"I'm not hungry."

"Oh—then you'll just sit with me."

But he did have some dinner. Afterward, however, instead of doing his homework in his own room he brought it into the living room where she was reading the newspaper. She would sneak an occasional glance at him. He seemed deeply immersed in his work. But when she got up to go into the study to read some journals, he said, "Mommy?"

She turned quickly, impaled by the urgency in his voice. "This." Eyes on her, he pointed at the open book on his lap. When she came over, he quickly glanced over the open pages, then touched at a caption beneath a picture. "Which one's—this?"

She looked at it; it was obvious that he knew. She said, "I want you to think hard and tell me."

He thought. "Tom?"

"That's right." She decided not to force things tonight, so she said, "I'm going into the study to get something. I'll be back."

She came back with three journals. But how do you concentrate? How, with all the pulsing in her skull? She kept turning pages, her eyes going to him occasionally. At times she would stop at something that interested her, but couldn't read more than a few paragraphs. He was, she finally saw, simply sitting there, homework apparently done. She glanced at her watch. She had let him stay up almost an hour later than usual.

"Okay, time for bed."

"I'm not sleepy."

"I didn't say you're sleepy, I said it's time for bed. Come on, come on. Come on." The words seemed to be forcing him up. "When you're in bed call me."

She watched him walk up the stairs. She could hear Mrs. LeVine call out good night to him from her room but didn't hear him answer. She gathered up the journals and went up to the study; two walls were almost covered with books—one, mostly with medical and psychiatric books, the other with a hodgepodge of things they simply liked. She and Mark loved to buy books. Her favorite chair—Mark's was across the room—was in the nook between the two walls, with the white, overhanging balloon of a lamp above it. She sat down and leaned her head back and closed her eyes. She was exhausted but not sleepy.

Funny, she'd never understood what patients meant when they said that.

"Mommy."

He was sitting up in bed, against the headboard. She sat by his side and touched the few strands of hair that had fallen over his forehead. "You know I love you?"

He looked at her. Then he nodded slightly.

"You'd better believe it. I love you so much." She put her arms around him. He came to her easily. "I love you so much, and I'm never going to leave you. I don't want you ever, ever to think I'm going to leave you. You understand? You hear me? I love you." She squeezed him hard. "You hear what I say?"

She felt his nod.

84

"You remember that. Always remember that. Now let's lie down." She helped ease him down on his back. Then, something that always used to make him laugh, she tucked the light blanket under him on both sides, until it fit him tightly, mummylike. He began to giggle. She kissed him under his chin and he began to laugh and squirm and then thrash, kicking the blanket all around. Then she settled him down, fixing the blanket right.

"I love you," she said again, kissing him lightly on the cheek.

"I love you too."

She pressed her cheek hard against his, kissed him again. "Good night. Have a good, good sleep." She stood up.

"Mommy?" His voice was suddenly different again, edged with anxiety. "Where will you be?"

"Right here in the house. I'm not going anywhere."

He looked at her wide-eyed as she stood facing him from the doorway. Back in the study, that look, that terrible look of fear, was still with her. She could hear the sounds of his twisting, and had to keep herself from whirling around and running back to him.

Instead, she dropped into the chair, her hands flying to her face. For some reason she couldn't cry. She wanted to feel the pain of her fingernails digging into her flesh, wanted to block out every thought.

Slowly she let her hands drop. She stared at them as they gripped her thighs.

Oh, that innocent little victim. That poor, poor little guy.

There was no way of even pretending anymore that it might still be normal mourning—too long, too intense. It was becoming—that most terrible of words, so ugly, relentless—pathologic.

What do you do?

She sat there in thought. Gradually her hands loosened, she could feel her whole body easing.

She just wouldn't let it happen to him! And Bill Mackey wouldn't let it happen!

She had an appointment with Mackey at five o'clock the following day. He listened wordlessly, arms folded on his chest, as it poured out of her—Mark's lies about his parents, getting into med school right away, working on tankers, all of it.

Afterward, almost completely spent, she said helplessly, "Why couldn't he tell me the truth? Why couldn't he say, 'My parents owned a luncheonette'? What's wrong with that? Why did they have to be a professor, a stockbroker? I mean—who did he have to impress? Me? My father was a bartender. My mother, a hairdresser. I mean, so what? And tankers. What's wrong with working at Bessinger's?"

He looked at her thoughtfully. "Carla, if Mark were alive and you both were in here as a couple, or I was seeing him alone, maybe—just maybe—we could get at some of the deep, deep reasons. But we can't do that. So we only have what's obvious. And I'm sure it's as obvious to you as it is to me. For some reason, and who the hell knows what it was, he had to be a big man to you. He had to"—his voice deepened to express it better—"he had to have parents who were crème de la crème, he had to get into ten medical schools right away, he had to work on tankers."

"It's so, fucking maddening."

"He obviously had more problems than you can count. And what's so terribly frustrating is—there wasn't a clue. I couldn't have dreamed this about him in a million years.

"And Matt. I'm so worried—"

"Well, now you're talking about something. We

can't do anything about Mark. All we can do is go round and round in circles. Your job—and my job's to help you—is to try to come to terms with what you now know about Mark—and leave it at that. Work on yourself and let me help you work on Matt. He's your big problem. And he's someone we can do something about."

"Bill, I can't begin to tell you how much I appreciate what you've done, what you're doing. But tell me—how do I come to terms with something I believe? At the beginning I couldn't accept Mark's suicide in the sense that— Well, I've gone into that. It wasn't like him. All our plans. You know. Of course, I know better than that; I know that people do lots of things that are completely out of character. But Helene Tysdal—"

"You're not back on her, are you?"

"Well, her and Darby Houses and Wayne Delman and all the lies— They make it—I don't know—like anything's possible, that he could have been murdered."

"Well?" He shook his head slowly as though there wasn't much he could do. "I'm telling you to think of Matt, and you're thinking about being a detective."

"I am thinking of Matt," she replied angrily. "Bill, that isn't fair!" Then she caught herself. "I'm sorry. You're the last person in the world I should accuse of not being fair."

"No, go on. About your thinking of Matt."

"If Mark didn't commit suicide, I don't want Matt growing up thinking he did—that he caused it, that his father didn't love him enough to live. That when things get rough in life, the answer's kill yourself."

"What are you teaching him? That when he needed a mother she wasn't there?"

Tears suddenly burned at her eyes. "Oh, Jesus."

"I'm just laying it on the line for you, Carla. All I know is I can't help you if you're not going to help yourself. And I can't help Matt without you. He needs your full attention, Carla. What you're doing is only harming him."

Mackey's first thought when she left was to call his wife and tell her everything Carla had told him. But he didn't dare talk to her about it on the phone. Anyway, she wouldn't want to hear. Never wanted to hear. We made a decision; stick to it, she would say, as she always did. Keep your balls. But just the same she was drinking herself to death, as he was, although he never let himself get drunk when there were people around like she did.

Jeannie, you can't get drunk with people around, he'd say; it's dangerous; just a few words could do it. "Fuck you," she'd said that one time, at the convention; and afterward in their room it was the first time he'd ever hit her—a real punch, right under the eye—so they had to fly home that night, sneak out of the hotel and fly home.

He sucked up a breath, pushed himself up from his desk and started out to the floor. Old Man Cartwell, who rarely came in anymore, was futzing around with the files, complaining to the secretaries about something, the loose flesh under his jaws swinging as he turned from one to the other. One of the secretaries looked at Mackey with a slight roll of her eyes, and somehow this made him feel better, stronger, more confident. He calmed the old man and gave him a few minutes, telling him about the plans for expanding the drug abuse program. Then he walked down the corridor toward the lecture hall where he was to give a talk to some of the senior staff.

He made, on a sudden decision, a quick detour. He felt himself tensing up.

He stopped at one of the rooms and stood in the doorway. Samuel Devereaux, looking out the window, turned and smiled at him. "Bill? Good to see you."

Mackey felt his heart contract. How he'd hoped for a miracle—that he'd find him sunk deeper into senility.

Chapter 15

The instant Carla hung up, she berated herself. Why was she doing this to herself, to Matt? Hadn't Bill Mackey pleaded with her? "Carla, the boy needs you. Don't scatter yourself, don't go rushing after shadows in the wind!"

And yet—the call. Why had she made the call?

She glanced at the name she'd scribbled on her scratch pad. Impulsively she had called the woman in Bessinger's personnel office who had answered her letter. The woman had given her the name of Mark's department supervisor.

But what did she hope to learn from him?

No. She wasn't going to go searching anymore. No more looking. Over with. Done. Let Mark just rest in peace. She had Matt to think of. Only Matt.

She crumpled the paper in her hand to toss into the wastebasket. But she found herself holding on to it. Then, though swearing she would do nothing about it, she put it back on the desk.

She glanced at the paper briefly when she came back to her office later in the day. The following morning, she brushed it to the side so she would have more space for the stack of morning mail. She didn't even look at it during a short break between patients late that morning. But that afternoon, sitting at her desk before meeting with her postmastectomy group, something broke within her. She swept up the receiver, began poking quickly at the buttons.

"Mr. Petrecca's office."

"May I speak to Mr. Petrecca, please. This is Dr. Carla Keller."

"He's not at his desk right now. Can I do something for you, Doctor?"

"No, I'd like to talk to him. Do you have any idea when he'll be back?"

"I'd say in about an hour."

"Would you have him call me?" She gave her number and extension. "If I'm not in my office, would you have him ask my secretary to page me?"

The postmastectomy group was made up of new and former patients who met once a week to offer each other support and share experiences. Members drifted in and out of the group as they needed it. She would start off the session with some general comments, then someone would usually bring up a problem, such as her boyfriend wanting her to wear her bra during intercourse. This would evoke responses from the others, often recrimination. Carla would interject a few comments here and there, such as "Forget for a moment about how the others feel about him wanting this; how do you feel about him wanting it? You haven't really said. Do you agree with him in a way? Are you ashamed for him to see you?" But today she spoke up less, and wasn't sure whether it was because there was less reason to or because she didn't trust her thinking right now. Her mind kept going anxiously to her beeper. But it didn't start beeping until the session was breaking up. She excused herself quickly, took the call at an open phone.

"Dr. Keller?"

"Yes."

"One moment please. Mr. Petrecca will be right with you."

She looked around; people were walking by. She hunched around the receiver, cutting off the world with her shoulder, when he came on.

"This is Joe Petrecca."

"Mr. Petrecca, my name is Carla Keller. Listen, I'm at an open phone right now and I was wondering— Can I call you back in about two minutes?"

"Of course."

"Thank you so much. I'll call you right back."

She was out of breath, and still not sure how she was going to put this, as she made the call from her office.

"Yes, Dr. Keller, what can I do for you?"

Who? Oh, yes. Of course he remembered Mark Keller. Oh, he was very sorry to hear that; he hadn't heard; such a young man. And such a nice person. Oh, he was terribly sorry.

"I—was wondering if you could help me, Mr. Petrecca," she said. "I'm trying to locate any close friends Mark had when he worked at Bessinger's."

"Do you know their names?"

"No, I'm sorry I didn't make myself clear. No, I don't know anyone, that's what I'm trying to find out. I thought maybe you could help me. Or maybe you yourself—"

Well, as far as he himself was concerned, whatever he knew he'd be glad to tell her, but if she was looking for close personal friends he didn't think he'd be of much help. He'd known Mark as a very personable, bright young man who had been working his way up in new product sales. He had been destined for a high managerial position when he'd left for—what?—oh yes, medicine. Well, you couldn't beat medicine. But, it was a boss-employee relationship; and though as he said he would help her in any way he could, it wouldn't be as someone close to him. Offhand he really couldn't remember who his close friends were, but let him think. He would call her back. Or if he remembered a name, he might have that person call.

"You can call me here or at my home. Here's my number."

"I'll call you one way or the other, Doctor."

Shortly after seven that evening, a man did call. But it was someone her girl friend Jerri had given her name to, to call for a date. He knew Jerri from Penn, he said; he was in the English department while she, of course, was in chemistry. They'd had lunch together yesterday and that was when Jerri had mentioned her to him.

"I was wondering if we have any other mutual friends," he said.

They didn't. He asked if she liked opera, the theater, dancing; and though she tried to help the conversation along, she was aware she was being abrupt. But she was unable to stop herself. She hated this; she was so fucking mad at Jerri for putting her through it without warning. She had enough of it at work, from some of the married ones even, not outright approaches, but hints—a drink, relax.

"I thought we might go out for a drink this week," he was saying.

She eased out of it, trying not to make him feel awkward. She just wasn't going out yet, she said. Maybe in a month. Yes, please call back. And thank you for the call.

Immediately afterward she called Jerri.

"Jerri, I just got a call from some guy! Please don't give my name out anymore! You asked me, and I told you. I'm not ready, I don't want it."

"Who called? Sid?"

"I don't know what his name is! I don't care what his name is! Don't give my name out! I told you."

"Would I give it out to anyone who wasn't nice?"

"You don't hear a damn word I say! I said don't give my name out!"

"All right, all right, I won't give your name out."

"Please."

About an hour later Jerri showed up, in floppy sweater and jeans, her long blond hair stringy as though she'd just washed it.

"You," she announced softly at the door, "worry me."

Carla put her arms around her. "You're nuts. That's a long ride."

"And I've got cystitis."

"Oh, Jesus." She had to laugh, though she was also crying a little. "You're a good friend."

"Well, we'll see."

A little later, in Carla's room, after spending a few minutes trying to wheedle Matt into talking about school or television or *something,* Jerri said, "Matt seems fine."

"Come *on.*"

"He was doing so well." Her face was pained.

"Well, he's gone backward. But Mackey's seeing him again. And I'm seeing Mackey again. Jerri, it's a mess, it's a real fucking mess."

"Do you want to tell me?"

"Do you want to hear?" It came across almost icily, like a dare.

"I want to hear."

"I told you about Darby House, right?" She knew, of course, that she had. But it was as though she needed a familiar place to start. "That," she said in a deliberate way, "is just the beginning."

And now, after making sure the door was completely closed, her voice low, she told her everything—his lies about his parents, the tankers, all of it.

Jerri kept staring at her for long moments after. Then, in a drawn-out monotone, "Jesus Christ on a cross."

"I don't know how I'm keeping my head together."

"Honey, you've *got* to keep it together." And then came the words she'd known she would hear. "Nobody could have guessed he was off his head, but this proves it. He was sick, that's why he killed himself. It's the only reason he would have done it to you and Matt. And your doctor's right. You've got a job to do with Matt, and a big part of that is simply to get on with living."

"I am living. I'm working, I'm functioning."

"You're shit. You keep this up and you won't be functioning. I don't want to scare you, but if you make yourself sick who the hell's going to take care of Matt?"

She gestured. "What can I say? You're right."

"Of course, I'm right. He was a nut case! I loved him but he was a nut case! Where's the booze? Let's have something to drink."

"I don't want anything. You want something?"

"I don't want anything. I'm doing it for you. I'm—celebrating."

"Let me in on the big secret. Celebrating what?"

"As of now you're going to come out from under. And so, I swear to you, will Matt. You may be the best

95

shrink in the world but you're shit when it comes to yourself."

Carla couldn't believe she was starting to smile. Who would have thought one minute ago there'd be anything that could make her smile?

"Would you like something to drink?"

"No, I was making the sacrifice for you. Lady, I have to drive. And"—she looked at her watch—"I am going. Where's my bag?" She was looking around. "Where the fuck do I always leave my bag?"

The phone rang. Motioning to where the bag had fallen next to the couch, Carla answered it. She also waved for Jerri to wait. "Hello?"

"Dr. Keller?" A man.

"That's right."

"My name's Alfred Karpides. Joe Petrecca suggested I call."

She said, "Can I call you back?"

Jerri shook her head fiercely. Her lips formed: I am going. She bent over and kissed her on the cheek. Carla said into the phone, "Could you hold on one moment?"

"Sure."

She stood up and embraced her. Jerri said, "I'll talk to you tomorrow."

"Thanks for everything."

"For what? For what?" She was gone with a wave.

Carla sat down, holding the phone hard on her lap. She tried to think. She must get on the phone and say thanks, but I already found out what I wanted.

But even as she lifted the receiver she knew from the sudden tension in her that she would ask to meet him.

Bessinger, Inc., one of the largest mail-order companies in the country, took up an eleven-story building, set on four acres of ground about five miles across the Delaware River from Philadelphia. Alfred Karpides, a gangling man of about thirty-five, had a small office on the tenth floor. He greeted her warmly, ushered her to a chair next to his desk.

Last night was the first he'd heard of Mark's death, he said. He still couldn't get over it. He often thought of him, though he hadn't seen him since he left to go to med school.

"I really envied him—not so much med school, but just leaving here. It's not a bad place, but like any place you never know when heads are going to roll." He shook his head, then segued into a story of something he and Mark once did, which she really didn't follow.

Karpides was a good talker, but she knew he was waiting for her to explain why she'd wanted to meet him. When there was an appropriate pause, she said, "I would appreciate it if you would be very honest with me about this because it could be very important. Can you think of any possible reason Mark wouldn't want to tell me he worked here?"

"He never told you?" Instantly, as though wanting to soften this: "Well—it's not the greatest place, I guess. Although it's not bad. No, it's not bad. In fact, you could see he was on his way up. Everyone liked him."

"Do you know of anything unusual that happened here—something he wouldn't want to talk about? Was he—involved with anyone?"

"You mean like a girl?"

"I really don't know what I mean. I mean, anything important. Something so important to him that he couldn't say he worked here."

"I really can't think of anything. He never stole anything I know about. As far as I knew, he did great

97

here. He was unhappy but he did a good job. Everyone liked him. Lots of personality, always knew what to say, a good dresser."

"What do you mean he was unhappy?"

"He wanted to be a doctor. I used to tell him, 'You're cutting your own throat here if you don't keep it to yourself, if you don't make believe this is for the rest of your life.' Now, that's not all he talked about, but he'd let you know he wanted to be a doctor. I remember he used to be very friendly with the company doctor."

"Is he still here?"

"No, he died a few years ago."

He wished he could help her, he said, he really did. But there was nothing he could think of. And there was no one he could think of who might help her. Mark knew other people, of course, but he could honestly say that he and Mark were the closest—about the same age, always had lunch together; never socialized outside work, but were close.

"I'm really very sorry," he said. "I wish I could help. I'm really surprised though he never told you. It's"—he added it apologetically—"not a bad place."

She stood up and he slowly stood up with her. She held out her hand. "I really appreciate this. It's—just—something I wanted to find out. Our son asks me all sorts of questions about his father, and I'd like, you know, for him to know as much about him as possible. I don't know why he never mentioned it."

"Look, it's nothing to be proud of, nothing to be ashamed of. It's not a bad place."

"Well, thank you very much."

"I just want to say," he said, "he was one hell of a nice guy. I'm awfully sorry."

In the lobby she walked over to the security desk to sign out. As she approached it, she paused and stared at a portrait hanging on the wall near the desk. She frowned slightly. She walked closer to it, a portrait of an aristocratic-looking man with thinning gray hair. A little gold plate on the frame identified him as the cofounder and former president of the company.

She suddenly reached out to balance herself.

Samuel Devereaux.

Chapter 16

Ross heard his phone ringing as he approached his apartment; he sprinted the last few yards, unlocked the door, and grabbed the receiver.

"Daddy. Me."

"Hey me. How's my love?"

Ross wriggled off his jacket and sat down, putting his feet up on the cocktail table. His heart used to plummet when he heard Patty's voice on the phone, and it had always been with a sense of anxiety that he would call her, for the calls had always been tinged with gloom and her voice with barely masked hostility. But no more. For the past year their calls had been, well, conversations. She seemed to have found a balance, no longer resenting him or Margaret or Margaret's new husband.

Now she wanted to know what he thought of this: her guidance counselor didn't think she should pursue anything in college in the sciences; he felt her strength seemed to lie in subjects like psychology and English. There was a touch of hysteria in her voice, for she wanted to be a vet. Gradually he calmed her, telling her of the few wrong shots he knew that guidance counselors had called, that her marks were pretty good in the sciences, weren't they? So she should go for what she wanted. And now the conversation turned to what she'd been doing lately and what he'd been doing and what Mother had said about this boy who was real nice. Afterward, after thinking over the conversation—he was so damned angry at that guidance counselor!—he turned on the stereo and stood for several moments by the picture window, staring out at the night-glitter of the buildings and the streets.

Strange, how all the bitterness was gone and all the pointing to blame. For a long time back there—sometimes it was hard to believe they'd been divorced five years—both he and Margaret had felt taken, in a sense: she that he hadn't stayed on the paper in Chicago, where she had just graduated from law school; he that she hadn't wanted to come to Philadelphia with him, where he had a far better opportunity and where she could have taken the Pennsylvania bar. But it had taken them a while to realize that those were simply the final incidents in a marriage that had been slipping apart. The fact was that the two people who married at twenty—the guy who only wanted to be a biochemistry prof, the girl who spoke of wanting four children and never once of a career—were simply not the same two people in their thirties. It had been no one's fault; they'd even tried to hold on, longer than they should have, for Patty's sake.

Not only had he long ago stopped being bitter about it, he was glad that Margaret seemed happy in her new marriage. What's more, he'd found that he liked this life, not the bar scene—he hadn't been in a singles bar for years—but the freedom to do, to go.

He checked his watch; almost ten. He wondered should he call Jill, a local TV reporter and weekend anchorwoman he'd been dating off and on for the past three months; he was sure she was still out of town on assignment. He turned out to be right and left a message on her machine that he'd called. They were turning into just friends, which was fine. She was anxious to get married again, and he couldn't see that for himself right now.

He showered and sat down in the living room to read the newspaper. But he found his thoughts drifting to Carla.

Was she building a lot of this up in her mind?

But he couldn't see her as the hysterical type.

He saw her, rather, as a blend of opposites—all business but tremendously sexy, very sensitive and yet tough, book-bright as hell but also street-smart. In no way hysterical.

At the same time, he just couldn't see Wayne Delman in this.

But who knew? He had learned about Wayne being missing from one of the chemists he knew at Delman & Sharples. But the person he'd really wanted to speak to—and would have, except he'd been on a trip—was Jeff Malmquist, the advertising manager, a particularly good friend. Jeff worked closely with Wayne, might know a lot more about him than most people in the place.

Ross had called him that morning, but he wasn't due back until the afternoon. He would call Jeff tomorrow.

Delman & Sharples Laboratories, Inc., was located in a sprawling eighteen-story building near the outskirts of the city. It had been founded in 1891, as a retail drugstore (Delman & Crawford). They then branched out into the wholesale distribution of drugs as Delman, Crawford & Sharples. In 1928, Crawford sold out to Delman and Sharples, who were cousins, and several years later they began to manufacture

102

drugs. But the company didn't really begin to become a giant until after World War II, when they developed two top-selling antibiotics. Today, though they still had several highly regarded patented drugs, they mostly manufactured generic drugs. Until his recent suicide, John Delman, who was a grandson of one of the founders, had been a principle stockholder, as was his cousin, Stuart Sharples, grandson of the other founder.

The receptionist signed Ross in and gave him a visitor's badge. He took the elevator to the fifth floor and walked past bright offices and L-shaped cubicles toward the advertising and promotion department.

Jeff Malmquist motioned him to come into his office even though he was on the phone. After he hung up he reached over and shook Ross's hand, then sat back and clamped his palms to the sides of his head.

"This joint." He looked to the door and rose to close it, then came back to his desk. "I'm quitting. I'm absolutely quitting. Tell me how to start free-lancing."

"Just do it. There's plenty of work out there." For the first couple of years, before his first book and his magazine work took off, Ross used to write a lot of promotional material for Jeff. "Are you serious?"

"No." He sighed. "I'm just a talker. I've got too much time invested here. But it is getting to be a pain in the ass. More goddam rumors going around. One day good ol' Stu Sharples is selling out, next day he isn't, next day an Arab's buying him out, then another drug firm is taking over, then nobody's buying us out but a hundred people are going to be laid off."

"I thought they were making money hand over fist."

"I'm sure they are but, you know, what's enough? One of our problems is that everyone's making generics. We're not going to hold on to our position in generics very long. As for the drugs we do own, our

103

patents are running out on most of them. Everyone will be able to make them. The guy who ruined us, you know, was Delman—Johnny boy. He should have dropped dead twenty years ago."

"What did he do?"

"What did he do? He put a ton of money into fancy research that won't produce a drug for twenty years. We need new drugs now. Why Sharples didn't stop him I'll never know. But he's an asshole. A rich asshole, but an asshole." He let go another sigh. "But what am I bugging you for? A rich, famous author."

"Cut the crap."

"You are. I'm proud of you. I'm jealous as hell, but I'm proud of you. Christ, you're not even married. You got it all."

Ross laughed.

"Look," Jeff said, "you said you wanted to ask me something about Wayne. Another asshole, honest to God."

"A friend asked me to find out what I can about—"

"You don't have to explain. Just ask what you want. But I don't really know all that much about him."

"Nobody's heard from him yet?"

"Not that I know of. But you hear stories. Someone said he heard he called from Florida, drunk as hell. Someone else said he heard he was in Alaska. You know. Stories. What a pity! That poor son of a bitch could have had half this company."

"John Delman never changed his will back, did he?"

"No, I heard not."

"You'd think Wayne would have hated the old man. But I hear he was very upset when he died, blamed the hospital for him killing himself."

"He did that around here, too. But he had such a

buzz on all the time it was hard to make sense out of him."

"He was drinking a lot before he disappeared?"

"Does a rooster screw chickens? As soon as the old man went, he dropped off the wagon."

"Did you ever hear him mention the name Mark Keller? Dr. Keller? He was one of his father's doctors at the hospital."

"You know, the police were here asking that. No, I don't remember any names. Just that he didn't like anyone at the hospital."

"Did you ever hear him making any threats?"

"Like I say, he had such a buzz on . . . He'd walk around muttering things, but I don't remember any actual threats."

Someone, Ross noticed, occasionally came to the office's glass door to see if Malmquist was still busy. Hating to take up more of his time, and unable to think of anything more to ask, Ross stood up slowly.

"I appreciate this, Jeff. Thanks for seeing me on such short notice."

"You kidding? This is fun. Out there"—he jerked a finger—"is bullshit."

"By the way, will you be at the convention in San Francisco?" It was an international conference of primary-care physicians, and Ross was sure Delman & Sharples would have an exhibit there.

"Yeah, we'll have a booth and a hospitality suite. Why? You going?"

"Yes, I'll be covering it."

"Stop by. I'll see you there."

"Good."

Jeff Malmquist stood up. "Incidentally, maybe you can help me. We're going to be holding a seminar on the family doc handling psychosomatic problems. I need a medical advisor, someone to run it. And I need him fast, like yesterday. I don't want a psychiatrist for this crowd, what I'd like is an internist, a real humanist. You know anyone?"

"Let me give it some thought. I know a hell of a lot of internists, but I know more I wouldn't pick than I would pick."

"Speaking of Wayne," Malmquist said, walking him to the door, "we could have had a very good medical advisor on this. Wayne met him somewhere, thought the world of him. Fellow named Cohen. But he died in an accident. Understand he fell down a flight of stairs in his own home."

"Of course I knew he used to be president of Bessinger's," William Mackey said, "but why would I have thought to mention it?"

"I don't know, maybe when I told you I found out Mark had worked there," Carla replied.

"I'm sorry, I honestly never gave it a thought. Or if I did, I honestly don't remember. It probably never struck me as important."

"I'm starting to wonder why I'm still sane. It's hard enough, God knows it's hard enough, to try to understand why Mark would lie about working there. But not telling me he had a patient he used to work for? It's not as if he never mentioned Devereaux to me. He did. I knew about a Samuel Devereaux who used to be president or vice-president of something or other."

"But if he told you he worked for him, he would have had to admit never going to sea. No, that part's the easiest to understand."

"Bill, what do you know about Devereaux?"

"Nothing of very much consequence, I would think. Basically, that he retired about two years ago, and was a brilliant man. He'd been a widower a long time."

106

"Does he have any children?"

"A daughter. She lives in New York."

"Where does he live?"

"He's got a condominium here in the city. His daughter wants to sell it, I know, and have him come live with her."

"Can you ever see discharging him?"

"If she wants to try to take care of him. But knowing her I can't see that happening. I think she just wants to sell it."

"I'd like to talk to him, Bill. May I?"

"Why not? But I doubt if you're going to learn anything from him."

A few minutes later, looking into his room, she saw what he meant. Devereaux was sitting on a chair, staring fixedly on the floor. He didn't look up when Mackey spoke his name.

"He's been this way for days," William Mackey said.

Chapter 17

Mrs. LeVine was on the phone when Carla entered the house. Her hand over the mouthpiece, she said, "It's Mr. Robbins. Do you want to talk to him now or should I tell him you'll call back?"

"No, I'll take it." She slipped off her raincoat—it had been drizzling all day—then, as she walked to where Mrs. LeVine was standing by the wall phone in the kitchen, said, "Where's Matt?"

"In his room."

"How is he?"

"All right." But her tone, her look said otherwise.

Carla, her thoughts on Matt, took the receiver. "Yes, Ross."

"Just walk in?"

"Yes, but that's fine. How are you?"

"Good. Look, I don't know if this is anything more than a plain, simple coincidence, but I think it's something the police should know. I was over at Delman-Sharples to—"

"Where?" The word "police" had so startled her that she wasn't sure she'd caught the rest of it.

"Delman and Sharples."

108

Eyes widening as she listened, she felt in back of her for a chair, then slowly lowered herself into it. Then: "Wayne Delman and Stephen Cohen were close friends?"

"No, Jeff didn't say close friends. He said Wayne knew Cohen and respected him very much."

"Did he say anything else?"

"I asked him what he knew about Cohen and he said all he knew from Wayne was that he was a very fine internist."

Yes, she'd heard that. And had heard, too, that he was supposed to have been a warm empathic person whose patients worshiped him.

"I appreciate this, Ross, I really do. I'm going to call right now. Can I use Jeff Malmquist's name?"

"Sure. I told him I was going to tell you."

"I'm going to call right now," she said again.

But she hesitated before making the call. She didn't want to talk to Harris. But she was afraid to go over his head.

She dialed his number.

Usually the only time Harris woke up before his alarm clock went off was when he was anxious about something. But he couldn't think of anything that would make him edgy this morning. Still, he'd beaten his alarm by almost a half hour. What the hell was he doing up at five-thirty?

He tried falling back to sleep, but gave up after about ten minutes. He slipped quietly out of bed, trying not to disturb Marie, and shaved and showered down the hall in the kids' bathroom: nothing would wake them. But when he came back to begin dressing, she opened her eyes heavily. "Time is it?"

"Still early. Six. Go back to sleep."

"What—you doing?"

"I've got an appointment. Go back to sleep."

Downstairs, he went outside and got the *Inquirer* from the lawn and read it with his coffee. Before leaving, he stood by the staircase listening for sounds, wondering whether he should wake the boys. Then he remembered their saying it was a late day, there was a teachers' meeting. He got his raincoat from the closet and walked out to the car. It was a neighborhood of row houses and single-car garages and two-car families, so there was an unwritten law that you never parked in front of a neighbor's house. Pretty nice people here, especially these few blocks.

He became more aware of his edginess as he drove.

Ever since that damn call from the shrink, he had to admit. But why should that bug him? Except it meant some more running around, making calls. It was becoming one of those cases that were just a big fat pain in the ass.

Except—the truth, now—except how he'd just love to come up with something to wipe the whole department's face in, to get the headlines for a change, to have Marie proud of him, the kids coming home from school saying, "Hey!"

In center city now, he parked his car partway up on the sidewalk of a narrow street and lowered the visor with his identification on it. He walked around the corner to a medical office building and, after checking the directory on the lobby wall, took the elevator to the fourteenth floor. These goddam doctors! Best time to see him or even talk to him, his secretary had said, was before hours.

Dr. Kauffman, all long white coat and white hair, was busy at something at the receptionist's desk in the empty, almost dark waiting room. He glanced up just long enough to smile and say this would take just a moment, then continued what he was doing for some five minutes more. Finally he stood up and held out his hand.

"Nice seeing you again. Let's go into my office."

Harris followed him past several examination rooms. Kauffman had been one of Stephen Cohen's closest friends and had taken over most of his practice. And so he'd been one of the first persons Harris had checked with to find out if Cohen had known Mark Keller.

In his office, his face showing concern, Kauffman said, "You're still not satisfied about Dr. Cohen's death?"

"I'm just checking on something else that's come up. Another name."

"I can't believe for one second that Dr. Cohen was murdered. I mean, if it was for robbery—well, yes, nobody's safe. But as I told you, something in his personal life? No. I just can't believe it."

"Wayne Delman. Do you remember Dr. Cohen ever mentioning that name?"

"Wayne who?"

"Delman. Like Delman and Sharples, the drug firm."

"Wayne Delman," he repeated quietly, frowning. Then he shook his head. "No."

"Let me put it another way. Wayne Delman is one of the Delmans in Delman and Sharples. Did Dr. Cohen ever mention doing any kind of work for them?"

Kauffman thought. "Once he said something about doing some consulting. If I recall correctly, it had to do with some promotion for one of their products. I do remember that, but I don't remember the product or anyone's name there."

"Wayne Delman," Harris said.

"No. Doesn't ring a bell."

111

"Maybe he was a patient. You have most of Dr. Cohen's records, don't you?"

"Well, they're in with mine. I wish my girl was here. Let me see what I can do."

Soon Kauffman called from somewhere in another office. "No Wayne Delman. You sure you don't mean John? There's a John Delman here."

"Can I see that?"

Kauffman walked back with a folder. He opened it at his desk, began to read aloud. "John Delman . . . sixty-two . . . Devon." He looked up. "Is this who you meant?"

"I'm sure that's his stepfather."

Kauffman read on, silently. Then: "Yes. Says here. Referred by W. Delman. Let's see. Apparently just one visit."

"Would you tell me what it was for?"

Again Kauffman read silently. "Depression. In fairly good health otherwise, I would say."

"May I see that?" When Kauffman hesitated, he said, "Mr. Delman's dead. I really just want to check on the W. Delman."

Kauffman handed him the single sheet of paper in the folder. The W. Delman was definitely a W. Delman. He read on a little. In tight little handwriting, Dr. Cohen had noted the fatal auto accident, a loss of appetite, frequent crying spells, insomnia . . .

Harris handed it back. For the first time he felt a real sense of excitement about Wayne Delman. Why not—with him disappearing after the deaths of two men who had treated his stepfather?

Carla walked out of her office toward the elevators. She had to pick up Matt to take him to Bill's, and she was a little late. She'd just been on the phone with Howard Tompkins, who had called to say he would be

112

away for several days and he wanted her to know that he'd have the final figures on the sale of Mark's interest in the Darby House restaurant within a few weeks.

She hated keeping Bill waiting.

"Doctor." Mary was standing out in the corridor. "Phone."

"Get a message and I'll call back."

"He says it's important. A Detective Harris."

She walked back quickly. She closed her door and took the call standing up. "Yes, Mr. Harris."

"Sorry I didn't get to you sooner, but I've been on the run all day. Look, I don't make it a practice of filling people in every step of the way, but I feel you have the right to know this. Now it may turn out to be absolutely nothing, but I was over to see a Dr. Kauffman this morning . . ."

A few minutes later she was staring at the phone. Apparently Wayne Delman had taken his stepfather to Dr. Cohen's about a week before he went into the hospital. Bill Mackey had been seeing John Delman, so the visit was either about a physical problem or else to get a second opinion.

But the diagnosis was still depression.

Although Harris didn't come right out and say it, she knew what he was thinking—that, after his stepfather's suicide, Wayne Delman had turned on Cohen with the same hatred he'd shown to Mark.

She glanced quickly at her watch. Oh, God, she was so late!

She called Mackey to ask him to wait. And to explain why she'd been delayed.

"You still miss your daddy terribly, don't you?"

Matt looked at him, his lower lip quivering.

"You're afraid your mommy's going to leave you

113

too, aren't you? That *she'll* die. Of course you don't want your mommy to die. You want her to be with you all the time, don't you?"

Shh. Shh. No crying.

"Why do you look so scared, Matt? You can tell me. I'm your friend, aren't I?"

Shh. No crying.

"Now I want you to draw for me again. Draw whatever you want to draw. You want to draw your mommy walking away from the house?"

Shh. No crying.

Chapter 18

The next morning she was brushing her hair in front of the long narrow mirror in her bedroom when a little dry choking sound whirled her around. Matt was standing in the doorway in his pajamas. Instantly he broke into tears.

"My tummy hurts."

She'd been afraid it wouldn't simply go away, that it would happen next on a school morning; but she forced herself to stay calm. "Again? Oh, I'm sorry. Let's take a look."

He sat with her on the bed. He was sobbing convulsively as she lifted his pajama top.

Again wherever she touched, it hurt; even near his hips and up on his chest. "Oh," she said slowly, knowing this wasn't going to work. "I think it's going to be better once you have something to eat."

"It won't! My tummy hurts. My head!" He began rubbing at his head screaming.

"Matt, stop it!" She grabbed his wrist out of frustration, dread: everything was growing, spreading. She released him immediately, touching his face gently.

"You'll see, you'll be better, sweetheart. I promise you."

"I won't! I won't!" And with that he leaped up and ran to his room. She followed slowly, walking past Mrs. LeVine, who was in her robe and looking on, concerned; and she sat next to him as he lay sprawled face down on his bed. "Come on, sweetheart." She rubbed his back, biting her lips and trying not to cry, thinking of those drawings Bill had shown her yesterday: those terrible, dark, foreboding drawings. "You'll see, you'll feel better. I promise you."

He began kicking and punching the mattress.

"Matt!" A sudden snap in her voice. "Stop it! Now stop it!" He gradually eased up. Then she said, certain about what would happen next, "It's getting late, you've got to get dressed and go to school."

He whirled, his face savage. "My tummy hurts!" he screamed. "My head! My head!"

"Matt, stop it! Stop it!"

He stared at her wildly as he lay there, half turned around, sucking in breaths.

"Doctor." Softly, from the doorway.

She looked around. Mrs. LeVine gave a slight motion of her head. Carla walked out to her, her legs trembling. She followed Mrs. LeVine a little way down the hall. Mrs. LeVine, a plump gray-haired woman, had gone almost plaster-white.

"I—don't want to butt in," she said. "But, you know, Friday—it's Friday. Maybe if you let him stay home today, he'll have the weekend to get over it."

It was what she wanted to hear, the mother part of her, not the smart-ass psychiatrist part who read in the books that you mustn't give in to it, who would have told a mother to stick to your guns.

What she wanted to hear because she was so much at fault.

116

"I think," Bill Mackey had said, "that he either senses or overheard that you think Mark may have been murdered. He hasn't come right out and said it, but he's a very, very sensitive youngster and that's what's coming through to me. You can see by the drawings he's more afraid than ever something's going to happen to you too."

"Don't mean to butt in," Mrs. LeVine was saying again.

"Don't ever say that," Carla said, taking her hand. "Please."

"I just feel so bad."

"I know. And how I appreciate you." Carla embraced her, held on to her hard. Then she walked back to Matt's room. He was lying with his face in the pillow, shaking with dry sobs. She sat with him. "All right, you can stay home. And you'll see, you're going to be all better. And tomorrow"—she put her hand on his back, and a cheerfulness came into her voice—"tomorrow's going to be your day. We're going to do whatever you want. Hey, how about a movie? Would you like to go to a movie?"

Harry Boy whinnied and flung his head about as William Mackey reached in his stall to stroke his muzzle.

He knows the smell of fear, Mackey thought. "Here fellow, here fellow . . . that's it," and though Harry Boy grew calm and came closer, Mackey was almost afraid to stroke him anymore—his hands felt too icy.

He walked out of the barn into the sunshine, looking for things to do. He dreaded going back into the house. Jeanne was already half plastered, her lipstick—almost as red as her hair—smeared at the corners.

Usually William Mackey's home was a haven from

all the stresses of work. But no more. Certainly not for the past few months.

He and Jeanne had bought this farm twenty years ago, soon after he came to Cartwell. It was close enough to the city—about twenty-five miles—and just the right size, some twenty acres, with an early nineteenth-century stone house and even a red barn. He only worked a small part of it, just for vegetables, a hobby more than anything else; and though he no longer had the Angus—he'd given them up after the last of their children moved out—he got tremendous satisfaction out of the few horses he had kept.

Occasionally he still rode; Francine, their eldest, was the real rider. He used to love to ride with her, but she was living in Paris with her husband. Johnnie, their second, worked in Texas, and Liz, their youngest, was an occasional rider. But her children, twins, would be ready for ponies soon.

Jeanne had stopped riding long ago.

He walked toward the house, picking up a few scraps of paper along the way. Jeanne was rinsing off dishes at the sink.

"Liz is late," he said, adding, "Do you mind if I tell you about your lipstick? Right here." He touched the corner of his mouth.

She glanced at herself in the mirror, then looked long and hard at him. She began rinsing the dishes again. "You learn how to put lipstick on in psychiatry school?"

"Oh, Christ!" He had to get out of the room.

"Big shot," she called after him. "Big shot shitting in his pants."

He came back. "Don't you have a heart anymore? Nothing? *Nothing?*"

"No. You took it from me."

His stomach rumbled; he rubbed it. He'd been

118

having stomach pains the last couple of days. She watched him rubbing himself.

"Why don't you be a goddam man?"

"Tell me, what's a man to you? What is a man? Tell me! I want to know."

"A man makes a decision and doesn't say later"— she began to imitate a whine—" 'I shouldn'ta done it. Oh, what am I gonna do, what am I gonna do? I'm gonna kill myself.' "

He had grabbed his revolver once, put it to his mouth. She had looked on without saying a word.

"You're a son-of-a-bitch bastard, you know that? But, lady, if I'm in trouble—you're in trouble!"

"How many times have I got to hear that from you? How many times? I wouldn't be in trouble and you wouldn't be in trouble if you'd just stop shitting in your pants."

He whirled and went outside, slamming the door. He stood there, shaking, fighting for control.

He sat down on the porch steps. She was right about one thing. Had to keep his head. Must. Had to.

He lifted his eyes, wondering if he heard a car turning into the lane. Yes. He stood up. The kids' station wagon. It pulled up in front of the house and Bob and Liz got out. He clapped Bob on the back, not wanting to shake hands, to have him feel his cold hands, and he kissed Liz on the cheek.

"Hey, let's see the guys," he said as they opened the back doors. The twins were in car seats. He lifted one of them, while Liz took the other. Bob gathered all the paraphernalia to take into the house.

"How's my little fellow," Mackey said to the baby, hugging him and kissing him in the crease of his neck. How he loved that sweet, sweet smell!

And as he carried the baby into the house, the last of his doubts faded: he didn't care about Matt, he wasn't

119

going to let that keep him up anymore; he didn't care about Carla. Didn't care about anything, nothing, just that he would keep doing whatever he had to do, *whatever,* to be safe, to keep his honor, to make these children know they had *some* grandfather.

Every so often during the movie, a matinee, she would slip a glance at Matt. He seemed intent on it; his face showed expression at many of the appropriate places, but it was hard to tell if he was really enjoying it.

He hadn't complained of anything that morning, which was good, of course—except it could mean that he would be "sick" only on school days.

Relax, she urged herself; be grateful he didn't complain, that he seemed to be immersed in the movie.

Still, she would have felt a lot better if he'd taken her up on inviting a friend.

The movie was ending now, the music loud. As soon as the lights went on she looked at him with a smile, hoping it would trigger a smile from him, but he was looking at the few people walking up the aisle. She said, "Did you like it?"

He nodded slightly.

"I really enjoyed it," she said.

Outside she asked him if he wanted something to eat, and he shook his head. Silently they headed toward home.

"Carla."

She turned. Ross was walking quickly toward them. "Hi. I saw you from the corner. You," he said, looking at him, "have to be Matt. You were two feet shorter the last time I saw you."

"This is Matt."

"How you doing, Matt? Ross." He held out his hand. After some hesitation, Matt took it.

"Matt and I were just at the movies."

He wanted to know which one, and then he asked Matt if he liked it. Matt may have responded with a nod, but it was hard for her to tell.

"Well, look," he said, "you're going this way, and I'm going that way. But I just wanted to say hello." He looked at her, asking with his eyes how she was. Then he held out his hand to Matt again. "It was good seeing you again, Matt. I'll talk to you soon," he said to her.

She nodded with a trace of a smile. "It was nice seeing you."

She shook his hand. Later, walking on, she wasn't sure which of them had kept holding on.

Chapter 19

Edwin Haywood, after a last-minute check on some papers in his attaché case, put his wire-framed glasses back in his jacket pocket and looked out at the night as his private jet, a Gulfstream 111, approached Heathrow Airport. As president of the Decton Corporation, one of the world's largest engineering firms, he tried to visit the company's key offices, as well as some of its farflung subsidiaries, every few months. He did too much he could delegate to others, he knew well enough, but he would never change. Didn't want to change. In many ways, the man of fifty-eight was no different from that boy of seven who would have had to be half-dead before letting anyone else run errands from Goldman's drugstore.

Even his taking on a new responsibility at Cartwell. He should never have agreed at the last board meeting to head up the committee on enlarging the youth center. Should have passed it on to someone else. But there was that feeling the new building just wouldn't turn out right, or on time.

Soon after the plane landed and was approaching the

terminal, Haywood was on his feet. He always did that, as though somehow he could make it get there faster. Yet he shouldn't be in any hurry tonight. It was almost midnight and his first meeting wouldn't be until morning.

After the plane eased up to the terminal building and the whine of the engines died, the pilot and copilot joined the cabin attendant to say their good-byes. Patrick, his bodyguard, stepped out first; out of second nature, he paused and looked around. A tall, cherubic-faced man in a three-piece suit, he was the only other person Haywood had brought along. With all the kidnappings of executives, Haywood rarely went anywhere abroad without him.

They cleared customs easily. Two men waited for them; the younger took their luggage. A Rolls-Royce pulled up barely half a minute after they stepped out on the curb. It sped them to London, drawing up, soft as a whisper, in front of a Hyde Park hotel. The doorman greeted Haywood by name; the desk clerk waved to him from a distance as the older of the two men handled the checking in.

Haywood stood impatiently at the back of the elevator as it whisked them to the top floor. He wanted to make a couple of calls, was anxious for the others to leave. Patrick went straight to his own room but the other two waited in the suite until the porter had set down the luggage and tested the TV in the bedroom. Nobody seemed to pay any attention to a young woman sitting in the bedroom. Tall, with long blond hair and a thin archly held neck, she sat with a fashion magazine on her lap.

He made his two calls from the living room, both to friends, one outside London, the other near Rome. He carried his jacket into the bedroom and hung it up. He noticed that her eyes followed him as he went by her but he didn't so much as turn. His back to her, he said from the closet, "Are you comfortable there?"

"Yes. Quite."

He went into the bathroom in his robe and turned on the shower. It felt good after the long flight. Just as some people start singing or talking to themselves in the shower, he found that he did some of his most freewheeling thinking there. Mostly thoughts, however, that weren't worth two cents later, although occasionally there was something that he'd hurry to scribble down. Now he found himself thinking in a fragmentary way about his father. It always came as a little surprise whenever he thought of him, though it shouldn't in England; his father had been born in England, probably still had family here.

The poor, sad son of a bitch. Red hair that turned almost white at thirty, and the constant cigarettes and yellowed fingers. Disbarred at thirty-two—for what reason, Haywood never knew: his mother had taken off with him and wouldn't let him even bring up his father's name. And all she'd done was marry some other loser.

He'd seen his father only once after that, three days after his eleventh birthday and only a few months, it turned out, before the poor sucker died.

"So you're a chess player, eh?" his father said. "Let's see how good you are."

It took him only five moves, and a part of him regretted it immediately. So, he'd never shown his father the stunt where he could remember any number of digits you called off, hundreds, three hundred one time before he got bored; could rattle them off front-ward or backward. It was one of the things, he was sure, that got him the scholarship to Penn; the dean who'd handled the interview, his eyes became this big.

Sometimes he felt that learning to do that had helped give him a philosophy, was one of the things that helped guide him the rest of his life. He had tried, at first, to memorize just eight digits. And it was the most he could do. But then over the months it became fifteen, thirty—he'd begun to see them in his mind, as on a blackboard—and finally it was endless, as far as he knew. Maybe it was the awareness that he had unknown abilities waiting to be tapped, plus being poor and not wanting to be, plus maybe something genetic that gave him absolute belief in himself, a drive to push forward—whatever, there was no way he was going to remain a civil engineer working for someone else. So, he started his own company. Soon he had offices abroad. Then he began to diversify. He understood, early on, the impact high tech was going to have on the world; and against advice he invested in a small firm making pocket calculators, took it over, and developed it into a giant. Meanwhile, he'd gotten into the manufacture of personal computers and video games. Today the Decton Corporation owned or controlled scores of companies. They weren't all high tech, of course—one holding was a Caribbean resort— but he was always searching out the technologies of the future, often making his moves on a simple hunch and then dragging his executives after him.

He came out of the bathroom in his robe. The young woman sitting by the bed looked up again from her magazine. But he stretched out on the bed and picked up the phone. He hadn't reached his friend near Rome, and was trying him again.

He knew without looking at her that she was watching him for a signal. He'd had her twice before, never in London, though: once in Budapest, the other time in Vienna. It was a small twist in his character, he imagined, but one that gave him pleasure—knowing

125

that a woman had to fly to him for just a night or just a few hours, had to use a passport, perhaps cross a time zone; and, perhaps more than that, knowing it was one of those women who are admitted with quiet quickness to palaces and embassies, who stand and wait by the shoulder of financiers at gaming tables. Even more erotic, possibly: he never asked them their full names or where they were from.

At the same time, though, there was a touch of anxiety. Why should he feel any anxiety?

There was no reason for it, he'd failed only two or three times in his life, but there was still a sense of nervousness at the beginning, even with his wife after all these years, and even with these women: perhaps especially with these women who, discreet as they were, could compare you with the best.

He had his friend on the phone now.

"Louis, Ed. How you doing?"

"Hey. Where are you?"

"You don't think I'm in the States, do you? When did you know me to spend money foolishly?"

"Did I hear you're interested in a shipping line?"

He looked over at her and opened his robe completely. She immediately rose and reached in back for her zipper.

"Why? Do you have one in mind?"

Watching her, tall and occasionally flinging her hair as she undressed, he wondered would she remember. She remembered. She stood at the side of the bed, naked except for high heels, and began to rub a white cream on her breasts and then down her belly and on the insides of her thighs, and out on her buttocks, turning to look at him all the while, then putting first one high-heeled foot up on the bed and then the other as she rubbed in the cream, eyes always on him.

126

She stood there now, staring at him, hands molding her breasts, nipples between her fingers.

"I hear the Marsison Line can be had," Louis was saying.

"I think I'll pass on that one. Know of anything else?"

He nodded slowly to her. She sat down on the edge of the bed. Starting with his chest, her long fingers worked the cream into him.

He deliberately remained on the phone for almost ten minutes. He wanted her to see how long he could stay ready.

Edwin Haywood looked out the rear window as the Rolls moved with the flow and halt of the early-morning London traffic. The young woman had left at close to three in the morning, perhaps to go to the city she'd come from, perhaps to another. He was no longer surprised or worried about having barely felt his own climax; that frequently happened when he couldn't completely close his mind to the next day's work.

They were pulling up now to the entrance of a modern, seven-story building near Piccadilly Circus. Haywood waited until Patrick, who was sitting with the chauffeur, opened the door for him. They got off the elevator at the seventh floor, at the executive offices of Beacham Industries, Ltd., a subsidiary of the Decton Corporation. Hayward walked to the thickly carpeted office of the president, the older of the two men who had met him at the airport.

For the next half hour they discussed Beacham's latest acquisition, a brewery in Holland. They were just finishing up when Howard Tompkins entered the office. Haywood shook hands with the attorney, who sat down quietly without interrupting the conversation. Tompkins, a graduate of Yale Law School and a member of a socially prominent family that had lived on Philadelphia's Main Line for generations, had been Haywood's attorney for the past twenty-one years. He'd just spent three days on the continent, and had flown in from West Germany last night.

"Well, Howard, how's it going?" Haywood said, turning to him.

"So far, perfect."

Haywood watched as Tompkins reached down to open his attaché case. Sometimes, as now, Haywood was particularly aware of his mixed feelings toward him: envy of that lean, classically handsome face, with the shiny white hair. At times, in Tompkins's company, he even felt puffy and gross. But along with these feelings was an undercurrent of scorn. For his background. All those generations of "people with horses marrying people with horses," as Haywood once put it to his wife, had weakened Tompkins, he felt. Why else would he have such an underlying feeling of insecurity about his abilities? Haywood had sensed that about him at their first meeting, when Tompkins was a young lawyer whose only clients were the few his family had directed his way. And that, combined with his obviously tremendous legal mind, had attracted Haywood to him.

"As of yesterday," Tompkins said, after checking through a couple of papers, "we have forty-one percent of Krantz stock. We'll be over fifty by next week."

He was referring to an industrial-robot manufacturing company in West Germany. The Decton Corporation was trying to buy controlling interest in it, but the company was battling the attempt to take it over.

"I'm absolutely confident about it," Tompkins said.

"Good." Haywood had been annoyed with himself for months because he hadn't gotten into robotics sooner. The possible applications for reprogrammable robots were, of course, almost limitless—not only in repetitive or unsafe jobs in factories and labs, or out in space, but as far as the human imagination could go.

From what he'd learned, Krantz Autotechs was on the verge of new breakthroughs.

So that was the company, no other, that he wanted.

"What about the doctor?" he asked.

"He started making noises that he's gotten all sorts of other offers, but he won't be any problem."

"I mean when's he supposed to be here?"

Tompkins looked at his watch. "He was supposed to be here ten minutes ago." He went to the glass door and peered out. "No."

If there was anything Haywood hated, it was lateness. This, he thought, is a mark against you, mister.

Actually, most of his search committee had some reservations about the doctor. Not about his brains, but his personality, his ability to be part of a team.

Not that he always listened to his search committee. He generally trusted his hunches more.

Five minutes later, while they were continuing their conversation about Krantz Autotechs, there was a tap on the glass. A secretary stood there with a slender, ashen-faced man. Haywood was a little jolted as he walked in. He knew Dr. Montana was only forty-three, but he looked sixty-five. He would never recognize him as the man on the cover of *Time* and *Newsweek*. Yet it was only three years since the scandal had broken.

129

Chapter 20

Carla woke with a feeling of well-being, of having slept well, of having had a good dream which she could not remember but would like to reenter. As she lay there, she relived fragments of yesterday—all of it good, all about Matt: of his going out to play with a friend (only for about a half hour, but still . . .), of having a fairly decent lunch (not dinner, though, but that could be one of those things), and, most important, of not complaining once. Then gradually, she felt a spiraling uneasiness which widened into dread.

Monday. Today was Monday.

How would he be when it was time to go to school?

She glanced quickly at the clock on the night table. Almost six-thirty. Matt's alarm was always set for seven.

She took a shower and washed her hair. She blow-dried it carefully in front of the bathroom mirror, tilting her head first one way and then the other. Then she went through a much more prolonged procedure than usual to select her clothes. She settled on a dark gray skirt and a pastel cashmere turtleneck that felt good as she slipped it on. Matt's alarm went off as she walked downstairs to the kitchen.

She stopped, listening.

He had turned it off. Now she heard the flushing toilet, then the usual sounds of him padding around, and finally the comforting opening and closing of drawers.

Letting out a breath of relief, she went into the kitchen and set out plates, putting on coffee for herself and Mrs. LeVine.

"Mommy."

She turned. He was standing in the doorway, still in pajamas. The words came out with a cry. "My tummy hurts."

He was sobbing so pitifully she had to steel herself against turning the car around and heading home. She had let him stay home from school yesterday, after all, and had taken him to his pediatrician who, after examining him carefully and finding nothing, told her what she knew. You mustn't give in to it. You must be firm, gentle in a sense but firm.

God only knew how you managed that. Whoever wrote the textbooks should have had to do it.

But it was true, she knew it was true.

She parked the car on a little side street, away from the eyes of the children converging on the school. She turned to him. He was sobbing convulsively.

She said, "I know it takes an awful lot of courage for you to go to school, and I want you to know I'm real proud of you."

"I can't go! My tummy hurts! *My tummy hurts!*"

"Matt, stop it! Stop it! You've got to go! You hear me? You've got to go!"

"No!"

"You don't want me to have to walk in there with you, do you?"

He continued sobbing.

"Do you?"

He shook his head. Staring down, he began pawing at his eyes. Once in a while he would let out a little gasp and his body would shake.

She wanted to say, "Matt, I love you so much," but was afraid it would trigger the crying all over again. So she made herself say, "All right, now say good-bye to me."

Instead, he flung open the door and began striding toward the school.

Halfway there he accidentally dropped his books. He bent to pick them up, but they kept tumbling from his hands, and, in between, he wiped at his eyes. She watched, fighting against running out and helping him and then bringing him home; watched, letting herself cry at last.

She called at four, the time he usually came home, and Mrs. LeVine said very quietly yes, he was there, he'd just come in, he seemed—you know—all right.

"Has he said anything to you?"

"No."

"He didn't eat anything, did he?" He usually had milk and cookies.

"No."

"Where is he?"

"In his room."

She wondered if she should talk to him, decided against it, decided to try to act toward him as though it had been just a day. Oh, Christ, just a day! A day waiting for the school or Mrs. LeVine to call and say

that he had to be picked up or that he'd run away or—
A murderous, murderous day!

"Do you have everything you need for dinner? Can I pick something up on the way home?"

"No, we're fine."

"All right, then I'll see you about six-thirty."

She felt a little better now, knowing he was home; a thousand vibrating wires gradually slowed down in her. A member of the medical staff called to ask if he could stop by; it turned out he wanted advice on dosages of antidepressants, and for the first time that day she was able to give something her full attention. Afterward she met with another member of the medical staff to discuss her diagnosis of one of the patients he'd asked her to see.

But when Dr. Raphael, the director, came in from the next office to discuss what he felt was a bad attitude on the part of one of their residents, her mind was filled again, her thoughts racing to Mark and Samuel Devereaux, to Mark and Stephen Cohen, then back to Mark and Samuel Devereaux.

Who was Samuel Devereaux? Of all the psychiatrists he could have seen, how had he ended up with Mark? And again, always again, why hadn't Mark told her about him?

"So, I don't think I'll say anything to him just yet," Raphael was saying. "I'll give him this week. Well, I guess I'll be heading home." He walked to the door. "You know, I think I'll take the wife out to dinner. I'm in the mood for Chinese."

"Enjoy."

"Oh, I will, I love Chinese. Good night."

"Good night."

The instant he left, she picked up the phone. For the past few moments she had been wondering if there had

ever been anything in the newspapers about Devereaux. And if Ross, through his newspaper connec-
tions, could find out for her.

Matt had just a few french fries for dinner. Spitting
one of them out now, he sat back and stared at her, as
though defying her to say something. When she said
nothing—deliberately said nothing—he got up
abruptly and ran upstairs to his room, slamming the
door.

She looked at Mrs. LeVine. Then she stood and
went up to his room. She opened the door. He was
sitting on the bed, his arms crossed on his chest.

"Get your shoes off the bed."

He didn't move.

"Now. Get those shoes off the bed! All right. That's
better. Now I want to see you start your homework."

"I don't have any!"

"Then pretend you do."

He walked over to his desk and sat down. He didn't
move for several moments, but finally he reached
down angrily and opened his schoolbag, taking out a
copybook and pencil. The way he opened it and
looked it over, and the way he began to write in it, she
knew he had homework. She stood there for several
more moments. "I want you working at that desk
when I come back."

She went downstairs, the drumming within her
again. She sat at the table, pushed away her plate.

Mrs. LeVine said, "He'll be fine."

"Yeah. But will I?"

Spreading, it was still spreading. To school phobia.
To behavior in general.

*Children don't always show their depression the
way adults do.*

134

True enough. But always for other parents, for couples sitting by her desk.

She stood to take her dishes and silverware into the kitchen. She looked at the clock. Ross had called earlier to say that a friend of his had photocopied several clippings on Devereaux, that he'd drop them off.

Something had to be wrong with her, it really did. To be still so obsessed like this when she had such a disturbed child.

He came by about eight o'clock, in jeans, white sneakers, and a thin blue windbreaker. He seemed to sense her terrible distress. He handed her a manila envelope. "I was told there're four clips."

"Please come in."

"That's okay. No, I'll be on my way. It was just a short walk."

"Please. Just for a few minutes." It was wrong to have him do her a favor and then let him run off. Inside, she said, "Would you like a drink?"

"No, thanks. Really."

"How about a cup of coffee? I'm going to have some."

"In that case."

While he waited in the living room, she went into the kitchen. She started to go right back, but instead took the photostats from the envelope and began glancing at them. One was about a prediction on the economy that Devereaux had made to a financial writer, another about a groundbreaking ceremony, the other about his work for the United Fund, and the fourth about some sort of an awards ceremony. Then she found herself reading them carefully.

Sixty-nine. A captain in the Second World War.

Cofounder, of course, of Bessinger's. Board member of a number of companies.

She stopped all at once, frowning.

A few years ago Devereaux had received the man of the year award from an orphanage in the neighborhood in Brooklyn where he was born. Bay Ridge. Where Mark had lived.

Chapter 21

If she could only fall asleep, she had to get some sleep! She tried reading—some journal articles, a novel, the *Smithsonian*—but she couldn't concentrate, her mind only raced more. She tried TV two different times, pressing the remote with a kind of desperation, but even though she finally found an old movie that she would ordinarily find calming, she couldn't lose herself in it. She switched off the set again, then the night-table lamp, determined to make another effort to sleep but knowing that the very trying, the working at it, would keep her awake.

The rain, which had started about ten, soon after Ross had left, was not only patting at the windows but overrunning the rainspouts—there had to be a ball or leaves up there. She didn't want to think about the time. The last time she'd looked, at least an hour and a half ago, it was going on two.

Mark and Devereaux from the same neighborhood—probably just a coincidence. But when you added that he'd been the one Mark worked for, that he'd ended up as Mark's patient, that Mark had kept all of this a secret from her . . .

It stirred up all the questions. But engulfing everything now, she realized, was her anger at Mark. For being crazy. For fucking up. For causing all of this.

She lay there, trying to calm herself.

Thoughts of Ross, little flickering pictures, kept breaking through. She didn't want to let him in all the way, though, as if that would be only in retaliation. So—just the little pictures. The look on his face when she had come back from the kitchen—his sensing that something else had gone wrong. And then the intent way he'd listened when she'd told him about the clipping.

He was in now completely, his chair pulled close as they talked.

"With everything that's been thrown at you, how can you call yourself paranoid?"

Should be proud of yourself, the way you're handling it all . . .

When she awoke, it was morning.

She left McCallum General at four to pick up Matt and take him to Dr. Mackey. She pulled into the garage, but left the door open; they would be leaving in just a few minutes. As soon as she entered the house, he began screaming to her from his room. "I'm not going! Not going!"

Mrs. LeVine walked down; apparently she had been in his room with him. She said softly, "He's been very upset since he came home."

He was sitting on the bed, staring at her with bulging eyes, face red, fists clenched. He looked as if he might spring at her as she came close. She kneeled next to him, tried to hold him, but he yanked himself away.

"Please, darling, talk to me, please talk to me. Why don't you want to go? Dr. Mackey loves you."

138

"I'm not going! Not going!" He broke into tears. This time he let her hold him, but only for a few moments. Then he tore away and stared at her, his chest heaving, obviously terrified she would try to force him to go.

"You don't have to go, sweetheart." She was touching his cheeks, his hair. "No more crying. Please, sweetheart, please, no more crying."

He gradually calmed down, but turned away when she tried to kiss him. She went into her room and called Mackey. His secretary answered and put her through right away.

Mackey came on, urgency in his voice. "Carla, is something wrong?"

"Bill, it's a mess. He doesn't want to come in. He's been screaming, crying. The only way I could calm him was to say he didn't have to go in. What do I do? I don't know what to do."

"First, try to calm down, take it easy. Did you—ask him why?"

"Yes. I couldn't get a word out of him. He was hysterical."

"All right, let it go at that. Do you hear me? Let it go at that, don't try to force him. It could be just a thing he has against me. But he's got to see someone."

"I know. That's what scares me. He won't want to go."

"Let's worry about that when the time comes. The first thing is to get him to a top child psychiatrist. I feel very guilty about this, I should have insisted—"

"Bill, don't. Please."

"Do you have anyone in mind?"

She thought, then mentioned two she had heard very good things about. He said, "Yes, they've got very fine reputations. Let me just offer something for whatever it's worth, though. We've got three top people here. They knew Mark, which can help, can speed things up. And, of course, I can work very closely with them.''

There was one in particular he recommended very highly, he said.

William Mackey stared at the phone, as though it were a gun that had almost gone off. Why was he so shaken? Even if the child had said anything, what could he have said? That he didn't like Dr. Mackey? Was afraid of him? That Dr. Mackey made him cry and told him that mommy might die? That he talked about sad things?

There was nothing Matt could say that he couldn't explain away as part of the child's problem.

But there wouldn't have been a thing to be worried about in the first place if Mark hadn't lied to her. There would have been absolutely no problem. Not that he couldn't understand some of the lies—but why about where you were born and raised? Why that nonsense about tankers?

Big man. Had to be a big man. Father in stocks and bonds. Mother—whatever the hell he said his mother was. Why that?

Had to be a big man. Or was it all the result of making just one wrong turn? That was something he knew well—one wrong turn leading to other wrong turns, and then all your life paying.

He looked at the bottom drawer of his desk. He could picture the flat little pint bottle under the papers. Just go to the door and close it and come back and open the drawer and unscrew the cap, and then the good burn, and then just a few squishes of mouth spray. But he fought it off, not that he wouldn't do it later, but he was meeting with a committee of volunteers about the annual fund-raising ball and he needed a clear head, needed the pain that cleared the head.

"Hello," Samuel Devereaux said.

The word came out clearly. And the face that spoke the word looked fairly clear too.

Mackey, who had stopped by to look in after the meeting, stared at him, stunned. He had expected him to be in bed or slumped over in the chair, head too heavy to raise. But, though he seemed somewhat withered in that chair, it was as though he had broken through chains. And in a sense he had.

Where did he get the strength, the will, whatever it was?

"Hello," he said again.

Oh, old man, Mackey thought in panic. I can't help you anymore.

Chapter 22

That was awfully nice of Mr. DeTurk, Sandy was thinking as she walked out of the hospital to her car. She had stopped to look in on Mr. Devereaux before leaving for home, as she did all her favorite patients, and there was Mr. DeTurk standing by his bed, fluffing up his pillow. It really took her by surprise—he always seemed so gruff, barely the type. In fact her opening the door and catching him at it seemed to embarrass him.

Well, shows you. You just shouldn't judge people.

Sandy Picarcwiz got into her car and, as usual, held her breath until it started. It caught. Actually it was her boyfriend's car; he didn't like her taking public transportation nights, and he didn't need it since he worked at the McDonald's near her home. Manager. Most nights he'd pick her up but tonight he didn't really know when he'd be getting off.

She liked the idea of him worrying about her.

But he wanted to marry her, and she didn't know how she felt about that.

She loved him, she guessed; certainly she liked him. But if she got married now she'd have to keep working, and she didn't want to be a nurse's aide all her life. After all, she was only eighteen. She used to have thoughts about going to cosmetology school, but this job was making her see things differently. She liked doing hair, but *hair* wasn't like *people*. She found she liked working with people, the worse the cases the better. She couldn't see herself ever becoming an RN, but maybe a licensed practical.

There was really no difference between the two when you got right down to it; you still helped people. And like one of the patients said, a woman no less, you're too pretty to be an aide all your life.

That was no reason *not* to be an aide; still it was flattering.

Well, she'd see.

She headed for Jimmy's house, to say hello to his parents and wait for him. Then he'd drive her home. First though, they'd stop and make love. She didn't particularly like making love in a car. The only times she ever came, funny, were in Jimmy's house, when of course his parents weren't home.

Jimmy, who called himself an amateur psychologist, said it was because it was something like being married.

Maybe so.

That was so nice about Mr. DeTurk.

She stopped for a red light. She always kept the doors locked, but she checked to make sure. Locked. She turned on the radio, but turned it off because the motor was threatening to stall. She gave it gas, in place, and it ran smoothly again. She pulled away.

Jimmy, this car.

She turned onto Jimmy's street, looking for a spot. It was almost midnight. That was late, but in summer, when it got real hot, people would be sitting on their stoops.

143

She stopped the car near his house, picked up her handbag, and started to slide out. Suddenly something exploded against her face—a fist—then again.

She fell back into the car. She barely felt her panties being yanked down, barely felt her legs going open; felt nothing, now, but the hands around her throat, squeezing.

Chapter 23

Dr. Mary Sundstrum had a hearty, booming voice that Carla had always associated with big, horsey-set women. But a certain warmth and tone of reassurance also came across on the phone. "No, no," she said when Carla apologized for having been put through to her while she was with a patient, "I told my secretary to do that. Bill said you'd be calling. He called me about nine this morning and he said, 'Mary, you've got to see this child tomorrow,' and I said, 'Bill, *tomorrow!*' and he said, 'Mary, do me a favor.' Then when I heard the story, there was no question. You've really been through it. Will tomorrow be all right?"

"I can't begin to tell you how much I appreciate that."

"Well, no need to. Let me see in my book here. If I juggle things around, the best time for me would be five o'clock. Five o'clock?"

"Fine."

"Let me mark it down. Now I generally like to meet with the parents and child together for a few sessions before I see the child alone, but Bill has filled me in and I'd like to get started with the child. We'll meet together off and on as we go along. In the meantime I'd like to have a longer conversation with you just to make sure I have certain things right. Could you call me tonight?"

"Of course."

"Let me give you my home phone."

Afterward, Carla sat limply at her desk, every tension released from her body.

"We're going to do fine, Doctor," Dr. Sundstrum had boomed. "So you just try to take it easy."

And for the first time in a long while she felt that she almost could. Although she had never met Mary Sundstrum, she knew her by reputation. She had, however, met her husband on a couple of occasions—a pleasant, almost typically Scandinavian-looking fellow in his forties. Mark had introduced him to her. He was a psychiatrist, too, in the adult division.

Matt was crying and holding back as Carla, her hand locked in his, strode with him from the parking lot to Cartwell Institute's three-story Youth Center. Near the front steps she stopped and kneeled down, trying once more. "Matt, please, don't make me drag you in there. Nobody's going to hurt you."

"I don't want to go," he wept.

"But why? You don't tell me why." All she could get out of him was an incoherent jumble. "Scared." "Bad man." "Don't want to draw." Nothing made sense. "I told you, she's a wonderful, wonderful lady. Lots of children go to her. Please, Matt, just walk with me, don't make me drag you."

But he kept crying softly, even though he stopped resisting as they walked in and took the elevator to the third floor. Maybe she was projecting her own feelings, but the lobby and then the elevator seemed particularly hushed. The morning paper had carried a front-page story of the rape-murder last night of a young nurse's aide from here—such a pretty girl, from her high school graduation picture—and everyone seemed subdued, grave, even the few who smiled.

Dr. Sundstrum had apparently just stepped from her office with a child and was standing in the waiting room talking to the mother. After they left, she turned with a smile and held out her hand to Carla; then she looked at Matt with that same smile. "I think we all ought to go into the toy room," she said.

She looked almost the way Carla had imagined, though much thinner: tall, with short graying sandy hair.

There was something about her appearance and manner that bolstered the sense of reassurance that had come across on the phone; and this was enhanced even more by the look of her office, which, floor scattered with toys and coloring books and walls Scotch-taped with drawings, suggested healthy, vigorous children. Carla could see she enjoyed getting down on the floor with them.

And Matt, clutching at Carla, seemed to relax gradually as Sundstrum knelt before him, talking to him, asking him did he like that engine over there, or what about that fire truck? And soon Sundstrum had him playing with the truck. She looked up at Carla. Her lips said: Say good-bye.

"Matt, I'm going to be leaving for a few minutes."

"No!" He stood up. "I don't want you to go!"

"I'll be right outside. Or I may take a walk down the hall."

Sundstrum spoke to him soothingly: of course

Mother would be back, and look at this over here, this little motorcycle with the man who comes off; and as Matt began playing with it, she raised her eyes to Carla, who walked out, closing the door quietly.

She sat for about ten minutes in the waiting room. She couldn't believe she could feel this calm, this good about Matt. She stood up, hesitating to leave in case Sundstrum or Matt wanted her, but she had the absolute feeling that they wouldn't. And while she was here she might as well do what she would only have to do later by phone.

She walked across the enclosed, windowed bridge that joined the Youth Center to the adult hospital. She went to the front office on the first floor. The manic-depressive patient whom she had admitted here to be stabilized on lithium had been discharged last week, but she would be admitting a new patient—a middle-aged man she'd been treating for depression following the amputation of his right leg. He was being discharged from the surgery floor and there were no available beds at present in McCallum's small psychiatric unit. She hated putting him in a psychiatric hospital but he was definitely suicidal and had no one at home to look after him.

She arranged for him to be admitted at the end of the week, then started back to Dr. Sundstrum's office. But she found herself drawn to Helene Tysdal's room. Although Mrs. Tysdal wasn't lying in bed, it seemed they had simply lifted her up and transferred her to a sitting position. She sat tied in a chair, silent, rigid, eyes wide and fixed.

The head nurse, a bony-thin blonde in her late forties, came and stood with Carla in the doorway.

Carla went out to the hall with her. "I'm curious. What is she being given?"

"She was on Thorazine, now Haldol. She always

148

did very well with Thorazine, but it's hardly touching her, so Dr. Mackey switched over."

"What about electroshock?" Mackey, she knew, frequently used it when drugs failed.

"It's never done any good with her. And the last time she was in she gave us a real scare with it. She stopped breathing and things were pretty hairy until we got her back."

Carla went back and looked at her for several moments. The nurse was still standing there when she came out. As they walked away together, Carla said, "Did you happen to know the girl who was killed?"

"Oh my, did I. She worked on this floor."

"Oh, God."

"We're all absolutely destroyed."

Carla shook her head as she walked on. Then, though aware it would only be frustrating, that there was no way she could learn anything from him, she walked around the corner to Samuel Devereaux's room. He wasn't there. She looked around, wondering if he was in the lounge. The head nurse, who had returned to the nursing station, said, "Can I help you, Doctor?"

"I'm looking for Mr. Devereaux."

"Oh. I'm sorry. He died in his sleep sometime last night. We found him this morning."

Mary Sundstrum, sitting on the floor with Matt, watched as he worked at a puzzle. Then he began playing again with the motorcycle, pushing it around while making grinding sounds in his throat. He liked this much better than puzzles. But he liked the balloon figure of a clown even more; he went back to it and socked it and it rolled on its back and bounced up. He hit it several more times, laughing.

She drew in a breath, feeling herself grow tense.

149

"Matt?"

He didn't seem to hear her. He was with the fire engine again, scooting around on his knees with it.

"Matt?"

He looked over at her now.

"Mommy doesn't spend much time with you, does she?"

Chapter 24

Henny, who had just begun, yelled to the others as he stood against the tree, "Hey, wait up! Hey!" But his shouts were swallowed by the woods. Those bastards! Asked 'em to wait! "Hey!" Petrified at the thought of getting lost, he put it back on the run, zipping up. "Hey guys! Yo! Hey!"

That morning, he and three friends had piled into a car to take a ride and had ended up forty miles away, in the Pocono Mountains. Then Mike, who was driving—he'd just turned sixteen and was the first to get a license—had said let's stop and do some exploring. And they were really having fun—until this, until they had to be wise guys.

Henny was standing still, trying to listen for sounds. Could hear 'em. Couldn't see 'em, trees and brush were too thick, but could hear 'em. The movement of branches. Now a few giggles; they were waiting for him to start forward so they could begin running away again.

"Babies! Are you guys babies! What babies!"

But he walked toward the giggles. As he'd thought, he heard them pull back.

"You know what you guys can do! Remind me to turn in my mother's coupons and get you some brains!"

Hell with 'em, he was heading back to the road. But where was the road? He started walking to his left, feeling a lot better because—oh, those babies!—once in a while when he stopped he could hear those sounds behind him. About twenty more yards and the woods suddenly opened up to the full afternoon sun and a rutted lane. This should take him out to some kind of road. In fact, now that he was standing out on the lane he could see a car parked down there.

It looked abandoned. The windshield, the hood, were filmed and streaked with dirt. He walked toward it slowly. Behind that coated, filthy windshield— what? Figures? His imagination?

Cautiously, fighting against running the hell out of there, he edged around the front of the car, then leaned forward from a little distance to look into the window on the passenger side—and took a fast step back with a gasp.

Now he was running toward his friends, who were just emerging from the woods.

They followed him back.

Yeah. Yeah. Two mummies. Yeah.

Carla was with a patient when she was summoned to the phone.

"This is Mrs. Goode at the school." The school nurse. "I hate to bother you at the hospital, Doctor, but there was no answer at home. Matt's complaining of a headache."

"Does he have any fever?"

"No."

"Does he say anything else hurts?"

"No."

Carla said, "I would appreciate it if you would give him a Tylenol and have him lie down. I'd like him to stay in school if possible."

"I know that. I just wanted permission to give him something."

Receiver back on the hook, she stood by the phone at the nursing station, wondering where she would get the strength to go back to the patient. Matt mustn't think this could always be a way out for him; but at the same time, how did she really know that this time it wasn't something? And even if he wasn't physically ill, that didn't mean he didn't hurt. So many people weren't aware that psychosomatic pain really hurts, that it isn't the same as faking pain.

She was going to take him back to his pediatrician, even though she was sure he would still find nothing, that Bill Mackey and now Mary Sundstrum were right.

"He'll be all right," Mary Sundstrum had said. "But you've got to . . ."

And then everything Bill had told her.

Seriously depressed. Got to make him feel secure. Give him lots of attention. Has picked up that you think somebody did something terrible to his daddy.

"No, I wouldn't advise any medication at this time. His depression is based largely on reality, and we should deal with that. You can do far more than any medication could begin to do."

He should see me four times a week, she had added.

And you, I would advise that you keep seeing Dr. Mackey.

Detective Harris threw his hat on his desk and dropped into the swivel chair. Even the goddam chair was squeaking again. No matter how much oil he shot into the thing.

A squeaky chair, a trial that had gone fuck—how could the judge take some goddam ex-con's word over his?—a car that needed a new transmission, and a wife who had him lined up for another of those freak parties where everyone either was married to or living with a different color, or wrote or *painted,* for Christ's sake.

He'd had a couple calls. One was from a good stoolie, but it was absolutely nothing; the guy just wanted him to know he hadn't come up with anything yet on a series of holdups. The other slip of paper he just crumpled up and tossed in the wastebasket. That was an ex-con he'd busted several times who kept calling every few weeks to say he was still staying out of trouble.

He was on one knee now, the chair tilted on its back, squirting oil again and working the seat up and down. Standing up, he saw the sergeant motioning to him. He followed him into his office.

"Ray, this fellow Wayne Delman? He's not missing anymore."

"When did he show up?"

"Today. Dead."

The state police had just contacted them. His partially decomposed body had been found in his car in a heavily wooded section of the Poconos. With it on the front seat was the body of a young known male prostitute. The young man had apparently shot Delman and then himself.

". . . about seventy miles from Philadelphia," the young female newscaster was saying sonorously against the backdrop of a state police barracks. "The bodies were found by four young men who were walking through the woods. With me now . . ."

Carla, who'd just come home and had been in the kitchen when she'd heard Wayne Delman's name on

154

the six o'clock news, stood with a hand to her mouth as the reporter interviewed two of the youths.

As another story came on, Mrs. LeVine stared at her from the chair near the TV set. "That's absolutely dreadful."

Dead. The growing names. Mark. Stephen Cohen. Nora.

Then Devereaux, and now Wayne Delman.

She called Ross after Matt went to bed, to find out whatever he knew about the murder and also simply to talk to him.

"I just heard about it," he said. "I was going to call you. I'm absolutely floored."

"Did you have any idea he was a homosexual?"

"No. Not at all. But that's not what really gets me. It's the prostitute bit. What the hell did he need that for?" He paused. Then, concern in his voice, asked, "How are you doing?"

"Up in the air. It doesn't answer a single thing for me. It doesn't mean he wasn't involved. All it means is that now I'll never know."

"What are you doing right now?" he said, so abruptly it surprised her, and before she could answer, "Look, it's only nine, a little after. I'm only eight blocks away and I have this craving for beer. Can I pick you up?"

"Thanks so much, but I don't think so."

"It'll be a one-hour night, and you'll be doing me a big favor."

"Thanks. Really."

"And you might be doing yourself one. Just to get out a bit."

She thought about it. She was, she realized, afraid to leave Matt even though Mrs. LeVine was here. He might still be up, or might wake up, and want her.

"I can be there in, say, fifteen minutes. And you'll be back in one hour exactly."

"Well." She was still trying to think. Then, "Make it a half hour."

He came for her promptly and they walked two blocks to a restaurant-bar. It was almost empty. They took a booth; like the others, it was centered by an overhanging Tiffany lamp.

He said, "Would you like something to eat?"

"No, no. Thanks."

"What would you like to drink?"

"I was thinking—beer, maybe a brandy. No, I'm really not up to it. A Perrier."

"You sure?"

"Yes, that's fine."

After he gave their orders, he said, "I can't get over Wayne. As I said, it's not because he turned out to be gay or bisexual—though that does surprise me—but how he ended up."

She said quietly, "You still don't think he could have killed Mark?"

"It tells me I didn't know him, that's for sure."

"There're a lot of things I'll never know now. Did I tell you the old man Mark used to work for died?"

"No. When?"

"Day before yesterday. A heart attack. So that too. Ross, that man could have told me so much. I know it."

Their drinks came. They looked at each other until the waiter left.

"I know it," she repeated. "I'm a broken record, I know, but there's got to be a reason Mark didn't tell me he worked for him. Sometimes I tell myself it was because he was crazy. But it's not true. I lived with him. I know. There was a reason. And I just know that old man could have told me something important."

"I'm sure you're right."

"And I've never been more sure Mark didn't kill himself. I can't prove it, but I feel it, stronger than ever." She saw him frowning. "What are you thinking?"

"That I wish I could say you were wrong."

He'd never come right out and said anything like that before; she'd never known what he really believed about Mark's death.

"Tell me what you mean."

"What I'm saying is that I'd really like to think that Mark simply couldn't take things anymore and decided to cut out. I want to think that because then it's over, and it's a matter of you and Matt getting your lives back on track. This way it goes on and on. But so many damn strange things have turned up about Mark. And I guess it all boils down to this, I trust your feelings. They make sense."

"So what do I do?"

"What you have been doing. Keep after the police."

"Oh Christ, them. Then there's Bill Mackey and now Matt's new psychiatrist—Sundstrum. 'Pay more attention to Matt. You're not paying enough attention, you're running around digging for things and you're not giving him what he needs.' "

"Carla, I really don't see what you're doing wrong. I really don't."

She wanted to reach across the table and squeeze his arm. She felt she was going to cry. "I feel so damn guilty, Ross."

"About what? What have you done?"

She shook her head. "I don't know. I just feel so damn guilty."

"For Christ's sake, don't."

She sat back, took a quick nervous sip of her drink.

157

Her hand began to tremble and she set down the glass. His hand came over and held hers. She squeezed it briefly, smiled. "Thanks."

He leaned back. "For what? I haven't done anything."

"Yes, you have. You've been kind. I know I can call on you."

"Well, that you can."

"So, thanks."

"Okay." He smiled. "You're welcome."

She watched him sip his beer. Each bone in his face seemed placed just perfectly to give it strength. She wasn't aware, until now, that she had relaxed a little. She found herself wishing she wouldn't have to leave this place—the quiet colors of the Tiffany lamps, the bartender leaning on his elbow talking softly to someone—leave it to go into the blackness outside. It frightened her. Yet night had never frightened her before, even as a child.

"You're thinking," he said.

But she'd piled enough on him tonight. "I'm thinking," she said, looking at her watch, "that I'd better go."

"Would you like another Perrier? Or are you driving?"

She smiled. "No, that's it. But would you like another beer? I don't want to rush you . . . "

"No, I'll—just—drink—alone at home. And play the organ."

"Oh God, what an image."

"I forgot to mention my black cloak."

She squeezed his arm again, with a slight laugh. They walked quietly through the dark streets. Her heart had begun to quicken the moment they'd stepped outside. She found herself dreading leaving his calming presence. As they walked, she felt their arms begin to brush. Then she felt his hand fold gently over hers. He squeezed hard: it seemed to say, I'm with you. He relaxed his grip, occasionally touching her fingers. She could feel, it seemed, the complete texture of his skin. They said nothing.

At the house she took the key from her handbag but he took it from her, unlocked the door and pushed it open.

"Thank you so much, Ross."

"No. Thank you."

"Well, thanks to each other."

He kissed her on the cheek. His lips stayed there a moment, then his cheek pressed against hers. There was a faint, but somehow sharp, smell of aftershave on the grain of his cheek. She stepped back, but then, heart beating rapidly, let herself be led into the foyer. She sank against his chest as his arms closed around her. She barely reached his chin. She wanted those arms to stay tight around her, to enclose her from the world.

"Don't," she whispered.

But she let him lift her face. His lips were on hers now, gentle, barely open; they stayed just a few seconds, then went to one cheek and to the other. Now he held her again, knowing that was all she really wanted. She stepped back, looking up at him.

"Good night," he said.

"Good night."

"You're a courageous lady. Remember that."

"I'll try."

"I'll talk to you tomorrow."

He gave her a quick little kiss and was gone. She closed the door, bolted it, then leaned against it for a while. She felt dazed, confused.

He'd joined the whirl of everything that was happening to her.

Chapter 25

It was a little jolting, even though Ross had known that the story would probably be accompanied by pictures, to see Wayne Delman's face staring up from the front page of the morning paper. It was a younger face than he knew, with a smile he'd hardly ever seen. Next to it was a rogues' gallery shot of the killer—a young man of twenty-three, with a wisp of a goatee.

The bodies were, as the story put it, "partially nude." Wayne had been shot three times in the head, his killer once in the head. According to the police, the young man's fingerprints were on the gun, which was found between his legs on the front seat. He had lived in Philadelphia, had been arrested several times for prostitution, including once for rolling a "client." The autopsy had not been completed as yet, but the preliminary estimate was that they had been dead "about two months."

That would place their deaths around the time of Wayne's disappearance, two weeks after Mark's death.

He closed the paper and put it aside. The article on hemophilia he was doing for the *New York Times*

Magazine was taking forever. Not that he'd been working on it all the time; he'd had to stop to do a fast, short piece on biomedical engineering for a medical journal. Still, it felt like forever. And he was finding it hard to get his mind back on it now.

He felt so sorry for Wayne. It was goddam sad. How a person can screw up his life!

But soon his thoughts went back to Carla. He'd been thinking about her off and on all morning. Kaleidoscopic thoughts. Those big eyes. That raspy voice. The feel of her deep in his arms. The touch of her lips—it had been just a touch; he'd had to hold back from pressing in hard. And honest to God, like a kid, the feel of her hand as they'd walked.

But clouding everything was his concern for her. She was going through so much! Not only fighting on her own to get to the truth, but there were her problems with Matt, and all of that crap from the past, from Mark.

She talked of going crazy. Hell, anyone would go crazy from all that . . .

He looked at the word processor. But he still wasn't up to working. He went to the kitchen, where he always kept hot coffee. He didn't drink too much, but he liked it ready when he wanted it. He poured a cup and brought it back to his desk, black.

He took a few sips when the phone rang. It was Jeff Malmquist, calling from his office at Delman & Sharples. "Can you believe you were just in here talking about him? And all these months, here I've been thinking the guy's going to walk in here any day like nothing happened. That poor, poor bastard."

"That's exactly how I feel. I feel terribly sorry for him."

"You know? I knew that's how you'd feel. As far as I'm concerned, he was a real nice guy. But you can't talk to anyone around here. You ought to see all the creeps coming out of the woodwork."

"What do you mean?"

"The fag jokes. It's really sickening. In fact, we just had a real lulu. Eileen Troy? Wayne's secretary?" Ross recalled an attractive black woman. "Someone must have said something to her, or she overheard something, I don't know what, but the next thing I know she's screaming at a couple of people that he wasn't a homosexual, no way could he be a homosexual, she knew him like nobody knew him. She was so hysterical she had to go home."

"Obviously he was bisexual."

There was a long pause. "Ross. Look, I did call about him. But there's something else. Remember we were talking about my going free-lance? I've decided I really want to. Would we be able to get together one of these days? I could use some tips, some leads."

"Fine. Whenever. As I told you, there's a lot of work out there."

"Let me tell you what's happening. There's a rumor which I've heard is more than a rumor. It's that we're being sold. Well, I may chicken out, but I really don't want to just hang around, praying they're going to keep me on."

Several minutes later, Ross was quickly dialing Carla's number.

Carla looked up from her office to see the director of the consultation/liaison section standing in her doorway. It struck her right away that Dr. Raphael seemed uneasy.

"How's everything going?"

"Fine."

He came in partway. "How's your little fellow doing?"

She had told him Matt was seeing a psychiatrist, simply because she had to leave early, by four, to take him. "He's coming along."

"Look—ah—is there any way you can schedule the appointments later in the day? Or have someone else take him?"

"I'm trying to schedule them later. I'll work something out."

But he still seemed reluctant to go. He looked as if he were about to say something else, but changed his mind. "Well, I'll see you."

She stared after him. She was sure he had also stopped by to talk to her about her work, about something obviously being wrong, but had decided to hold off a while—as if he hoped she would take what he said about Matt as a general warning. Maybe she was being paranoid again, but she doubted it: too many times she'd come in late for a meeting or hadn't realized that a question had been directed at her or had felt her mind start to wander during a discussion.

Even now, with this, it was hard focusing her mind on patients.

She looked at her schedule for the afternoon. She had three appointments; then she would see Bill Mackey while Matt saw Sundstrum. She also had to talk to Sundstrum about changing the time. This four o'clock business was impossible. And there was no way she could send Matt with Mrs. LeVine or anyone else. It was a struggle getting him there as it was.

She would talk to her. Sundstrum would work something out.

Carla managed to finish her last patient at ten of four. She walked quickly back to her office, unbuttoning her lab coat as she entered. There were several messages on her desk, which she glanced at quickly.

One was from the husband of a patient; she would call him from home this evening. Another was from Ross. Her forefinger tapped out his number.

"Ross? Carla."

"How are you?"

"Fine. You?"

"Good. And Matt?"

"Oh, the same. I'm taking him to the institute now."

"I won't hold you. Listen, I just heard something. It may be just a rumor, but if it's right, it's quite a coincidence."

"Ross, what is it?"

What?

For moments, she held the phone from her ear, as though her arm had gone weak.

Delman & Sharples being bought out by Bessinger's?

Samuel Devereaux's company? The company Mark tried to wipe out of his past?

Chapter 26

She hated the way Bill sat behind his desk, staring at her silently with that goddam maddening psychiatric silence.

"Well, isn't it?" she demanded. "Don't you think it's—strange? Weird? After all, Bessinger's? Devereaux? Aren't you surprised? . . . *Bill*," she pleaded, "don't treat me like a—patient, like I'm sick."

"I'm listening, Carla."

"Oh, shit, I don't want to hear you're listening, I know you're listening, I want to hear you say something. Isn't it strange? I mean, of all the companies in this world? Bessinger's?"

He still said nothing.

She pulled in a breath, trying to calm herself. She thought of all the times she had done just this with patients, waited for them to talk out all their feelings, not wanting to interrupt, to cut them off, to cause them to digress.

But it was so hard, on the other side. It was so damn hard.

"And that woman"—Ross had mentioned the incident with Wayne Delman's secretary—"do you blame me? I don't see how I can talk to her, or why she'd want to talk to me, but can you blame me for wishing I could? After all, if she knew him that well, maybe she'd know something about him and Mark."

He kept looking at her. When he saw she wasn't going on, he said, "Let's say that Wayne Delman really did kill Mark. Let's just say it. And let's say that this woman knows all about it. Do you think she's going to tell you?"

"I didn't say that, Bill. And I didn't say I was going to try to talk to her. I said I only wished I could. Maybe—she might even know something that could put my mind at rest . . . Bill," she said, and again her voice was a plea, "do you have any idea what it's like to find you've been married to a blank? A face, words, some things we did together—but other than that, a blank?"

"Carla, you said not to treat you like a patient. I'm really not. This is what I'm trying to do. One," he tapped a finger, "I'm trying to keep you from *becoming* a patient. Two, I'm trying to help you not to get all involved in whether Bessinger's buys the drug firm, or whether it's United Steel or General Motors or your tailor. I'm trying to keep you from getting involved in what Wayne Delman said or didn't say to his girl friend. After all, his father committed suicide while he was in our care, he had a grudge against all of us, probably all of psychiatry. Most of all I'm trying to help you help Matt. But I don't seem to be able to convince you that you're hurting him, not helping him."

She lowered her head. She tented her hands over her face.

"Would you," she heard him say, "like to see someone else?"

She looked up, alarmed. "Bill, are you giving up on me?"

"My God, no. I just want you to feel free. Maybe you think that because we're friends—"

"Bill, no! Oh, no."

It frightened her, thinking of starting all over with someone else. And why change, when all of this was her fault, not Bill's?

Slowly, Mary Sundstrum went through page after page of her appointment ledger before looking up at Carla. "I'm afraid I'm completely booked for the next six weeks. I don't see how I can change anything around before then."

"Nothing at all in the evening?"

"That's what I've been looking for." She began flipping pages at random, looking here and there. "No. Solid."

"Well . . ." Carla rubbed at her temple, as though it was hard to think. "We'll see you tomorrow."

Mary Sundstrum watched them walk away, Carla holding Matt by the hand. She returned the ledger to the top drawer of her desk. For a few seconds she tried convincing herself that she couldn't have switched anything around, but she was too trained in being honest with herself to hold on to that thought. But she didn't feel anything more than a fast twinge of guilt. She had stopped feeling terribly guilty about the boy. After all, one of the things she was trying to do was save his mother's life.

She called her husband on his extension to see when they would be meeting for dinner.

Carla told him, as she drove, not to sit against the door; she was afraid it would fly open. But she had to ask him twice more before he moved. It was obvious that he didn't want to sit closer to her.

"And put the seat belt on. Matt, the seat belt, please? . . . Matt!"

Reluctantly he swung it around him. But he had trouble buckling it and let it go. She said nothing. She wanted to scream but forced herself to say nothing.

How do you handle all of it? How?

"Matt"—it burst out of her anyway—"put that seat belt on! I told you to put it on!"

This time he did. And the instant he did she felt a quick rise of tears. How pathetic he was! How lost!

"How about something to eat, darling? Mc-Donald's?"

He shook his head quickly.

"How about it?"

Again the quick shake of his head.

But she pulled into McDonald's anyway. For a while after she parked the car he didn't move, even though she'd opened her door. However, when she slid out, he opened the door on his side.

She watched him as he walked ahead of her on the parking lot.

They were both going to make it! They were going to make it because they came from fighting stock, from the loins of one hell of a tough little guy who won twenty-three out of twenty-six, all of them over his weight, and who even jumped over a bar to—

And was shot to death, it hit her. Shot to death.

She woke in the dead of night, thinking of the rumored sale. It stayed with her all through the morning, but she wasn't going to do anything about it. No more. That was it. Over. But then, after lunch, something broke inside her like a wave and she dialed the number of Pauley & Staub, the investment firm.

168

"Is Saul Osterman there, please? This is Dr. Carla Keller."

"I'll ring him."

He sounded surprised. "Hi there, how are you?"

"Saul, can you spare me a minute?"

"You want to come over?"

"No, no I mean on the phone."

"Oh, sure."

"Saul, have you heard anything about Bessinger's buying out Delman and Sharples?"

"No, when was this supposed to have happened?"

"I'm sorry, I didn't make myself clear. Someone told me that Bessinger's might be buying them out. And I'd like to find out if it's true. Would you have any way of finding out? I'd really appreciate it."

"Well, I'll check around."

"Do you know anything about Samuel Devereaux? He founded it. Was president. He just died."

"Yes, I read it. No, I really don't. All I remember reading was that he was supposed to be quite a philanthropist."

"Do you know who took over as president?"

"Not offhand, no."

"Saul, I hate to bother you, I really do. But this could be important to me. If Bessinger's is really buying them out, could you find out who the president is?"

"I'm sure. We should have their annual report."

"Thanks so much. As I say, I hate to bother you."

"No bother. I'll get back to you as soon as I can."

Hanging up, she debated about the next call, the hard one. She got out the phone book and looked up the number. Then she dialed slowly, still not sure she was going through with it.

"Delman and Sharples."

She was still debating. Then, "Eileen Troy, please."

After two rings: "This is Eileen Troy."

"Miss Troy, you don't know me. My name is Keller. Dr. Carla Keller."

"What did you say your name was? Dr. Keller?"

"Carla Keller."

A pause. "Was your husband Mark Keller?"

Chapter 27

Edwin Haywood sat near one of the drawing-room windows, waiting for Patrick's car to appear on the circular drive. Each morning his bodyguard came here from his home to accompany him to the firm's office building in center city. Haywood rarely left the house later than seven. It was eight minutes to seven now.

A few minutes later, he stood as his bodyguard pulled onto the drive and got out. Haywood's chauffeur, also waiting, walked out of the house, parked the car in back, and returned with Haywood's Rolls-Royce.

"How've you been, Patrick?" Haywood had come outside only when his Rolls pulled up.

"Fine, sir." Patrick waited until Haywood got in the back and then sat with the chauffeur. When they reached the Decton Building, Patrick got off at the fourth floor to go to his own office while Haywood went up to the eighth.

Haywood was the first person to arrive on the executive offices floor. It was five days after his return from Europe, and his first appointment would be with Howard Tompkins, who'd returned yesterday morning. They had seen each other at the Academy of Music last night—there had been a fund-raising affair for Cartwell Institute—and afterward they and their wives had gone to Haywood's club for a quiet toast to Decton's finally having acquired control of the West German robotics company. It had happened a few days sooner than even they had thought.

Tompkins showed up promptly at eight-thirty. "Here," he said, drawing a folder from his attaché case, "are the signed contracts—Dr. Severn's, Dr. Michelson's, Dr. Podowsky's." With Dr. Montana's, which they got in England, that made the key four. The other two the search committee had recommended, Dr. Schemenko and one of his assistants, would be more of a problem; but Tompkins felt more confident about helping them defect.

"So just two to go," Haywood said. "Very good."

But from the way he placed his hands on his desk, it was apparent he was ready to move on to other things. And as soon as Tompkins left, he was on the phone. After all, that was just one of his projects.

Walter DeTurk, chief of security at Cartwell Institute, liked spring best of all the seasons. He used to like the fall best, because of the hunting; but even though he still loved to hunt, the fall had come to stand for the beginning of winter, which he hated, especially here at this place. Maybe even because of this place. It was bad enough being with nutsies all day, let alone being with them when the days were as gray as old bath water. In spring, though, the grounds burst into color: the forsythia at the entrance, the blazing cherry trees, and the apple blossoms.

He pulled into his spot on the parking lot and got out and looked around, taking it all in.

Well, now to the nutsies.

He walked to the entrance, a solid figure in short sleeves, carrying his suit jacket over his thick arm. He barely nodded at the guard near the front door. He walked down a long corridor to his office, hung up his jacket, went to the men's room for ten minutes with a security systems trade magazine, came back freshly scrubbed, and began going over the reports from the night men.

He stood up from his desk to make the first of his rounds, then sat back drumming his fingers on the desk top.

He didn't like the way Mackey was taking his time about reporting to him, was acting real big, sooo big. Well, big his ass.

He had thought he would stop in at his office for the report, but he was tired of going to him. He called interoffice, instead.

"Dr. Mackey's office."

"DeTurk. Doctor there?"

"Yes, one moment, Mr. DeTurk."

"Yes, DeTurk."

He leaned back in his chair. "You know, I haven't heard from you lately about what's going on with Keller."

Eileen Troy got to the hotel first and was waiting, as they'd arranged, by the large bulletin board in the lobby. Carla walked over to her from the revolving door, a woman in her late thirties, very black, who accentuated her skinny, rather grotesque features with large earrings and touches of color that made her strikingly attractive.

"Thank you so much for coming," Carla said.

Eileen Troy said nothing. They found two chairs, off by themselves.

"I really appreciate your coming," Carla said again.

She shrugged. "I'm a curious lady, Doctor. You said you wanted to talk to me about Wayne and your husband. All right, I'm here. First, what do you know about Wayne and me?"

"Just that I heard you said you knew him better than anyone."

"Oh. That. The scene." She smiled slightly, but seemed to be swallowing back a lump. "I'm glad it happened. It's out. You don't know how I always wanted it to be out. But not this way." She rubbed her palms. "So. So, Doctor?"

"Well, I called you out of desperation, really. An awful lot's been happening in my life since my husband died. I wouldn't know where to start to tell you. What I want to find out is how Wayne might fit into it. And if he doesn't, I want peace of mind on that."

"Wait a second, wait." Her eyes flared. "Do you think there might have been something between them? Doctor, Wayne was no homosexual! I don't care what the papers say, what the police say, he was not that way!"

"No, that isn't what I meant."

But she didn't seem to hear, or else simply wanted to let it all out. "Look, I'm no fool, I'm no kid, and I'm certainly not naïve. I know about bisexuals. I wouldn't be surprised if there were even trisexuals. But even if Wayne was a bisexual, no way would he be with garbage like that. And why in the woods? You know he had a place no more than fifteen miles from where they found him? Not his, really, a friend's. An A-frame. His friend went to Europe and gave him the key. So why—in the car? It doesn't make sense."

"Did you ever tell the police this?"

"When I first heard he was missing, I drove up there. It was locked up. There was no answer, no car. Later I called the police about it. Anonymously. They must have checked the place. . . . So, why not there? Why the car?"

"What are you saying?" Carla said, after a moment.

Eileen looked at her, as though she hadn't considered the question. Then she said, almost to herself, "I don't know what I'm saying." She shrugged. "He was with him. And he was killed by him. So what I'm really saying, I guess, is that I thought I knew him. We were so close; God, were we close. There wasn't anything we couldn't talk about. He was the finest, kindest, gentlest person I'd ever met in my life. He wouldn't hurt a fly, nothing, no one."

"I guess," Carla said quietly, "you're telling me something I wanted to learn from you."

"Which is what?"

"If you thought he was capable of—well, violence."

"I don't understand what you're saying."

"I know. I'm talking all around it. Look. I know in my heart my husband didn't kill himself."

Eileen frowned, as though she still didn't understand. Then softly, "No. Oh, no. Absolutely no. He felt your husband, others there, were responsible for his stepfather committing suicide; he was angry, he was frustrated, but killing someone? . . . No. God, no. Let me tell you something about Wayne and his stepparents. During the past few years he began feeling terribly, terribly guilty over them. He had a drinking problem—he was working on it, by the way, he'd joined AA—and they'd apparently had a rough time with it, his father cut him out of the business, let him have just a job. And Wayne felt terribly guilty. Why do you think he couldn't tell them about me? Then his stepmother was killed in an auto accident; you can imagine how he felt. And he was upset at how hard his stepfather was taking it. He even insisted on taking him to another doctor."

"A Dr. Cohen? Stephen Cohen?"

"I can't think of his name offhand. I don't know who his stepfather had been seeing before that, maybe your husband, but he took him to this other doctor—a GP or internist friend of his. But his stepfather only went once before he went into the hospital. So you can imagine what Wayne went through when he committed suicide. He not only had all this guilt, but this second doctor told Wayne he shouldn't ever have been hospitalized."

Carla's immediate reaction was: What a cruel thing for Cohen to say.

Chapter 28

She snapped awake at about four in the morning—as she had almost every morning for the past couple of weeks—an hour when the darkness seems thickest, fears never more real, problems never more maddening. What was it she used to say to patients who couldn't sleep? Try relaxation exercises, let your muscles go limp, try to think soothing thoughts, listen to soft music, don't try to solve problems, know that nobody ever died from lack of sleep.

Had she really ever said that? God, she'd had no idea how it felt to have every inner part of you in a frenzy.

She slipped out of bed, went into the bathroom and took out a small bottle of Valium. She had gotten it a few days ago but had resisted taking any so far. But that was silly, she had to calm down; more than that, this was going to be a particularly busy morning, she had an eight-thirty staff meeting, then was giving a lecture to internal medicine residents on masked depression. She had to be fresh, had to get a few more hours sleep. She washed down a pill and went back to bed.

She lay there, trying to think calm thoughts.

Mark.

Don't think of Mark. Try to sleep.

Wayne Delman. Stephen Cohen.

Don't think of them. Time enough later.

No homosexual, Eileen had said. And not with garbage like that. And why in a car in the winter woods, when there was an A-frame?

But it had been Eileen's heart talking, her hurt, her love, her despair.

Yet, wasn't that what everyone said about *her?* That she just couldn't face the fact of Mark's suicide?

There wasn't one single thing, from what she read in the papers, that linked Wayne Delman and his killer in life. According to the killer's friends, including his roommate, they'd never once heard him mention Wayne. He'd simply left his apartment one night to "turn a trick" and never returned.

And what of the killer himself? He hardly seemed the type of person who had feelings that would make him kill out of jealousy or "love" and then turn the gun on himself out of remorse or a tragic sense of loss.

She lay, struggling to sleep.

If someone could kill Mark and make it out to be—

And if it wasn't Wayne Delman who'd sent that clipping with the warning, then who? And why— again, again, again—a clipping of Stephen Cohen?

She opened her eyes, though only slightly, to bright sunshine. But she let her lids drop closed again. She started to sink back into sleep, relieved the night was over and with it the terror, and even the importance, of the beeswarm of thoughts and questions. She slept for a while longer, then her eyes opened again. And this time they sought out the clock on the bureau. Jesus God! She leaped to her feet, swept off her pajamas and

178

began seeking out clothes. How had she ever slept to twenty of ten?

She came downstairs, stuffing her blouse into her skirt. Mrs. LeVine looked at her from the kitchen.

"You should have wakened me!"

"The alarm went off and you slept through it and I thought that's what you wanted."

"Oh, God, I'm so late."

"I'm sorry."

She went to the closet for her thin topcoat. "Did Matt get off all right?"

"No, he wouldn't go."

"Oh, Jesus!" She came out of the closet without it. "Where is he?"

"In his room."

She hurried upstairs. He was sitting in his pajamas on the edge of his bed, staring at her as though he had been anticipating this. He immediately began to cry. "I feel sick."

"Get dressed! I'm taking you to school!"

"I'm sick!" He screamed it at her, his face distorted.

"Just get dressed. And fast." He rose slowly, stood there. "I said fast!"

He took a maddeningly slow step toward his clothes, and for a moment she had the impulse to run over and hit him. God forgive her, he *was* sick, sick in a way he didn't know, and she wanted to hit him! "Matt, I said fast. I'll be downstairs."

When she came down, she said, "Mrs. LeVine, please wake me if I sleep past the alarm. Don't ever let me sleep past the alarm."

It must have come across more harshly than she meant, or maybe Mrs. LeVine was upset at the way she was handling Matt; she simply stared at her with a slight lifting of her head. Jesus, she mustn't lose *her*.

"I'm sorry if that came across wrong. It's just that—I mustn't be late."

She made a fast call to the office—something about her car—she'd be there in about an hour. Then, between glances at her wristwatch, she waited near the staircase.

He walked down slowly, holding his schoolbag, his eyes wet. He seemed so little all at once, as though he had been gathered into himself, had shrunk. His schoolbag seemed bulkier than he was.

She brought him to her. He resisted a little, then let himself go limp. "Oh, Matt, I love you! Do you believe I love you? I love you and want to help you! Believe me I'm only trying to help you!"

She had missed not only the staff meeting and lecture, but also appointments with three patients. Dr. Raphael nodded from his office as she walked by; one of the psychiatry department's two secretaries handed her a medical journal that had been routed to her; her mail and two phone messages, from physicians who had referred patients, were on her desk.

She made up one of the appointments, and decided to work in the evening to make up the others. The lecture would have to be rescheduled. At a quarter to four, just as she was walking into her office, her phone rang.

"Carla. Me." The gravelly voice of her mother. "Matt called me. What're you doing to that boy? He's sick, you're making him go to school? He needs a doctor, not school!"

"Mother, he's seen a doctor." She tried to stay calm. "There's nothing physically wrong with him. I would never let him go to school if I thought there was."

180

"He needs a doctor, not school! Why don't you take him to a doctor?"

"I just told you." She was straining to keep her voice low. "He's seeing a doctor."

"What kind of doctor is that, lets him go to school? He's sick! You crazy? You treat crazy people you become crazy? That boy cried to me! You're a doctor?"

"Mother, I can't talk to you here. I'm at the hospital. I will call you from home."

"Hospital! You belong in a hospital! I think you've gone crazy!"

"I will talk to you, Mother." And with that, eyes closed, she lowered the receiver to the hook. A quivering ran through her. The phone rang again. She let it ring, then was afraid one of the secretaries would answer and her mother would harangue her. She picked it up. "Yes."

"Carla?"

"Ross. I thought it was someone else."

"You all right?" Which meant you sound lousy.

"Oh, my mother called. Where does a psychiatrist go who's got mother problems?"

He gave a short laugh. "At least you've got a sense of humor."

"Do I? I wish. Giving me a hard time about Matt— he's sick, I'm making him go to school, I'm crazy."

"Oh, Christ."

"Well—it's all right. Doesn't bother me that much. I just don't need it. Anyway, how are you?"

"Fine. Look, I was just thinking. I told you I was going to San Francisco, didn't I?"

"That's right, you did." Still, it came as a jolt. He had mentioned it in passing when he'd sat with her the evening he'd brought over the clippings on Samuel Devereaux, but she hadn't thought more about it.

"I'm leaving tomorrow and I wanted to know if we could have dinner tonight."

She felt something drop in her, as though someone bound up to her security or even to her very sanity was going away. "Thanks, but I really can't. I came in very late and I'm going to have to take Matt to the doctor and then I'll be coming back here. I won't even have a chance to eat."

"Well, what time will you be through? We can have a late dinner."

"I'm not sure what time. I'd say about ten."

"Great. How about it?"

"You're sure it's not too late?"

"No, it's not too late. Are you kidding? Do you want to call me when you get home?"

"What if I call you when I'm ready to leave here? We can meet somewhere."

"Fine."

It wasn't until she put down the phone that she realized that for those few moments she'd been able to put aside Matt, her mother, everything.

Mary Sundstrum kneeled in front of Matt as he kept sobbing and looking away from her. "Don't you like to see me, Matt? We're going to be playing more games today, we're going to be having fun." And as she talked to him she gave that little look at Carla, and Carla took a few steps away. "I'll be out here waiting for you, Matt."

The instant the door closed behind them she walked quickly to Mackey's office for her visit. He was standing in his waiting room, and he gave her a big smile. They took their usual seats, his behind the desk, hers next to it.

"I'm getting in a real mess at work," she began. "I got up at, what, a quarter to ten. Matt hadn't gone to school, I had to take him, I missed a staff meeting, appointments, a lecture. Raphael is already on my neck, this isn't going to help, and oh, yes, my *mother* called. 'You're crazy, you're not doing right by the boy'—the whole shit. You know, I know better but she affects me like I'm twelve."

"I don't think she really does, does she?"

"Well, not really. I just about hung up on her. Maybe I did hang up on her. But it's a pain, I don't need that now. Oh, and I've got to go back to the hospital, then I'm seeing Ross for dinner."

"That's good. That I like to hear . . . What do you think of him? You've never said."

"He's—quite handsome. I enjoy being with him very much. We kissed. I never would have believed I'd be kissing someone, enjoying it."

"Good."

"He's going to San Francisco on an assignment. When he told me he was leaving, I found I—for a moment I didn't want him to go."

"You mean you're going to miss him."

"I don't know. I don't know how I feel. I'm terribly confused."

He waited for her to go on. When she didn't he said, "Do you feel guilty seeing him?"

"I don't feel guilty. I don't know, maybe I do. A little. I guess I feel guilty. And afraid."

"Of what?"

"Of getting involved. What else?"

"Why? You're a healthy, normal—"

"Oh, Bill, we're not going through the healthy, normal bit again, are we? I don't know how normal I am, but I know I'm healthy. I'm lonely and I need someone to hold me and maybe I'd like to go to bed with him, but I don't want to find out. I've got to get Matt straightened out before I think of myself."

"You won't get him straightened out until you've straightened yourself out."

"I fell into that one, didn't I?"

"Only a thousand percent."

She sank into silence. He said, "What are you thinking?"

"That I've been afraid to tell you something," she said quietly.

It was true. She'd been skirting it so far. After the last session, how could she tell him she'd called Eileen Troy? And yet, what good were these sessions if she couldn't tell him everything?

"I called that secretary at Delman and Sharples. And I met her."

He said nothing, and his face showed nothing. He simply seemed interested.

"It's not just that she can't believe he was a homosexual, but she can't believe he wouldn't tell her. They had that kind of relationship." And she went on about the A-frame and then about Wayne Delman and Stephen Cohen.

Afterward she looked at him for a reaction. Still nothing. Finally he said, "What do you think about it?"

"All night all I could think of was that if someone could make Mark look like a suicide, why not?—" She gestured.

"Don't be ashamed. Say it."

"I don't know, make it seem like this fellow killed Wayne and then himself. Bill, it's crazy, I know."

"Are you aware what kind of plot that would be? Hook up this Delman with a male prostitute, force them to drive sixty, seventy miles, then kill them in such a way that the police would never suspect anything?"

"It's crazy, I know it's crazy, but I kept thinking it."

"And today?"

"I've been so busy. But—once in a while, yes." She stared at the floor, then said in a strangely calm voice, "Maybe all of this is driving me crazy."

William Mackey stood staring out his window long after she left. Then he went to his desk, sat down heavily.

No, mustn't drink. Had a meeting.

He looked at his watch. His hand was trembling. He grasped it with his other hand.

Phi Beta Kappa. Fellowships. Author—books, papers. A fine name. How had he come to this?

But that wasn't the point anymore. He knew for sure now. She wouldn't stop. She would never stop. Never, on her own.

Chapter 29

After dropping Matt off at home—why had she aggravated herself by trying to coax him into looking at her when she'd said good night?—she drove back to McCallum General. She was to see two patients, but was called to the room of a third—a divorcée who was to undergo cosmetic surgery the next day and had gone into a panic. After a long tearful outpouring, she agreed with Carla's assessment that she ought to hold off, that she didn't really want a face-lift but was hoping it might win back her husband.

She called Ross at about twenty to ten. "Hi. I'll be leaving in about ten minutes."

"Great. What time should I pick you up?"

"That's not necessary. I can meet you. Just tell me where."

"What do you feel up to?"

"It really doesn't matter. Italian. Chinese. American."

"If you'd like Italian, there's a great place only a couple of doors from here."

"Fine."

"I'll tell you what. I'll wait for you outside my place and we'll park it together. It can be a problem around here."

"Okay. I should be there in about—I'd say a half hour."

She walked out to the parking lot with one of the cardiologists. They spoke for a few moments, then he got into his car and roared off as she was backing out. She stopped long enough to fasten her seat belt, then started again. As she headed toward the street she was aware of the glare of headlights in her rear-view mirror and she adjusted it to soften them. Then she turned onto what she thought was the one-way exit lane to the street, but found she'd made a mistake and was on the entrance lane instead.

Too late to back out, though. The other car had just turned in behind her.

Blind leading the blind, she thought.

Out on the street, she turned right. She found herself in back of a truck; she signaled to pull out and then passed it quickly. She came back into the same lane. It was a warm night, and she put on the air conditioner, the first time this spring. She closed her window and adjusted the vents on the dash so the air blew on her face. Just enough to cool off. Then she turned them away again.

She was so glad she wasn't going straight home. She was tired—no, beat—but she was really looking forward to seeing Ross. In fact, unwinding as she drove, she felt kind of rejuvenated, fresh. She refused to let her thoughts linger on Matt, on anything; just that there was a nice hour or two ahead.

In center city she turned down the street that led to Ross's apartment building. It was a fairly narrow street, with townhouses on each side. She slowed, thinking that if she saw a parking spot she would take it. Nothing. Although you were only supposed to park on one side, there were cars on both sides.

Now that looked like a spot. Over there, just around the corner.

Could be a fireplug though. But she'd try.

She turned into the street and saw it was a spot. It was pretty small, though. She edged past it, stopped, then backed up. Two turns and she had it. She pulled up the brake, slid out, and hoisted on her shoulder bag. She tested the doors to make sure they were locked. She started toward the corner.

Her head whipped back as an arm locked around her throat. She tried to scream but couldn't. She began kicking and flailing back with her arms, struck something, a face, nose. The breath was going out of her. Her teeth found something, cloth, a jacket sleeve, sweater, she bit. Bit hard, her head going from side to side as she dug in. A cry, and the arm fell away, and she ran, one shoe flying off, stumbled, kicked off the other shoe, ran. Ran, screaming. Screaming.

Some doors came open. And someone was running to her. Ross, from the sidewalk in front of his building.

He grabbed her. She wanted to rush past him, get into the building. "It's all right," he kept saying. "You're all right now." Then he led her into the lobby. The desk clerk quickly came around.

"I"—she could hardly talk—"mugged."

The man ran back to the desk, picked up the phone. Ross led her over to a chair. Several people gathered around.

"My—shoes." Suddenly it was important she have her shoes.

"Where are they, lady?" someone said.

She waved toward the outside. A couple of men ran out. Soon they came back with one shoe. A few minutes later several patrol cars pulled up, lights flashing. Even while one officer was questioning her, a few of the others had already sped off to scour the neighborhood.

"Did you get a look at him?" The patrolman was holding a clipboard.

"No."

"He came up from in back?"

"Yes. He had—his arm around my throat."

"Did you see his hand? What color?"

"No. But I bit him."

"Bit him?"

"I bit his arm. I—I had another shoe."

"Are you hurt?"

"Just my throat—sore. I'm all right."

"I think you should go to the hospital."

"I don't need a hospital, I don't want a hospital."

"Did he get anything?"

"No."

"Lucky. Lucky all around. Look, we need your name, address. And a detective will be talking to you. I don't know when."

She gave her name and address. Then she said to Ross, "I want to go home." But when she stood up, her legs almost crumpled.

He said, "Come up to my place. Just till you settle down."

"I—want my shoe."

Ross said to the patrolman, "If you find her shoe, we'll be in apartment twelve twenty-eight for a while."

She walked with him to the elevator, weakly, the others looking on. In his apartment, she sat on the sofa, hard.

"Let me get you something to drink."

She nodded. "A little scotch. I really need a drink."

He brought her a scotch and ice and a little soda. She sipped at it. "I bit him. I really bit him."

189

A few minutes later the doorbell rang. It was a detective, a young man who looked barely out of his teens, carrying her shoe. He asked just about the same questions as the patrolman.

"It's a typical mugging. But they don't usually miss the bag."

"He could have asked me for it. I would have given it to him. I really bit him. How's scotch for hydrophobia?" It was strange, suddenly she felt a little giddy, wanted to joke.

"Do you think you drew blood?"

"I don't know, but I really bit him."

When the detective left, Ross sat across from her with a drink. "You're never going to have dinner with me again, are you?"

"Never. You know, I've read of muggings, I've read of them, but I've never been mugged. You know I feel a little slaphappy? Shaky but slaphappy."

"You could have been hurt."

"How about killed?"

"You're very lucky. Can I bring you in something to eat?"

"God, no. I couldn't touch anything. But get something for yourself."

"No, I don't want anything."

She sat there quietly. She had become very solemn; it was all finally sinking in. Then after several moments she frowned. "A car followed me out of the hospital."

"What do you mean followed you?"

"Followed me. I saw the headlights in the mirror. The thing is, I took the wrong way out and it followed me."

"Maybe they didn't know the way."

"Maybe. I don't know. But it did follow me."

"Did you notice anything while you were driving?"

"I forgot about it. I—I wouldn't have parked if I'd thought anything of it."

"You just saw the headlights? You didn't see the car?"

"No."

"Do you want to tell the police?"

"What will they do? They think I'm loony enough. And I just might be."

"Come on."

He went over and sat next to her. He took her hand. It was cold. He rubbed it.

He said, "I hate leaving."

She'd forgotten he was going. She tensed.

"I want you to know where I'll be," he said. "The Mark Hopkins. I'll stay in touch. And if you want someone to talk to, call me."

"I will."

"You won't, though."

"Why do you say that?"

"I didn't know what else to say."

She smiled, then took a deep breath. It was as though she felt his hand on hers for the first time. She rubbed his, then put her hand down.

"I'm going. I'm very tired."

"I'll drive you home."

"I don't want you walking back."

"No problem."

"I really don't want you walking."

Her feet felt for her shoes. She bent over and put them on. "It's funny. All I cared about was my shoes. I almost got killed and my only worry was my shoes."

She stood up. Her legs were still weak. And there was a sudden ache in her back as though she'd pulled something. Suddenly, as he stood up with her, she felt a torrent of panic rush through her, as though she

191

dreaded facing the night and the house and whatever else lay ahead of her.

And those headlights!

He seemed to sense it. She let his arms go around her. She held his forearms, her head on his shoulder. She wished she could close her eyes for a long, long time.

"No, please." But she let herself sit on the sofa with him. His arms stayed around her. She huddled against him. She felt his hand stroking her back. Then she felt his finger touch her chin, to lift it, and she said, "Please," and the arm went around her again and she stayed close. "Tell me something."

"Such as?"

"Anything. About you."

"I played basketball in college. Do you want to hear that?"

She nodded.

"I played basketball in college. I have a daughter who's—she'll kill me—I think, sixteen. She's very beautiful. My wife remarried. I enjoy my work."

He fell silent, but it was a while before she noticed. It was so good sitting like this, her cheek against his chest. "I'm going to be leaving."

"All right."

But this time when his finger touched her chin, she let him lift it. She watched his face come close, then she closed her eyes. Her lips were hard at first, closed, but they opened as if to the pounding of her heart and she felt his tongue and drew it in, and she sucked on it, and held him tightly. Then she turned her head away fiercely. He let her stay that way against his chest. But he seemed to know when it was time to lift her face again. This time her lips were soft, her mouth open. She drew in his tongue, then pressed hard against his mouth. She felt his lips now on her eyelids, her

192

cheeks; she held her head back, turning it as he kissed around her throat, under her ears, sought out the tender swirls and hollows, then her lips again.

He unbuttoned her blouse. She watched him. She arched to let him unsnap her bra. He was looking at her breasts now, then touched them with the tips of his fingers and then covered them with his palms. He kissed her gently on the lips.

"No."

He'd started to lead her to the bedroom; she braced herself. She didn't know why, but she didn't want the bedroom. She looked at him looking at her. Then she drew him to her and kissed him. She stood there as he slipped down her skirt, her panty hose. She stepped out of them, then her bikini.

He eased her back on the sofa. She closed her eyes as he undressed. She could feel him coming closer. She touched his bare arms, then held his head to her, to each breast. Little spasms caught her at the gentle touching of his teeth, the sucking. His lips were on her belly now, then in the hollows of her thighs. She opened, convulsive with the dartings, the probing. She clutched his head. He lifted himself to her, and she slid her arms around him. She took him in, lay still for a minute, then joined him, pressing up in spasm after spasm.

No night, no death, no hurts, no wrong, just this, this, this, God *this*.

Chapter 30

She stood by her door, watching him start down the street. He turned several times, and each time they waved to each other, and once he made a move to come back to kiss her again but she smiled and waved him away. Then she closed the door, making sure, twice, it was locked. She stood with her back against it, then walked upstairs. The house was quiet. A small lamp was on in the living room and the overhead light in the dining room had been dimmed.

She went up to the second floor and, in the soft glow of the hall night light, looked into Matt's room. She took a few steps in, arched her head to see better; he seemed deep in sleep. She went into her room, and there, as though suddenly conscious of the weight of her body, sagged onto a chair.

Thoughts, images crowded each other—the headlights, the arm around her throat, running, Ross.

She felt so confused, dazed, frightened.

But why, she wondered, no wrenching guilt? Why, through her terror, just this terrible sense of sadness—

these feelings of loss that her marriage hadn't been what it seemed?

She woke during the night, woke biting that arm and trying to tear away. For moments she couldn't shake the dream, but then she realized she was shivering, sheathed in sweat, clutching a drenched sheet to her.

She dreaded letting go of the sheet, even though it was like a glaze on her.

Gradually, though, she felt her heart easing, became aware she'd started thinking of Ross. But the thundering instantly started again. She wished he'd already gone and was back!

In the morning she called Detective Harris from the office. She had hesitated because she knew what he would say, but she wanted him to know about the attack. And he reacted as she thought he would. Those goddam animals, it was a shame, no one was safe, no, no one would follow her in a car to mug her on a downtown street, that was just a mugging pure and simple, you gotta watch yourself, though how much can a person watch, you can walk just outside your house and bingo.

And afterward, sitting at her desk, she was aware that he'd relaxed her a little, that this was what she'd actually wanted to hear. But almost instantly something struck her with such impact she wanted to grab for the phone again.

Mark, Stephen Cohen, Nora, Wayne Delman— hadn't all of the crimes been made to look like something else?

She was paged; she had a call. Ross said, "I had to hear your voice before I left."

"I'm so happy you called. When are you leaving?"

"About an hour and a half. Hey . . . " His voice trailed off. There was a long silence. Then, "If thoughts can melt telephone wires, I just put them all down."

She laughed.

He said, "What are you doing in about three-quarters of an hour?"

"I'll be here."

"I want to see you. Just for ten minutes. Five minutes."

"You've got to make a plane."

"I've got time. So, three-quarters of an hour? In front of the building?"

His Porsche drew up a few minutes early. She was already there. She walked down the steps and he opened the door on the passenger side and she climbed in. He drove off.

"Where are you going?"

"To San Francisco."

"I mean with me."

"To San Francisco?"

"I wish."

"God, do I wish."

He found a spot on the parking lot. He sat angled toward her, his hand on her shoulder. "Did you call that detective, like you said?"

"Yes. He said all the right words. Mugging. Life in the big city."

"Did you tell him about the car following you out of McCallum?"

"He doesn't see that fitting in at all. A plain and simple mugging. Can you believe I made all that fuss about my shoe?" Then, "I scared myself a little bit this morning."

"What do you mean?"

"Mark, Cohen, the others—I was thinking. Their deaths were all made to look like something else."

He looked at her, frowning. Then, shaking his head quickly, "I'm not going on this damn trip."

"Don't be silly. You're going. You have to go."

"I don't got to do nothing!"

"You're going. Forget it. I'm sorry I said that. I scared myself, but it's nonsense. I'm absolutely not scared anymore. I was mugged. If someone wanted to kill me, they'd kill me."

"Oh, shit." He looked away, his face agonized.

"Ross, I'm sorry. I shouldn't have told you. It was just a thought. Christ."

"I'm not going."

"That's silly. I don't even want to hear it. What are you going to do if you're here? Walk around the hospital with me? Shadow me? Now stop it. If you want to get me angry—"

He held out his hand to her face, cupped her chin. She loved the tender way he was looking at her. His fingers touched her cheek.

He said, "I want to hold you and kiss you."

She put her hand on his wrist. She stroked it, then his hand. How she wished it weren't broad daylight! He leaned forward and put his lips to hers, eased them open. She could feel his breathing. His hands, under her hair, pressed her head to him. Her arms quickly encircled him, squeezing with a burst of all her strength. She sat back.

"I've got to go." She hardly had a voice. "And so do you."

He looked at her.

"You're going to be late. Please. And don't worry about me. Please don't."

He was still looking at her as he started the motor

197

and released the brake. At the front of the hospital, she slid out and came around to his side. She kissed him quickly on the cheek.

"What I said, it's nonsense. I was mugged. Now I'm of age and can vote. Have a good time. Call me."

She walked quickly up the steps, then turned. He wouldn't drive off until she kept waving him away.

This time DeTurk didn't look at the trees, the flowers. He pulled into the institute's parking lot, yanked up the brake, and strode into the building.

One of the guards was waiting for him in his office. He jumped to his feet as DeTurk walked in. DeTurk closed the door and stared at him in fury.

"I-I wasn't making it up, Turk. I wasn't lying."

"I don't give one good goddam."

"But lemme show you. Lemme." And with that he pulled up his sleeve and showed the purplish teeth marks on his arm.

Chapter 31

Matt kept sobbing as they drove home. But all she could get from him was that he "didn't like" Dr. Sundstrum.

"But why? You don't tell me why."

"I don't like her!"

"Does she say something you don't like? Does she do something?"

"I don't like her!"

"Matt, that's no answer."

"She's bad! I don't like her!"

"Why is she bad?"

"She just is! I don't like her! I don't want to go anymore!"

"You play games with her, don't you play games?"

Still sobbing, he nodded slightly.

"You like to play games, don't you? And you color pictures?"

"I don't *like* her!"

His voice rose to such a piercing scream that she wanted to stop the car and grab him and shake him. She fought for control. What in God's name do you do?

Sundstrum had said today she would be trying an antidepressant. But if that didn't work—and Sundstrum still seemed to doubt it would help much—what then? Hospital? God, no, she couldn't see him needing that yet; that would be the very last thing she'd agree to. But he *was* deteriorating—his behavior, his schoolwork, just about everything.

Try someone else?

But why would it be different than with Bill and Sundstrum, really the best? Would she just be doctor-shopping, instead of facing up to her own role in this?

She pulled into her street, then into her garage. As she started up the stairs, she heard voices. Oh, Jesus. The last thing she needed right now was hell from her mother.

The International Congress of Primary-Care Physicians—mostly general practitioners and internists—was sponsored by three medical schools, its aim being to improve the skills of family doctors, particularly in dealing with medical problems they might ordinarily refer to specialists. So the program for the five-day meeting included sessions on such topics as "The Family Doctor and the Psychiatric Patient," "Office Surgery," "Neonatal Emergencies," and "Gynecology in General Practice."

The sessions Ross was covering for the medical news magazine, which wanted his by-line as much as his expertise, were generally more science oriented and would blend into a single article that was tentatively titled "Advances in Science and the Family Doctor." The piece he was doing for the *New York Times Magazine,* on the other hand, was a profile of a general practitioner who, after acquiring a PhD in chemistry, became the much-published head of a team of genetic researchers, but who still maintained a part-time clinical practice.

Ross had interviewed him last night, a few hours after landing, and would see him again before the conference was over. But this was just the beginning. A week or so from now, he would spend several days with him in Milwaukee, his hometown.

Today he attended four sessions, then took his first stroll through the exhibit area. It was lined with festive booths—exhibits by pharmaceutical firms, medical instrument companies, book publishers, and medical services of various kinds. The aisles were jammed with doctors with name tags, most of them carrying plastic bags bloated with gifts from the exhibitors. Afterward he went with several physicians to Delman & Sharples's hospitality suite, one of several that pharmaceutical firms had set up. It was crowded, noisy, most of the doctors clustered somewhere near the bar, the few in serious conversation huddled in a corner or standing out in the hall. He chatted with Jeff Malmquist, then worked his way through the crowd to say hello to Stuart Sharples, the dead man's cousin. He had met Stuart Sharples twice before, in connection with Delman & Sharples's grant for his television show.

Later, in his room—he was to meet two physicians for dinner in a few minutes—he called Carla. He'd spoken with her last night, and felt good about how she had sounded.

"Hi. How are you doing?"

"Good. How are you?"

"Fine. Were you sleeping?" It was seven o'clock there, which meant ten o'clock in Philadelphia.

"Nooo," she said, meaning she wished she were. "My mother, brother, and his wife are here. They're about to leave."

"They giving you a rough time?"

"Not—everyone." Which he took to mean they were standing nearby, and that she was referring to her mother. "But, it's all right. How's the meeting?"

"Okay. The interview yesterday went very well."

"Oh, I'm glad."

"Hey, I miss you."

"Me too."

"You miss you?"

She laughed. It was good hearing her laugh. He said, "I'll hang on till they leave."

"It's hard to say exactly when."

"Well, look, I'm going out to dinner. Don't let her give you a rough time."

"Don't worry."

"I wish you were here."

"So do I."

He said nothing for a few moments. Then, "You just were."

"I know," she said quietly

The moment she hung up, her mother said, "Who was it?"

She deliberately didn't answer; she was too angry at her, just wanted her to go.

"I want you to start going out, meet a man," her mother said. "What that man did to you, what he did to that boy, how he couldn't want to live—"

Carla had told them nothing about what she'd learned the past few weeks; she hadn't wanted to worry them, didn't want all the phone calls it would trigger.

"Mom," Frank said.

With her brother and sister-in-law leading the way, they started drifting toward the door; they were driving back to Trenton. Her mother said, "You take care of yourself, hear? And you see to Matt," which meant take him to another doctor, don't make him go to school when he's sick—all the things she'd said two dozen times all evening. And, worse, she had said them to Matt, which would only encourage him to stay home. "You take care of yourself, hear?" her mother said to her again.

She took Carla in her thick stubby arms and Carla kissed her and held her, trying not to be angry anymore, knowing she meant well. Then she and her sister-in-law embraced, and now she and Frank hugged each other. Frank kissed her hard on the cheek. He said quietly, "You do what you think is right. You got the brains, you know what's right." And she hugged him again, thinking: If I told you, you'd think I'm crazy. She went with them out to their car, waiting until they drove off—her mother and sister-in-law waving—and then went back in, again testing and retesting the door to make sure it was locked.

She put away the last of the dishes—Mrs. LeVine was already in bed—and then went up to her room and got into pajamas and robe. Matt's bed had begun squeaking, as though he were thrashing about, and she went to her doorway and listened. It stopped after a while. She went into the study, looked through the shelves, then settled on a journal, the most recent *Archives of General Psychiatry*. But she closed it on her lap, unable to concentrate. Her thoughts went to Ross. They were such good thoughts. But they couldn't hold out what was really pressing into her mind. Mark. How she'd always felt uncomfortable about her background compared to his. Wasp. Money. Culture.

She remembered the first time he'd told her his

mother had gone to Smith, his father to Harvard. He'd mentioned it so very incidentally, which for some reason had impressed her even more.

To have a mother who went to *Smith,* a father to *Harvard!*

From things he'd said, and from what his background had implied to her, his was a family that served tea sandwiches and champagne at weddings—she'd never *heard* of a tea sandwich until she was at least seventeen!—and there wasn't all that hugging and kissing when relatives got together, or even all of the crying when someone died. None of the women shrieked at good news or bad, with a clap of the hands and a look toward heaven. And certainly he'd never had an Uncle Dom and Aunt Dora—so embarrassing in front of Mark—who would scream at each other half the night, then end up hugging and maybe even playfully slapping each other on the head.

Her feelings about her background seemed so weird now. Unbelievable.

"You're Calabrese and be proud of it," she remembered her father saying to one of her brothers.

But in the ring, she'd learned later, he had called himself Kid Doyle.

That drew bigger crowds them days than Kid Vignola, her mother explained.

She came back to her office for lunch break the next day, deeply disturbed. How could she have done that? Twice during the same session she had called a patient whom she knew well by the wrong name. But it wasn't just a matter of the name that troubled her, but that even as the woman talked about her problems as a kidney dialysis patient, her thoughts would occasionally drift.

You can't do this to patients! It isn't fair, it's all wrong!

Her phone rang, but she was too upset to answer. She let one of the secretaries take it. Then her phone buzzed.

"It's a Mr. Saul Osterman, Doctor."

She swept up the receiver. "Yes, Saul."

"Do you have a minute?"

"Of course."

He had checked on the rumor that Bessinger's would be buying Delman & Sharples and had found that it was only partly true. Actually Bessinger's parent company, the Decton Corporation, would be purchasing it. From what he understood, the sale would probably be completed next week. "I've compiled a report on Decton. It's a multinational corporation. It's hard to tell how many subsidiaries they own outright or have an interest in or what."

He began to read off several of them.

The fourth name stunned her.

Darby Houses?

Chapter 32

Why hadn't she gone straight to Saul's office? Why had she done this to herself? She was so anxious to see that report. But instead of simply breaking Matt's appointment with Sundstrum, as she should have, she had brought him here to Cartwell and would have to take him home before going over to Saul's.

Although Matt would be in there at least fifteen more minutes, she kept glancing at Sundstrum's door, as though somehow she could urge it open.

She sat, rose, sat down again, went out to the hall.

Darby Houses and Mark and Devereaux and Devereaux's parent company and the purchase of Delman & Sharples—all somehow linked in a fuzzy, giddying whirl. But how? Why?

Door, please open.

"Carla, dear."

She had been staring at the office, hadn't seen Mackey walking toward her down the hall.

"I'm on my way upstairs, but I saw you standing here. Look, I spoke to Mary," and he nodded at her office, "and she said she'd see what she could do about changing the time. She's very booked, but she said she'll do what she can. I think she'll be able to do something."

"It better happen before I lose my job."

She was aware he was looking at her as though she troubled him. He said, "Are you taking anything? Valium?"

"Just once. Valium. To sleep."

"That's silly. I told you. Take them. What are they?"

"Fives."

"Well, take them."

She realized he was looking at her hands now, and when she looked down she realized they were clenched together like claws. She released them, held them apart; but it was as though they needed each other.

"Take them," he said again.

She felt the impulse to tell him about Saul's call. But she didn't want to risk any more rebukes, didn't think she could take any more guilt.

Starting to leave, he said, "Are we seeing each other tomorrow? Or the day after?"

"The day after."

"Do you want to make it tomorrow? This evening?"

What he was really saying, she knew, was that she looked like she needed help fast. "No. Thanks."

He kept looking at her, with such apparent concern that, almost against her will, she found herself saying, "I got a strange call this afternoon."

And then, his gaze urging her on, she described Saul Osterman's call. As it all came out, she was relieved. There was no rebuke, he just listened. He listened very carefully.

She managed to find parking almost directly in front of Saul's building. It was dusk by now, and she had to sign in at the lobby desk. Saul was alone in the huge suite of offices.

"I appreciate your staying so late, I really do."

"Don't mention it."

He brought out a large sheaf of computer printouts. "Like I said, this is a multinational company that's very, very difficult to figure out. There're not only subsidiaries, but subsidiaries of subsidiaries. Some companies are owned outright, in others they're the principle stockholder, that sort of thing. I don't know if you could ever figure it out completely, but Decton is obviously the parent company."

"What do you know about Decton?"

"It has a very limited number of shareholders—it's not on the market—so it's a closely held corporation. The president and major shareholder is a man named Edwin Haywood."

"That's a very familiar name. Where have I heard it?"

"If you read the financial sections, you'll know him. I've also read about him in the *Wall Street Journal* and, I believe, *Fortune*. But he manages to remain relatively unknown to the public. Let's see if there's anything in one of these who's whos."

He went into the conference room and came back with a who's who of business executives. He had it opened to Haywood's biography. She sat down with it and began to read. Fifty-eight, two daughters, Wharton, president of this, that, belonged to this, that—

All at once she stopped, eyes sprung wide.

She came out of the night into the house in a half daze, never asked Mrs. LeVine about Matt, never went to see him; just went to her room and dropped the printouts on the bed and stared at them. And yet, why such a reaction to Haywood being on the Cartwell board of directors? He was prominent, wealthy. It made sense; he was just one of many.

But still. A jolt. A tremendous coincidence.

She sat down next to the printouts, unaware that Mrs. LeVine had come into the room until she heard, "Doctor."

She looked up at her. And instantly sensed, from her face, more trouble.

"Do you have a minute?"

"Yes, what is it?"

"I hate to do this, but I have to. I'm going to leave. So I'm—giving you two weeks' notice."

She felt her shoulders sag. This too? "May I ask why?"

"There's no special reason. I just think—I don't want to work anymore."

"I see. Well. What can I say?"

Mrs. LeVine seemed to be waiting for her to say something else. When she didn't, she said, "Well, I'm sorry."

Carla watched her walk off. She was sure she was leaving because she disapproved of the way she was handling Matt; and suddenly she was so angry she didn't really care. She would care tomorrow—oh, Christ, would she care—but right now she was too angry and had too many other things on her mind.

But it was hard for her to concentrate on the printouts. She began going through them again; then she remembered the thick handsome brochure on Cartwell Institute that Mark had brought home—a combination history and annual report.

She was sure she'd put it somewhere among all these books. She ran her finger along the spines, couldn't find it, tried again. It would probably be tucked— Here. She drew it out and began skimming. She found what she wanted near the back, a list of the board of directors and their professional or business affiliations.

She went back and forth from the booklet to the printouts.

Afterward she sat slumped in a chair, her clenched hands pressed against her mouth.

At least twelve of the fourteen directors of Cartwell were executives in subsidiaries of the Decton Corporation.

Chapter 33

Carla drank her morning coffee quickly, standing by the sink. It had been another night boiling with questions that kept her awake—almost until dawn. Mrs. LeVine had taken Matt to school and now was looking at her with concern.

Carla, walking past her, said, "I'll call you this afternoon."

"You'd better take it easy, take care of yourself. You're getting circles."

Carla came back and gave her a quick embrace. "I'll try."

In the car, waiting for the garage door to open, she wondered if she was clearheaded enough to drive. She opened her window all the way as she pulled out. The air blowing on her face helped a little as she drove.

One of the things she'd found herself thinking about off and on throughout the night was why Stephen Cohen hadn't thought John Delman had needed to be hospitalized. She was sure, just as she had been when she'd first heard about it, that it had been simply a matter of opinion. Even psychiatrists—and he hadn't been a psychiatrist—even the most skilled psychiatrists often differed about when to hospitalize a patient.

But why—and this was what she'd suddenly found a bit troubling—would a physician with Cohen's reputation for kindness tell Wayne Delman something so unfeeling after his stepfather's death?

Maybe he'd been annoyed that John Delman hadn't accepted his opinion.

She was approaching McCallum General now. She'd begun to debate whether to call Detective Harris. She was just curious—curious to see if Cohen's record of the visit might give any indication why he'd felt Delman didn't need to be hospitalized. But she was hesitant about calling.

She told herself it was because she'd only be making a further nuisance of herself, wouldn't learn anything anyway. But she sensed that the reason was something deeper than that.

That it was crazy—and wrong—that it was crazy and wrong to question Bill Mackey's judgment. And Mark's, as a psychiatrist. Whatever else Mark had been, he'd been a fine physician, gentle, empathic, bright.

But he'd been so different in so many other ways from what she'd thought, why not in his medical judgment as well?

But, no, this was crazy.

So she managed to hold back. But only until the afternoon.

No, Harris said—and there was a trace of annoyance in his voice—he hadn't made a copy of Cohen's chart for John Delman. "I didn't see any reason to. Why do you ask?"

"I hate to trouble you, but could you possibly find out a few things for me?"

212

"Such as what?"

"Well, whatever he put down about diagnosis. And how he planned to treat him—medication, dosage, whatever else. Also, whatever medications Mr. Delman was already on."

"Let me ask you, why do you want this?"

"Just— It might answer some questions."

"That's not telling me very much, is it, Doctor?"

"It's because I don't know anything more. All I know is that I've got some questions and this could answer them."

Silence. Then, "What is it you want again?"

He called back about an hour and a half later. The diagnosis was simply "depression since wife's death." Dr. Cohen had prescribed Elavil, seventy-five milligrams a day, and weekly counseling with him. John Delman had been taking Valium, five milligrams three times a day.

"So, does that answer anything for you?"

"I'm not really sure. Let me think it out."

"Sure. You think it out." And this time there was no mistaking the sarcasm. She sat back in her chair, a hand to her temple. Cohen had prescribed a proper drug for depression—a tricyclic antidepressant. But Valium was for anxiety. Physicians sometimes made the mistake of prescribing tranquilizers like Valium for depression, but she just couldn't see Bill Mackey doing it. Or John Delman, who should have been so knowledgeable about drugs, going along with it.

Unless there was more to this than the chart revealed.

Maybe, for instance, John Delman hadn't been taking the antidepressant Bill prescribed—noncompliance was common among psychiatric patients. Perhaps he had wanted to deny being clinically depressed and had put himself on a "mild tranquilizer."

213

Or maybe John Delman had been one of those depressed people who show symptoms of anxiety rather than depression. And though a tranquilizer like Valium might relieve the symptoms temporarily, it wouldn't touch the underlying problem. So maybe Bill had simply misdiagnosed the case and then put him in the hospital to correct it.

All she knew was that if Bill had prescribed Valium, there had to have been a reason—or else the chart was incomplete.

Later that day, when the door closed on Matt and Sundstrum, she felt a tremendous unease. It had nothing to do with Sundstrum or Matt, but rather with the place. And yet as she wandered through the halls now, with doctors and nurses walking about, and aides pushing dinner carts, and a pretty young nurse combing an elderly woman's hair, there was a brightness about the place, a caring, that made any dark thoughts about it seem stupid. Absolutely stupid.

What was she thinking anyway?

She wasn't sure, except there were too many dead, too many ghosts, too many coincidences.

Like here—what had once been Samuel Devereaux's room.

Who were you to my husband?

And here—Helene Tysdal's room. What did you see? And why your companion?

She found herself slowly drawn into Helene Tysdal's room, and she sat gently on the side of her bed. Helene was lying back on a pillow, her body stiff, face cavernous, eyes staring.

So frustrating, so maddening. Here, a woman, an athlete who had come back from many psychotic episodes, now so dreadfully lost within herself.

Why can't we make you better now?

214

She sat there for a while longer, as though hoping her presence would stir something in the woman, then finally stood up. At the doorway she looked back, hoping that somehow those eyes would have moved. She walked out to the hall, looked at her watch to see when she would have to go for Matt. Eight more minutes. She started to head there, but instead, walked—again, drawn—to the nursing station. She was curious to know if they'd begun to try anything else on her. Had they increased her Haldol? Begun a new drug?

No nurses were about.

She looked across the counter at the rows of metal-cased patient charts on the stand. She ran her eyes across them. On one adhesive strip was printed: H. Tysdal.

Two nurses passed at different times. She knew both of them by sight; one smiled at her, the other said, "Doctor?" She nodded at them.

She glanced at her watch again. Matt would be coming out in about three minutes. She looked once more at Mrs. Tysdal's chart. Would anyone care?

She really had no right to do this. But what harm?

She waited another minute or two. One of the nurses started to walk toward the station but then, as though suddenly remembering something, turned and walked in the other direction.

What harm? Really.

She went behind the counter and opened the chart. Her eyes skipped about. Here, Haldol. They'd upped the dosage a few days ago. She began flipping through the pages, pausing now and then to read.

At first, in her haste, she didn't notice it.

Then her eyes went back to it swiftly.

A rush of blood through her head filmed her eyes. She read through a blur.

When she looked up, her legs almost sagged. A nurse had quietly taken a seat behind the counter. But she was busy writing, didn't look at her.

Carla put back the chart, began to walk off. The back of her neck felt prickly, frozen. Had the nurse waited until now to stare after her?

She wanted to look back, but fought against it.

Did it make any difference that this wasn't the same nurse who had told her about Helene Tysdal?

That had been the blond head nurse.

The head nurse was the one who had told her that electroconvulsive therapy had never helped Helene Tysdal. Yet that was what had brought her under control before her companion was murdered.

Chapter 34

Grasping Matt's hand, she hurried down the front steps and across the parking lot to her car. It was only when she was in the car that she let her body go limp, then had to fight the urge to sag against the steering wheel. Her hand shook as she sought the ignition.

She had to get out of here, get far from here.

Bill Mackey? Deliberate wrong treatment for John Delman? Holding back treatment from Helene Tysdal?

Dear God, *Bill Mackey?*

Mrs. LeVine sensed something wrong the moment she saw her walk in. She had just answered the phone, but now covered the mouthpiece and said with some concern, "It's Mrs. Cassidy. Do you want to talk to her?"

No. Yes. She just couldn't think. She held out her hand for the receiver. "Yes, Jerri."

A pause. "You sound dreadful."

"No, I'm all right. It's— Look, can I call you later? I just got in."

"Sure. But all I want to know is if Matt will be here."

For a moment she didn't know what Jerri was talking about. Then she remembered. Jerri's son Jason was having a birthday party tomorrow evening; Matt had gotten the invitation last week. "Look, I— You know how he is. I don't know from one minute to the next anymore. I'll try."

"Tell him Jason wants him to be here."

"I'll try, Jer."

Hanging up, she almost closed her eyes in despair. Her mind was so full, yet she couldn't help remembering past birthdays, Matt's and Jason's. Jerri had had Jason only six weeks before she'd had Matt. By then Jerri and Don and she and Mark had moved out of the brownstone the four of them had lived in. But the move was just to a regular apartment building nearby. So, all the same children came to both boys' parties. She thought of the noise, the laughter, sometimes the crying and fighting; but most of all, right now, she remembered how Mark and Don would move about through the horde of children and mothers, taking movies or recording children's voices on their tape recorders. And then later, when the boys were older, how the men would join her and Jerri in taking the kids to the zoo, or that one restaurant in particular where waitresses in cowgirl costumes would huddle around the table with a birthday cake and shoot cap guns the exact number of times as the boys' age.

As Carla headed to her room, Mrs. LeVine stopped her with: "Will you be ready for dinner soon?"

"I—I hope you don't mind. I'm really not feeling well. I'm going to hold off."

It was true; she suddenly felt she might throw up. And she was clammy and cold. She went into the bathroom and sat on the edge of the tub, her face in her hands.

Bill Mackey, you bastard! You no-good son-of-a-bitch bastard! You bastard, you bastard!

It had to be—she couldn't see any other answer. She'd been thinking, thinking, thinking, and there was no other answer. Stephen Cohen had been right— maybe that was why he'd been killed—John Delman hadn't belonged in any hospital. No, oh, no. Bill Mackey had let that poor son-of-a-bitch become sick enough so he could talk him into going into the hospital. Someone—she'd been thinking, thinking, and it had to be this; it had to be Decton or someone in it— someone wanted the drug firm and had to kill Delman to buy it.

It had to be, had to be.

And they'd bought off Mackey.

But what about Mark? Had he been killed because he'd learned, like Stephen Cohen, that John Delman didn't belong there? But what about his investment in Darby Houses? And what of the other mysteries in his life?

"Doctor?" Mrs. LeVine called through the closed door.

"Yes."

"Are you all right? Are you feeling any better?"

"A little."

"Mr. Robbins called before."

She nodded. "Thanks."

But she still felt a little swirl of nausea in her stomach. And just as clammy and cold.

And Wayne Delman too? Because he suspected?

But who could she tell? The police? Harris? "There's this highly respected psychiatrist, this huge corporation—"

Sure. They'd really go for that.

"And what evidence do you have, Doctor?"

219

She stood up slowly. What do you do? She went to the sink and wet her face. She kept rubbing water into it, trying to ease the nausea. But then she looked up slowly, sensing a fresh hot gushing from her heart.

What about Mackey telling her to spend more time with Matt? And Sundstrum too?

Sundstrum too?

And when she kept on probing, digging further, those headlights, the attack . . .

The operator at the Mark Hopkins in San Francisco came back on. "I'm sorry, the room doesn't answer."

"I'll call back."

She wouldn't, though. It was almost twenty after one and she had to try to sleep. She turned out the light on the night table and lowered the pillow. She lay with her eyes open.

She was breathing hard, her heart leaping every few beats.

How could she make herself heard? Believed?

The next morning she delayed making the call to Mary Sundstrum, hated talking to her, hearing that voice. But when she did call she got her answering service.

"Dr. Sundstrum's office."

"This is Dr. Carla Keller. I'm calling to—"

But just then Mary Sundstrum picked up the phone. "This is Dr. Sundstrum."

"Yes, this is Carla Keller. I'm calling because I'm afraid Matt won't be able to make it today. He's got a fever."

"Oh, I'm sorry. I hope he's feeling better soon. Should I leave the next day open?"

"I don't know. I don't know what to say."

"Well, I'll leave it open. And you call me tomorrow."

She sat at her desk, icy hands clenched long after she hung up. Could she be wrong about Sundstrum? Would she deliberately harm a child? Ruin it? Cripple it emotionally? A woman—a psychiatrist—*her*?

It was so hard to believe. And yet she had to believe it for the sanity of her child.

Was everyone in that place evil? *Everyone*? But then what about that Dr. Greenberg, who'd pointed out the painting of the clowns? Certainly he wouldn't have done that if he was involved with Mackey.

"Carla?"

Her head snapped up. Dr. Raphael was standing in her doorway, frowning. "You haven't forgotten the meeting, have you?"

"No, I'll be right there."

But she had. She stood up and touched her hair. It felt greasy, or maybe her hands were greasy with sweat. She wiped them on a tissue. Then, as she walked down the hall, she suddenly stopped and looked around.

A lab technician had walked by, carrying a tray of vials and syringes.

Last night she'd had a thought. About the Haldol. How did she know Helene Tysdal was even getting the antipsychotic drug?

One way to find out was to draw some blood and test for it. If Helene was getting the drug, it should show up in her blood.

But who could she trust to draw blood?

No one.

It was only during the meeting that she thought she herself. But that was insane. And dangerous. And impossible. With all those people around?

*   *   *

221

She was walking to a patient's room after the meeting when, after a long pause in the hallway to think it out, she walked quickly to the elevators and went down to the basement. There, in a chemistry lab, she took a blood collection syringe and a rubber tourniquet and put them in her handbag. Then she remembered something else and asked for a tiny amount of alcohol and some gauze.

But she would never do it, she knew.

Not only crazy, dangerous, absolutely insane—it was illegal; she could probably be charged with assault. And it was years since she'd taken blood; probably it would take her forever to find the vein.

She would never do it.

Still, she felt better having the things with her.

Shortly after five Jerri called at the office to say that Matt was doing fine. She had picked him up at the house, as they'd arranged earlier, and though he was very quiet and didn't join in much with the other kids, she sensed that he was enjoying Jason's party. "I'll bring him home when it's over. That should be about eight."

"No, don't you bother, I'll pick him up."

"Sure? It's no problem."

"No, I'll be there. He—seems all right?"

"I'm telling you. Look, he's not acting like the master of ceremonies, but I can tell he's having a good time. So relax."

"Thanks so much."

"For what?"

"Picking him up. Everything."

"Oh, shut up."

She sat there now, eyes squeezed shut. If Jerry only knew she hadn't given Matt five seconds' thought in—maybe hours. At least not about the party. Maybe,

222

now and then, about what a crazy mother he would have if she tried this. Even just for *thinking* it.

But she wasn't going to try it, that was settled long ago. So why was she still doing this to herself? Why was she tormenting herself?

Why? Dear God, how could she even ask that? Mark murdered. All the others murdered. Matt emotionally crippled. The attack on her—and the chance they would try again, but were holding back for a while because they didn't want to be obvious. Then there was the whole maddening idea of psychiatry, with all its power, in the hands of venal multinational conglomerate. And what appalling power it was—the power to determine who was mentally ill, who would be labeled for life, who was no longer capable of controlling his own affairs, who would get a lobotomy, who would never be secretary of state, president. And more, so much more!

A horror! But that wasn't even enough of a word for it. There was no word.

"Good night." Dr. Raphael gave a little wave.

"Good night."

A horror. Unbelievable. But what could she do? Was she wrong in not telling the police? But even if they asked for a blood test—which they wouldn't, they wouldn't—and even if Helene Tysdal had never been given a drop of medication, Mackey would be crazy not to hold off long enough to get Haldol into her.

"Good night, Doctor." One of the secretaries.

She nodded; she was afraid she'd lost her voice, that her nerves had closed on it. She stood up, suddenly not wanting to be the last to leave, to be alone. She stripped off her lab coat, put on her suit jacket and lifted her handbag to her shoulder.

"Good night, Doctor." The other secretary. She hadn't seen her.

"Good night."

In the car, she put her handbag on the seat next to her. She headed for home, then thought maybe she ought to go over to Jerri's, wait there until the party was over. She turned in that direction, realized maybe they were having dinner, and decided to go home first. Ross might call. So she ought to go—

She couldn't reach a fucking decision!

A fucking decision!

For moments she was panicky; then she settled on home. But all at once she made another fast turn, driving with her hands hard on the wheel, her heart beating fast, strength flooding through her. She fought against thinking. Must think of nothing, nothing. But absolute terror broke through her at the sight of the iron grille archway.

She made herself drive through the entrance; drove slowly, taking each yellow hump in the road as though it were a mountain. It was giving her time to think, to change her mind.

She parked in the lot, leaving the motor on, and stared at the building. Her eyes still on it, she turned off the ignition. But she kept the key in it, sure she would change her mind. She kept staring.

It looked so normal. Staff walking down the steps, smiling, chatting. Visitors going in and out.

She drew out the key.

What harm—just to see? To get a glimpse of her? To—decide then?

She slid out of the car. She walked up the steps with a group of visitors, two of whom went over to talk to the guard who was already talking to several other people. She waited by the elevators off the lobby, then decided to walk up the one flight to Helene Tysdal's floor. There she suddenly felt her bladder was going to go; she'd barely realized she was in pain. She went into the female patients' bathroom; it gave her a chance to sit and think. And to try to control her breathing. She was breathing heavily through her mouth.

Strange what she was suddenly thinking. Of all the times to think of this: how when she used to come here, even when she had seriously ill patients here, people who depended on her, she sometimes felt she really didn't belong. That Mark belonged. And Mackey, of course. And Cartwell and all the other top people. But not her.

Top people!

Her bladder still hurt, though there was nothing more to relieve. She stood up and flushed the toilet and fixed her clothes, knowing that her body, not just her brain, was telling her to leave, to go.

Go home, Carla.

Yes. She would. No way could she try this.

But when she went out to the hall, she stood there, trying to decide. She walked slowly in the direction of Helene Tysdal's room. Two nurses, one of them the blond head nurse, were at the nursing station. Several patients, a few with visitors, were walking in the hall. Others were seated in a large alcove that served as one of several lounges on the floor. She walked by the nursing station; they were busy talking with each other. Helene Tysdal's room was three doors away. She glanced in without stopping. She could make out her legs on the bed, stretched out under a sheet.

She walked around the corner. She saw another bathroom and went in, buying time. She put her hands on the edge of the sink and stood leaning on her arms. Her heart seemed to be beating up at her.

Now? Will you go home *now?*

She waited almost ten minutes.

What are you waiting for? Go. Go!

225

When she came out, she saw from the corner that just one nurse, the other one, not the head nurse, was at the station. She walked toward her, and this time the nurse smiled at her. Carla smiled back, walked toward the stairs, but then stopped at the pay phone on the wall of the lounge. She opened her handbag. The syringe was right there. She took out a coin, leaving her handbag unzipped. She put it in the phone, dialed its own number. She kept watching the nurse as the busy signal sounded; occasionally she would move her lips.

A few minutes later the nurse was walking away. Where? Carla stretched to see, saw her enter a room. She hung up quickly, but waited. Then she walked slowly toward Helene Tysdal's room. She was prepared to go past it, started to, then came back. She walked in with a tremble of a smile.

Helene was lying on her back, eyes closed.

Carla sat on the side of the bed, not daring to close the door, but keeping her body turned so that it blocked—or she felt it blocked—what she was doing.

She whipped the tourniquet around Helene's thin arm, palpated the vein, swabbed on alcohol, and inserted the needle. But nothing, *nothing*, and she had to seek out the vein again. There was a soft groan, and this time she saw blood, it was rising slowly.

Christ, hurry!

Enough! Not enough, but enough. She yanked off the tourniquet, pulled out the needle, jammed everything into her handbag. She pressed a piece of gauze against the punctures.

"Hello."

She whirled. A nurse, the head nurse.

There was a slight frown, but then she smiled. "Have you gotten any response?"

"I'm afraid not."

226

"No, neither have we. I didn't know you were a friend of hers."

"Well"—she decided to come out with it—"she may have been the last person to see my husband alive. So, I feel close to her."

"Oh, my, yes. Well, look, I just wanted to see who was with her. Nobody ever visits her. It's a shame."

"Yes."

Carla waited several minutes after she left. When she stood up to go, she had to drop back down again. She sat holding on, waiting for the vertigo to pass.

The nurse came back immediately after Carla left. She looked down at Helene, then turned to go.

Instead she bent down and picked up a piece of gauze from the floor. She wouldn't have noticed it except for the specks of blood.

Chapter 35

After dinner, William Mackey went out on the porch with the newspaper. But he put it aside and sat with his head back, staring at the fading sunlight on the fields. Why did it grind at him that she was sitting inside, in the shadowy living room, with her perpetual drink and book?

It wasn't only that she was forever drinking or reading but that she was inside, away from him; that there was nothing they shared anymore, nothing of happiness, such as this light on the fields.

It was that, and her predictable reaction to the letter. Why had he told her about the letter?

"Dear Dr. Mackey," Samuel Devereaux's daughter had written, "I want to thank you for all you did to make my father's last few months as comfortable as possible . . . "

Why had he brought it home? What had he expected but that little glance up from her book, the silence? Why hadn't he told her instead about the call from the mayor today about chairing a task force on the city's mental health programs? Or the call from the Associated Press asking him to expand on his view that psychiatry had a vital role to play in the international peace processes?

Why not these or the other good things that happened in the day? Why was he still hoping for some kind of comfort from her, a sharing? And why didn't she need it from him? After all, there was nothing she hadn't known about, hadn't encouraged. Maybe she found it easier to loathe him than herself. Or maybe in that rummy brain of hers—when had she started drinking this heavily? two years ago?—maybe in that rummy brain, and in those books, she found a room all to herself, and an innocence.

He stood up, unable to sit still anymore. He walked toward the barn. One of the barn's cats, he was sure, had kittens. He wanted to think only of kittens, of where he might find them. He turned on the lights. He had a feeling they might be up in the loft; he'd looked just about everywhere else. He was partway up the stairs when the phone in the barn rang. It rang in the house at the same time, and he was sure Jeannie would answer it and buzz if it was for him.

But it kept ringing.

Shaking his head in anger, he went back down the steps and crossed to the other end of the barn to get it. "Dr. Mackey," he said.

Soon he was running to the house to change his clothes and race back to the institute.

She started to speed out of the grounds, forgetting how heavily trafficked the street in front of Cartwell was, and she suddenly had to swerve away from an oncoming car, brakes screeching. She didn't dare look at the driver, just gave her car gas and turned onto another street, then another, all at once forgetting the

229

way to Jerri's house, then remembering, then working her way out of the maze and onto the street that led to it.

Her eyes kept darting to the rear-view mirror.

She must have been crazy.

But it was done.

The nurse, she was sure, hadn't seen a thing. She'd seemed too pleasant, showed none of the surprise or shock she would have otherwise.

Still, Carla's eyes kept going to the mirror. Nothing back there. Not a car, other than two she'd passed. It was starting to drizzle. She put on the windshield wipers, but too soon, they left a smear. She tried some windshield fluid, and the smear gradually cleared under the blades. It began drizzling harder.

Strange, only now that she was miles from the institute was she feeling the first physical reaction to what she'd done. Little tremors went through her, then an onrush of weakness, a feeling she was going to faint. She looked dazedly to the side, intending to pull over, found a place and stopped. She rested against the wheel, arms folded under her head. It was beginning to pass. She waited, aware only of her heart, her breathing. She began to drive again.

There. Jerri and Don's street. She turned, slowing to find a parking spot, thinking the party might still be on and that their driveway would be filled with the cars of parents picking up their children. But the only cars were Jerri's and Don's; she parked behind them.

Before getting out, she took the syringe and removed the tube containing the blood. She tried to figure out how she could keep the tube from breaking. She wrapped it in a wad of tissues, then cleaned out the key and change compartment of her bag and placed it there, zippering it. Tomorrow she would take it to a lab. Only certain labs were equipped to check for Haldol. The lab at McCallum General was not.

She got out, holding the bag carefully by its long strap. She threw the remaining part of the syringe into a trash can next to the driveway. Her thighs were quivering as she walked to the door.

Jerri and Don were clearing away the last of the toys and boxes and papers that littered the living-room floor. Matt was sitting on the sofa. He stared at her as she walked in. He showed no expression.

"He's really been great," Jerri said in an exaggerated, loud voice, as though trying to convince himself as well as her. "Jason got cranky and went to bed."

"I'm sorry I'm late."

"Don't be silly. You're not late. How about a cup of coffee?"

"No."

"Birthday cake?"

She shook her head.

Jerri was looking at her strangely now. Obviously she saw that something was wrong, but she said nothing, just stared at her. Then, apparently thinking it was because she was concerned about Matt, she turned to Matt and said, "It was really fun, wasn't it?" He didn't answer. She said, "Let me get his gifts, he's got a few things to take home."

Don, who had gone out to the kitchen, came back. He kissed her. Then he, too, looked at her in a concerned way. His lips said silently, "He was fine," and she nodded with a flicker of a smile.

In the car, Matt sat pressed as usual against the far door. She didn't have the strength to say anything, even to tell him to put on his seat belt; she simply reached over and made sure his door was locked. All she wanted was to be home, to get to bed; that, and a call from Ross and long, long sleep.

It had begun raining harder; the streets were slick

231

and glittery black under the street lamps. It was hard concentrating on driving; it was as if she were hemorrhaging strength, as if all the sleep she had missed were trying to crowd in now. But still, running through her exhaustion, was the quivering of tension.

How had she had the nerve?

It was still so hard to believe.

And now that she had the blood, what? What if the drug was in there? What if Mackey was simply giving a medication that he knew had never been effective with her?

She saw that Matt had fallen asleep. She reached over to touch him. His forehead was soaking from the tension of his own inner hell. She had to get him to a doctor, the best. They would heal him, they would— But what if the damage, so subtly done, was irreversible?

She was so caught up in it, in fury and desperation, that she almost passed their street. But she saw it just in time and made the turn, then drove the three and a half blocks to their house. She turned in at the garage and pressed the remote control. The door lifted. She started to pull in, then stopped, frozen. She saw, in the mirror, a figure emerge from a car parked across the street. A man. Then another. They were walking rapidly toward her.

She put the gear into reverse and the car shot back.

For an instant, having jumped away, the men were on either side of the car.

She yanked the gear into drive and the car leaped forward.

Chapter 36

William Mackey strode quickly from his car, took the front steps two at a time, then made himself walk with a pretense of composure through the lobby and up the stairs to her room. Rivulets of sweat were running down his chest and back.

Miss Headley, sitting next to Helene's bed, stood up quickly as he entered, closing the door. Her face was ashen, fear pulling at her thin lips. He stared at her, then went to Helene and lifted her arm. A quick look at the two punctures and he dropped it. He whirled, fighting against leaping on her and smashing her in that stupid, ugly, goddam face. "Where the hell were you? Where were you?"

"I—I didn't see her come in." She'd begun to cry. "I saw her sitting here. That's when I came in."

"And you didn't see it?"

"Doctor, I would tell you."

He pushed his hand up past his forehead, held onto his scalp as though trying to squeeze in a thought. Mustn't fall to pieces, had to think. He said without looking at her, knowing the answer, "You told De-Turk."

"Yes."

"You told DeTurk," he said again, still pressing at his scalp. DeTurk would get her. There was nothing to worry about with DeTurk after her. Nothing. But what if DeTurk didn't catch up with her? Couldn't?

Had to think. Mustn't panic.

Had to call the police. But what do you say to them? He said, "Let's go to my office."

What do you say to them? Not about the blood. No, not about the blood. But what? A thought was forming. But he had to be sure about it, absolutely certain. And this stupid cow here had to get it right.

He sat at his desk, hands clenched against his mouth, Miss Headley staring at him wide-eyed.

A squad-car patrolman answered the call, a big man who took notes in a slow ponderous way. "So you first noticed her looking into different rooms," he said to Miss Headley.

"Yes. And it struck me as strange because she doesn't have any patients on the floor. So I asked her if there was anything I could do for her and she just walked away. She looked very disturbed and I followed her. I followed her here."

"She didn't do anything to any of the patients?"

"No. As I said, I watched her. It was very strange. She would look in, then go. Like she was inspecting."

"Do you know if she was anyplace else in the hospital?"

"No."

He turned to Mackey. "Did she actually hit you, Doctor?"

"Well, she hit my arms. Like I said, she came in saying we were keeping patients prisoners, we were killing them—you know, things like that—and then she began swinging at me. I grabbed hold of her wrists, I think Miss Headley grabbed her also but she broke loose and ran away."

"And you saw her drive away. Do you know the make?"

"I know she drives a Honda Accord. Maroon. I don't know the year."

"You wouldn't know the license."

"No. I'm very, very worried," he said after a pause. "I really wouldn't have reported this but I feel—I *know*—she's dangerous to herself and the child. Both of them need help desperately."

"And she's a psychiatrist?"

"Some psychiatrists get sick too, I'm afraid."

"You say this has been building up a long time."

"Yes, ever since her husband killed himself. But the real breakdown started when I told her I wanted her in the hospital, that she needed more help than I could give her as an outpatient. She was very, very distressed—about herself, about who would take care of the boy. Then she absolutely broke when the boy's doctor told her he should be hospitalized. It was just too much. But I blame myself. I should have tried to get them committed. But I wanted her to do it of her own free will."

"Christ, I got a sister-in-law . . . " The patrolman shook his head, as though he knew all about that. "Now you say she's been in contact with the police."

"Yes, she's had an idea in her mind that her husband was murdered."

"Do you know who she spoke to?"

"Someone from the station around here. Let's see. A black man . . . Harmon . . . Harris. That's right, a Detective Harris. He was over here once. One of our patients had an hallucination about someone kidnapping Dr. Keller's husband, and Dr. Keller took it very seriously. At the time, I didn't really know how sick she was."

The officer scanned his notes. "All right, I'll put this out on the radio. I'm really worried about the kid," he said with a shake of his head.

She took a sharp left on Eighteenth Street, so sharp the car started to swerve toward the far sidewalk, then slammed the wheel back and straightened out. Matt was screaming, curled into the far corner of the seat. She kept throwing wild glances at the rear-view mirror, and seeing two halos of light keeping up; she made a fast left down a narrow street, then a right, and now she was on Market Street. Ahead, through the rain, she could see the large overhead sign saying Schuylkill Expressway. She turned onto it, the twin lights following as she cut in and out of traffic, past the Art Museum on the other side of the river, past the row of boat houses, past—

God, what was this?

Traffic was slowing and she had to stop, cars lined in a halt on either side of her. And then she saw, just ahead but far to the right on the shoulder, the red whirl of a police-car light. Oh, thank God! She pulled Matt to her, started to climb out of the car with him, but now the cars were moving again; she had to get back in. He was hitting her. Sobbing, she eased the car forward, trying to get over to the right, but horns were blowing. None of the cars in that lane would let her through.

A truck had broken down, flares all around. An officer was talking to the driver.

She stopped, a line of fast-moving cars between her and the officer. She pressed hard on the horn. Other cars took up the sound; the officer looked around, then gave a quick motion of his arm for her to go on, and turned back to the driver. Cars sped past, horns blowing behind her. She couldn't get out, couldn't stay.

She inched the car forward, still trying to get over, horns blaring all around. The officer looked at her again, shot his arm forward, and now she was moving. She sped up, took the first cutoff, and screeched into the vastness of Fairmount Park. Somewhere she made another sharp right—not a street, it was too bumpy to be a street—onto a bridle path: somewhere perhaps to hide, to lose them. She careened forward into the blackness of the night and many trees.

She turned off the lights and sat there, heart rocketing.

She clutched Matt to her; he was screaming, trying to twist away. She kept staring back, waiting for those headlights to swerve in. Still holding him, she fumbled at the latch to the glove compartment, opened it, closed her hand around the flashlight, probed further, then clasped a screwdriver and brought it out.

She was tempted to leave here—certainly not to go home, but to a hotel, a motel. But she was afraid to drive out.

Better to wait until daylight, when there would be other cars, people she could scream to for help.

She held the screwdriver tightly as she pressed Matt to her. After a while he grew still, resting his head against the curve of her neck.

Chapter 37

The night started off wrong for Detective Harris. Someone, a state trooper, had usurped his usual spot on the small lot behind the station house and he had to park out on the street. He climbed out of the car, ran to the building through the rain and, after a stop at the coffee machine, walked upstairs.

His eyes were strained, tired, his legs heavy. He'd been up all day, before dawn after waking and lying in bed, his mind a motor. It had been one of those mornings when he couldn't see himself looking at another mutilated body, or hearing another old person cry about stolen life savings; was sick of the white-black shit, of the hours, of the grind with no promotion, of just scratching along, knowing that even some of his friends thought he was making it big from the hookers, the pimps, the porno shops. And now he had to face the night shift.

He hadn't shaken that feeling of gloom completely, even though he'd worked like hell most of the day paneling the basement. But he would, he knew, once he dug into the job; he always did. Still, it seemed this was happening more often, and lasting longer.

Tonight that son-of-a-bitch trooper didn't help.

He stopped to look at his box—nothing—then walked with a few nods here and there to his desk. He sat down heavily. He was soon aware of the sergeant's fat ass settling partway on the desk.

"Ray, that lady shrink?"

"Who?"

"What's her name—that Dr. Keller. It looks like she's blown a fuse."

And because of his contacts with her, he was in on the case.

A couple of hours later, necktie pulled down and shirt unbuttoned at the throat, Harris had made the last of the phone calls he could think of making. At first he'd thought Dr. Mackey might have been overreacting. But two quick calls to Dr. Mackey and Dr. Sundstrum at their homes filled him with the first sense of real dread, and a few other calls compounded it. Her housekeeper, a couple of friends, even her mother—all of them portrayed her as a woman who had changed drastically, one who was not "herself."

So far—it was almost two in the morning now—none of the hotels or motels they'd contacted reported a woman of her description checking in with a small boy.

Where could they be—a psycho shrink and her kid who needed help so desperately?

Ross gave the operator his credit card number, then waited as the phone rang.

"Hello!" Mrs. LeVine's voice came on sharply, with a sense of urgency.

"This is Mr. Robbins, Mrs. LeVine. Is Dr. Keller there?"

The line seemed to go dead. Then, "No." And there was a tremor in it.

239

"Mrs. LeVine, what's wrong?"

She didn't answer right away. Then he heard the sound of crying.

"Mrs. LeVine!"

"Yes." She was gasping.

"What is it?"

"I don't *know!*" It came out in anguish. "She's not here, Matt's with her, the police have called, been over. I don't know where they are!"

"What are you talking about?"

"I'm telling you! They're not here and the police are looking for them!"

"But why?"

"I don't know! I'm telling you. They won't tell me. I'm scared to death. That woman! She may be a psychiatrist, but you don't need to read all those books to have better sense! I don't need this! Why do I need this?"

"They didn't say *anything?*"

"No! Just they want to talk to her. Look, I've got to hang up in case I hear!"

"Look, have her call—"

But she'd already hung up. He lowered the receiver, trying to fight off panic.

Downstairs, the doctor he was profiling for the *Times* was waiting for him for dinner and to continue the interview. But no way could he eat, or even bear sitting in a restaurant away from the phone. It took him fifteen minutes to get to the lobby and back. He must have sounded half incoherent—a sudden migraine. And now for an ordeal. Just sitting here staring at a phone was such hell.

He gave the phone a couple of hours to ring. Nothing. At ten he called again, even though it was one o'clock there. And again Mrs. LeVine answered as

240

though on the run. Her voice dropped in disappointment. No, they still weren't here. God only knew where they were!

He sat on the edge of the bed, an icy hand pulling at his cheek.

The last time he'd spoken with her was the day before yesterday—yesterday, she'd been out when he'd called, and afterward he'd been tied up in his interview until after midnight. She'd told him about the Decton Corporation buying Delman & Sharples and owning Darby Houses and its executives making up the majority of the institute's board. But, whatever the hell that meant, what could a huge conglomerate like Decton possibly have to do with her and Matt's disappearance?

What really worried him was the car she'd seen behind her as she'd driven out of McCallum General that night.

Should he fly out tonight? He had six more sessions to cover. And the odds were that she and Matt would show up sometime tonight, tomorrow, and there would be a perfectly logical explanation.

He began calling airlines.

She woke, blinking, confused, disoriented. Then, in a searing instant, she became aware of the blackness, the car, the damp chill, the pressure of something against her breast—Matt, Matt's body. She started to spring up, but he began to whimper and she held onto him, holding him to her hard, her cheek against his hair. She bit into her lip, trying not to cry.

This couldn't be happening! It couldn't!

Shh. Shh, sweetheart. Shh.

She rubbed at his back. She adjusted the coat—her

raincoat—which she had flung over him, and continued to rub his back, his head.

She felt him settle into her.

She sat, afraid to move, her muscles aching. The digital clock on the dashboard said two minutes after six. What should she do? She had to think; why couldn't she think? She could keep driving down the bridle path, see where it led. Or go back to the road. Or—leave the car and just run somewhere through this huge park with Matt.

But—why run? That was crazy. Why run when you've got a car?

But weren't they looking for a car? This way, just the two of them—

Matt stirred again. She was sure the beating of her heart was waking him. She touched his head again, kissed his hair. The little creases in the back of his neck were wet. Police, she knew, occasionally patrolled the park on horseback. But it was so vast, and it might be God-knows-when before one happened to come by. Still—wait, hold off. Wait, see, don't do anything.

It was so much easier not to do anything.

Daylight. It came as a jolt to her—she'd been watching the blackness and then all at once it was light out. Had she fallen asleep? Simply been staring? Whatever, it was light and she had to do something!

Gently she lifted Matt off her, put him on the seat, and covered him. He moved a few times but didn't waken. She was afraid to U-turn to return to the road, so she decided to try the bridle path first. She drove along it for a while, slowly, the car swaying slightly. The path, she saw, was narrowing between the trees; ahead were mounds of mud from last night's rain.

She backed up until it opened enough to manage a

U-turn. Then she stopped, facing the road some fifty yards away. Here, she was in a safe harbor; out there, what? The morning was brightening, and there was a steady flow of cars, most of them heading into center city. She drove up the path. She hadn't noticed that Matt had awakened. He was sitting up now, crying. She reached over to bring him close to her. Only the upper part of his body came, then he pulled back. He was looking out the window, sobbing.

"We'll be home soon, darling."

She was at the intersection now. Cars were flying by; she was looking for a chance to break in. There seemed to be no end to them. But here, maybe here; and suddenly, almost without caring, she swung into a small opening, gravel flying off the bridle path. Horns went off behind and next to her; someone raised a middle finger. But, with a little cry of relief, she stared far ahead. A police car was parked on the shoulder near a busy intersection, the officer working the traffic light. She gradually eased her way over—stopping, starting, always amid the blasts of horns—and then parked on the shoulder. Turning off the motor, she grabbed Matt, jumped out of the car, and ran to the policeman.

"Help me! Please help me!"

Startled, he put the light on automatic.

"I— Please—"

"Come here, come here." He ushered them over to his car, helped them into the back. As he leaned in, she tried to get out the story. Parts of it. Whatever came out of her mouth. A car chasing them last night from the institute, Cartwell Institute. Spending the night in the park. But it apparently was enough, for he closed the door and slid into the front seat. She thought he was going to drive off, but he only used the radio.

After a few moments he turned and said, "Are you Dr. Keller?"

"Yes."

"All right, just take it easy. Now, look, someone will be here shortly. I can't leave here right now."

"Oh, thank you." She let her head drop against the back of the seat, eyes closed. And her hand found Matt's.

But "shortly" stretched to fifteen minutes, then a half hour. The traffic thinned. He came back to the car. "It shouldn't be long."

"Why can't you take us to the police station? My son's cold, he's got to go to the bathroom."

"It'll be any minute."

A few minutes later a car pulled up behind hers. She was surprised to see Harris come out. Why would they have to send for Harris? He walked toward the police car. She got out, holding Matt by the hand.

"Are you all right?"

"I don't know. I guess. No, I'm all right."

"You're going to be all right. And he's going to be all right. Look, you leave your car here and I'll have someone pick it up. You can come with me."

"I can drive, I'm all right. I'll follow you."

"Let's do it my way. It'll be better."

"I don't—" Suddenly she stopped. *Sundstrum?* Mary Sundstrum? In his car? "No! What is this? No!"

She swung away from him, pulled open her door. He grabbed at her, but she flung Matt on the seat and closed the door and locked it. Locked both sides. Harris was banging on the window; the patrolman was in front of the car. The key was still in the ignition and she turned it swiftly; the motor caught and the car moved forward slowly, the patrolman backing off, his arms straight out against it as though trying to hold it back, Harris slapping at the windows. The patrolman jumped away as the car leaped forward.

She made a fast left, then another, not knowing where she was going, just trying to find her way out of the park. It was only later that she saw with a frantic glance that she didn't have her handbag—the vial of blood.

Chapter 38

As usual, Patrick got off the elevator at the fourth floor, leaving Edwin Haywood to be whisked up to the eighth. He walked to his small office, put his gun, a 9-mm Heckler & Kock P-7, in the bottom drawer of his desk, and took off his jacket.

He looked at some reports in his in-file which he hadn't gotten to yesterday.

During his first year—this was his fourth—he had felt that, despite Mr. Haywood's promises, he had left the FBI just to be a glorified bodyguard. But since then, he'd generally accompanied him only on overseas trips, where the kidnapping threat was greatest, and on a few particularly important trips in this country. At other times, one of Patrick's staff would go with him.

As Mr. Haywood had assured him, being coordinator of Decton's security forces was a full-time job. Although each subsidiary's security department was usually able to handle its own problems, Patrick wanted reports on everything; and there were many problems that required him to step in directly, such as the recent hijacking of trucks from their Marseilles and Rome plants, which he was convinced involved some of their own security people.

"Good morning, Mr. Crew." His secretary waved and then hung her sweater over the back of her typewriter chair.

"Good morning. How's your husband?"

"Much, much better, thanks."

"Good."

He called her in soon to dictate some letters—one to a chief of police in Oregon, thanking him for his help in solving the vandalization of one of their buildings; another to one of the attorneys handling their lawsuit against a former employee for the return of some materials. He was in the middle of a third letter when the phone rang. She took it, then handed it to him. "It's Mr. DeTurk."

"Yes, Walter."

Frowning now, he motioned that he would get back to her. She closed the door quietly behind her.

"For Christ's sake, where is she?"

Mackey's first thought was to grab the phone. Jeanne, she's gotten away, it's all over, finished!

But he slowly drew back his hand.

Still trying? Was he still looking for a word, for comfort, something?

She was in this with him, yet he was on his own, all on his own. And he had to think. The blood, what could he do about the blood?

He sat alone in his office, the night against the windows, his forehead pressed against his hands.

After about a half hour he straightened up, eyes narrowed. He sat quietly, thinking. Then he stood up and took an elevator to the basement. There, he walked along the gray-painted corridor until he came to the laboratory.

Mackey looked nervously at his watch, the third time in five minutes. Almost half-past eight—the lab technicians should have been at work long ago.

Maybe they weren't going to report it to him. Maybe they were afraid to and would cover up. He hadn't thought of that.

Why hadn't he thought of that?

He rubbed his eyes. He'd managed to catch a few hours' sleep on his couch last night, satisfied that he'd come up with a good solution to her having taken the blood. But he'd have to think of something else, would have to—

"Doctor."

The director of the laboratory was standing in the doorway to his office. His face looked anguished.

"You're not going to believe this! A lot of our specimens are missing!"

In and out of traffic lanes. Fast, squealing turns through the maze of roads that veined the park. Then out of the park and making her way into a suburb somewhere, past buildings she'd never seen before. And finally parking and letting her head fall back, her eyes closed, every part of her totally exhausted except her heart, her booming heart.

She reached for Matt who cowered deep in the seat, shaking with dry sobs. He struggled against coming close, but he came.

"I have to make."

"Yes, darling. Yes."

But she had no strength to start the car again; not yet, not yet. Nor the courage to drive through streets again, with police cars surely everywhere. But she was moving now, her fingers fumbling in the change box on the dash. She counted a dollar-something; she thought about a dollar fifty-five.

How could she have left her bag? And where? In the police car? Dropped it on the street?

Who could she go to for help?

Ross. Oh, did she need Ross. But who else?

Someone who could go to the police with her and say, "This woman isn't crazy, this is what's happening. They want to silence her. They want to do it by putting Matt away and doing something to her, like they must have done to John Delman, to make her crazy." Or kill her like they did Mark and Stephen Cohen and Nora and Wayne Delman and who knows how many others.

But who would believe it? Who would believe that a giant corporation was using a top mental hospital and distinguished psychiatrists to take over a drug company and God knows what else? Even if she did have that blood, even if it somehow indicated she was right, what would that—just *that*—do against a multinational corporation like Decton, a respected institution like Cartwell?

But she mustn't think of that. Her one and only thought had to be Matt, how to save Matt.

"I've got to *make!*"

"Sweetheart, I'm *looking!* We'll find someplace."

She drove onto street after street, looking at every intersection for a service station, a restaurant, a store. But she was in a prime residential area of large stone homes with curved driveways, huge hedges, and iron fences. She would have to go up to one of the houses and ask if—

Suddenly she sped off to the right, toward an Exxon sign at what seemed to be another intersection. She was about to pull in but then saw that this was a shopping area, with a Howard Johnson's down the street. At the restaurant, she parked the car quickly, hurried in with him. He had finished and was waiting for her when she came out of the rest room.

"Let's have something to eat."

"I—I'm not hungry."

"No, you've got to eat something."

They sat at the counter. He finally agreed on a glass of milk and a doughnut.

"What will you have, miss?"

"Nothing." She had to save something for calls. But who?

Jerri. Why hadn't she thought right away of Jerri? She had a pretty calm head, would meet with her; together they might think of something.

She had to make the call from the phone booth next to the service station; the phone in the restaurant was open. Matt stood at the door as she dialed Information—Jerri would be at school now. She dialed the number quickly, before she forgot it, but then the operator came on and asked for more money. She didn't have the exact change and had to feed in an extra quarter.

"University of Pennsylvania."

"Dr. Jerri Cassidy, please. She's in the chemistry department."

The phone rang about five times before someone answered. Dr. Cassidy was in class; would she care to leave a message?

"Would you please get her for me? It's very important, it's urgent!"

"I don't know if I can. I'm—just a student."

"Please get her! Please! It's an emergency."

"Hold on."

The wait was so long that the operator broke in and

asked for additional change. She had it, just about, but Jerri still might not come on. And she would need the change. She hung up. And regretted it instantly.

She was about to call back, then changed her mind. Maybe she should go to the police. But she mustn't go with Matt. She had to keep Matt out of Sundstrum and Mackey's hands, had to hide him while she tried to work things out. But where?

Her mother? Get one of her brothers to pick them up?

She put in a coin and made a collect call to her mother.

"Yes," she heard her say to the operator, "this is Mrs. Vignola. Who's calling? Carla? . . . Yes, this is her mother."

"Mom?"

"Carla, where are you? You're driving all of us crazy!"

"Mom, listen to me."

"Police, your doctor, everyone's been calling us! Where are you?"

"Mom, listen to me, I need you."

"You need a crazy house, that's what you need! Where's Matt? A crazy house, that's where you belong! A crazy house! You're crazy! Where are you? I'm coming with Joe!"

"Mom, I'll be all right." And with that, head bent, she slowly hung up.

She was so shaken she just stood for several moments, a hand on the glass to keep from falling. When she opened her eyes, she made a weak effort to put in a coin to call Jerri back—but happened to look down at Matt. And for the first time she became fully aware of how completely terrified he was, that she'd been doing nothing but adding to his fears.

She swept him up—oh, how long legged he'd gotten—and carried him to the car. There, stroking his face, she said, "Matt, I want to tell you something. First, I want you to know that everything's going to be all right. Nobody's going to hurt you and nobody's going to hurt me. I won't let them. Do you hear me? Do you believe me?"

He looked at her without saying anything. Then he nodded.

"And I want you to know this. You were right. And all I can say is I'm sorry I didn't believe you. But you were right. Dr. Mackey is a bad person. And Dr. Sundstrum is too. I don't know why some people are bad, they just are, but nobody's going to hurt us. Nobody."

She put her arms around him and drew him close. His arms stayed down.

"I love you so much, sweetheart, and there's nobody in this world who's going to hurt you. Nobody. Nobody. Nobody."

Her arms tightened around him.

She was about to release him when she let out a little half sob. His arms had come around her and were now squeezing her hard.

She slipped out of the car and went to the phone again. This time Matt simply looked on from the window.

Quickly she inserted coins, then dialed Information.

Why hadn't she thought of him before? He should have been the first one. He was the one who should talk to the police, who stood the best chance of convincing them; a man with his reputation—

Please let him be in!

"Yes, who should I say is calling?"

252

"Carla Keller. Dr. Keller."

"One moment please."

He came on the phone, heard her out just long enough to ask where she was.

Stay there, he'd send someone for her, said Howard Tompkins.

Chapter 39

Harris pulled into his parking spot, turned off the motor, then sat staring at the station house. How the hell could he go in there and tell them he had had the lady but she had gotten away? She's all of five-five, a hundred-eighteen, and she's got a kid, and still she got away.

He shouldn't have brought the goddam shrink. He'd wanted to do the best thing for the kid, so he'd called in the shrink, but the sight of the shrink had sent her off. No question about that. None.

Still, no excuse, no, none, for letting her get away.

He picked up the handbag from the seat, sat for several moments holding it on his lap; then he opened the door to the car and strode quickly to the building, up to Division. He went to his desk, set down the bag, then, seeing the lieutenant was alone, he picked it up again and walked over to his office. He stood in the doorway until the lieutenant, busy going over some papers, looked up.

Harris walked in a few steps. "The fucking broad beat it."

The lieutenant put down his pen, sat back.

"She jumped in her car and beat it with the kid."

"Where were you during all this?"

"I was walking her from the squad car, she'd been waiting in the squad car, I was walking her from the squad car to my car and she saw—I told you about the shrink—she saw the shrink and jumped into her car and beat it."

"What do you mean she saw the shrink?"

"I mean she saw the shrink—you know, the kid's psychiatrist, I told you I was bringing along the kid's psychiatrist."

"What the hell did you need the kid's psychiatrist for?"

"Lieutenant, we discussed it, remember? I thought it was best for the kid."

"Oh, Jesus Christ. Jesus Christ." He gestured at the bag—it was an abrupt, angry question.

"She dropped it." A lie; when she'd begun to run, that's all he'd been able to grab.

"Jesus Christ. And you lost her. How the hell did you lose her?"

He gestured helplessly. "By the time I got in the car, and the cop got in his, she was gone. We went all over, she was gone. But they'll find her."

"I don't want to hear they'll find her! I don't want to hear that shit! Don't let me hear that shit! Who wants to hear that shit?" He flung his pen on the desk, then picked it up and made an elaborate act of returning to his paperwork. Harris stood there for a moment, then went back to his desk.

Everyone, everyone in the goddam place heard!

His face, his neck, burned. He felt like taking this goddam bag and heaving it into his goddam office—no, right into his goddam face.

He waited a while, trying to cool off.

255

He couldn't shake the rage, though; knew he had to work through it.

"Murph," he called to a heavyset man sitting near the lieutenant's office, "will you go over this with me?"

Murph, who was on disability, and served as a clerk, came over to record the contents of the handbag. Harris took out one item at a time. A small purse containing thirty-eight dollars and seventy-three cents, one comb, one lipstick, one more comb, a small pack of tissues, an appointment book—he flipped through it—one hairbrush, a copy of an article on something called conjoint therapy, a letter from a doctor referring someone, a prescription pad, a note to a doctor reporting on a patient, a thin tube partially filled with blood—

He held it in his hand, turning it.

"Hey," Murph said, frowning, "they're probably right."

"Who? What about?"

Hadn't he seen the report yet? Put it on his desk about an hour ago. Cartwell was missing some stuff from its lab. They didn't know, but thought it was possible Keller did it.

Harris looked at the vial again, the blood swirling slightly.

He'd been frightened by her look as she clutched the kid—wild-eyed, disheveled. But this senseless grabbing of stuff from the lab scared him even more for the life of that boy.

After hanging up the phone, Patrick opened the bottom drawer of his desk, took out the gun and strapped it on. He put on his jacket, wishing to hell he could trust DeTurk to handle this on his own. He generally did, but after last night you had to wonder.

He opened the door to his office, pausing outside to tell Mrs. Willey to call his wife and say he might be late—he was to take her and the kids to his sister's for dinner. Also, if he didn't get back in time, of course, she should let Mr. Haywood's secretary know he wouldn't be available for the ride home.

He walked past the line of other offices, with their little frontages of secretaries' desks, and out to the hall, over to the elevators.

If he did ride with Mr. Haywood, he might mention it. But that depended, as always, on whether it seemed important for him to know.

Harris made several calls—to Carla's housekeeper, her office, a friend of hers at the U of P, her mother, two of her brothers—but no one, except for the mother, had heard from her.

They would call, they assured him, the moment they did.

And he didn't doubt it. For without exception they mentioned how drastically she'd changed lately, and said they were worried about her and the boy.

He sat back from his desk now, wondering why the hell he didn't go home. He hadn't slept in over twenty-four hours and felt like collapsing. It couldn't be just the case. Besides, it wasn't really his anymore—every cop in the city and suburbs was on the lookout for her.

It was, he finally conceded, the argument he'd had yesterday with Marie.

What a bunch of bullshit he'd had to listen to.

"You've changed, you're angry all the time, you walk around with a chip on your shoulder, I don't even know you anymore!"

Let's go for counseling, she'd said—to a marriage counselor, a psychiatrist, anyone.

Oh shit.

He didn't need help, they did.

Ross's suitcase was almost the last one to come down the chute and onto the turntable. He grabbed it, hurried over to the long line at the baggage checkout gate, then strode outside to wait in another line for a cab. When his turn came, he tossed his suitcase into the taxi and climbed in.

He stared out the window, his body trying to run ahead.

But run where? To do what?

"I'm going to have to use Nineteenth—at Twenty-first there's a detour," the cab driver said.

"Anything."

At the building, Ross paid him off quickly and walked through the swinging door. He checked his mailbox, only to see if there was a message from her. But the mail was all crap, and he lugged it and his suitcase onto the elevator. When he opened the door to his apartment it felt empty, hollow, as though a presence were gone. He yanked open the Venetian blinds in the living room and sunlight sprang in—but the emptiness was still there. He put down the suitcase and went to the phone. He began dialing swiftly.

He had to get this goddam story straight.

The first thing he'd done when he'd gotten off the plane was call her home, hoping for a miracle. But all he got from Mrs. LeVine was this crazy story the police had finally given her about why they were looking for Carla and Matt.

Carla attacking Mackey?

It was crazy, it didn't make any sense. If she had, if it was true, something had led up to it. But out of the clear blue?

"Hello."

"Mrs. LeVine, I'm sorry to bother you again. Look, I want to try to get certain things clear. Where was Dr. Keller seen last? At the hospital?"

"No. Matt was at a birthday party, and she picked him up. No one saw them after that."

"Where was this party?"

"At the home of a friend of hers, a lady friend of hers. Dr. Cassidy. Her son had a party. In fact, Dr. Cassidy just called again, wanted to know did I hear anything yet. She's so upset."

"Do you know if Dr. Keller said anything to her about—where she might be going?"

"Dr. Cassidy said no. Dr. Keller just took Matt and left."

"Is there anything else you can think of? Maybe something the police said?"

No, she really didn't know anything more than what she'd already told him. But she was so upset when the police spoke to her that maybe she didn't get everything clear. If he wanted to talk to the police, she had some numbers they'd left in case she heard from the doctor. One of them—here it was, a Detective Harris—had even given her his home phone.

Waiting—probably it was close to a half hour now—she became suddenly aware of how sun-bright and warm it had become in the car. Very gently, she lifted her arm from around Matt—he seemed to have fallen into an exhausted sleep—rolled up her window, then turned on the motor so that she could run the air conditioner. He stirred a little, wetting his lips, but didn't waken. Warm air came in at first, but then it cooled.

She sat back, feeling, it seemed, every part of her body in pistonlike motion. She felt such rage, frustration. What do you do when something so horrendous,

259

so unbelievable is going on and there's no one to hear?

It was crazy focusing even a flicker of thought on her mother now, when that was so insignificant. Who cared? But she did care, only because it was a rerun of her whole life—the caring, loving mother who was always there in sickness and made the biggest, steamiest meals, and gave the biggest kisses in those stubby arms, but who never once came to school on parents' day. And who asked why college when you don't need college to get a good job, and *medical* school?—you a doctor?

All her life, it seemed, she'd had to fight.

But—*this?* How do you fight this? How do you scream listen, please listen, without seeming mad, without them taking your child away, even giving him to the same people who were destroying him? The *same!*

Maybe—dear God, maybe she was wrong, going in.

But what else? And who better to turn to than Howard?

"Mommy."

"Yes, sweetheart."

"I'm thirsty."

There was a soda machine over by one of the service-station bays. She looked at her change. Just about enough. "Do you want to come with me?"

He slid out after her and followed to the soda machine. After some deliberation, he chose grape. The can rattled out and she pulled open the tab. He gulped it, then began taking small sips. After a while he handed it to her. There was still some in it and she raised it to her lips. But almost immediately, frowning, she lowered it.

A car was driving slowly past the intersection, and for a few frightening seconds she thought the driver was looking at her strangely. She was wrong—he was pointing something out to a couple of children in the back seat. But it startled her into taking Matt back to the car. She locked the doors, but kept the motor running.

After a few minutes she began to worry about the time going by; perhaps she had given Howard the wrong corner. Had she gotten both streets right? She couldn't remember. Or even if she'd told him which suburb.

Maybe she ought to call again. She counted her change: thirteen cents left. Maybe the service station would let her use their phone. She couldn't see anyone in the bays or, from where she was sitting, in the office. But she could, she suddenly remembered, make a collect call to his office. She would give him five more minutes.

Still, the voice, when it came, startled her. "Dr. Keller?" A man had materialized next to her window, was leaning toward it. Tall, blond, he was smiling pleasantly. "Mr. Tompkins sent me."

She quickly rolled down the window. "I didn't mean to jump like that."

"I'm sorry I scared you."

"Please. What does he say to do?"

"He wants us to go to his office."

"Should I follow you?"

"He thinks it's best if I go with you—in case we're stopped. Someone brought me; I'll tell him to go back. Would you like me to drive?"

"No, that's all right."

She was about to open her door to let him slide through to the back when her eyes went to the side-view mirror. A man was walking toward them quickly. Too quickly. For a moment she sat paralyzed, then shot a wild look at the man next to her. He immediately grabbed for the door handle, but almost with one

261

movement she pulled the gear into drive and her foot pushed the pedal to the floor. The car roared forward as though from a catapult, the steering wheel shaking in her hands, and she turned onto the first road, then another, then still another. Now in farmland, she was on a narrow road that undulated past distant houses and barns and silos, past ponds, past dots of grazing black Angus cattle on a hill, past scatterings of fine shiny horses standing probing the grass.

Howard Tompkins too?

The words seemed to roar through her brain.

Past a farmer, far off, on a tractor, past a little abandoned railroad station and grass-tufted tracks, past the decayed tooth of a gutted stone farmhouse, past thick trees overhanging the road.

Howard Tompkins? Howard *Tompkins?*

Everyone?

Past narrow private lanes—

Swing into one of them! Go up, pound on the door, I need your phone, call—

But who? Who could she call?

She slowed. Her foot, rather, suddenly seemed too weak to hold down the pedal. She reached distantly for Matt, unaware he was huddled into her, was digging into her thigh. She pressed him to her harder. It was to reassure him, but she knew he had to feel her shaking.

She had to take a chance on her own with the police. She was trying to decide which lane.

This one?

But by the time she'd decided she had passed it. She drove on, past acres of white picket fence. And then, like a speck in the distance, a car appeared in the rearview mirror. It could be any car, any; she'd passed several. But she increased speed, eyes going to the mirror. It was coming closer. She floored the pedal, even though she still didn't know. The other car kept up.

The road was becoming sinuous now. She had to keep braking at curves, the tires squealing and threatening to slide away. She kept maneuvering back, then slamming the wheel around again. Another curve. Now another. Here was another—but this time, as she straightened out, a truck was lumbering in front of her.

She tried to pass it, but couldn't on the curve. She swung out at a short straightaway, but another curve and she had to come back.

Now the other car was slowly beginning to fill the rear-view mirror.

She could see two men.

She pressed on the horn, kept pressing it. Move over! Stop! Please!

The other car was next to her now, stayed next to her even at a curve. The blond man was smiling at her. Then he motioned for her to pull over, with a hand holding a gun.

When she didn't right away, he aimed it at her face, still smiling. And the car kept angling her onto the shoulder.

Chapter 40

Immediately after his call to Mrs. LeVine, Ross flipped through the phone book and placed a fast call to Dr. Mackey at the institute.

"I'm sorry, he's with someone right now," his secretary said.

"Do you have any idea how long he'll be?"

"No, I don't."

Ross left his name and phone number, then called Harris at the Division. But the line was busy. He quickly dialed again on the chance he'd gotten a wrong number; still busy. He slammed down the receiver.

Don't panic. She'll be all right. She'll be all right because she has to be all right.

That lady with the rasp of a voice whom he'd always looked on as though from a distance, as always part of a star-touched couple, had become achingly important and real to him. And no one could tell him that the Carla he'd made love to only a few days ago, whose lips and breasts and damp locked legs and rhythmic meetings he could still almost feel; that that Carla, and the Carla who afterward stayed in his arms and exchanged touches and smiles, and with whom he sat outside the hospital and spoke on the phone, that she—despite all the pressures, those goddam pressures—had gone suddenly raving mad.

Oh, no.

He dialed again. This time the phone rang.

"Harris." The voice sounded flat, dull.

"Mr. Harris, my name is Ross Robbins. I'm a friend of Dr. Keller's."

Silence. He was calling, he continued, to see if he could find out a bit more about what had happened, if anything had preceded the incident with Dr. Mackey, if there'd been any kind of argument, quarrel—

"Hold on, hold on," Harris cut in. "What're you driving at?"

"It's just that I know her, and I can't see her acting that way unless something started it off."

"I see." But there was a note of sarcasm. "Well, if you're a friend of hers, you already know what started it off. You wouldn't have to ask me. She's one sick lady, buddy! Out there somewhere with one sick kid! Who's in danger! You hear me? You hear what I say?"

"Wait a second, why are you yelling?"

He didn't seem to hear. "Instead of worrying what the fuck started it, worry about the kid! Don't ask me what started it! Tell me where she is! You seen her the past few weeks? You talk to her? You've seen her and talked to her, and you call me to ask me what started it?"

Grimacing, Ross stood by the phone for a few moments after he hung up. Was *this* who was looking for her? He sounded like a madman. Like someone—like someone who *wanted* to believe she was insane.

*   *   *

265

Walking out of his office, Mackey paused just long enough to tell his secretary he had an appointment and would be leaving for the day.

"Oh, a Mr. Robbins called you."

"Robbins? Did he say what he wanted?"

"No. I said you'd call back."

"Put it on my desk. I'll see you tomorrow."

He strode out to his car. He pulled off the instant the ignition caught; the car bucked, threatened to stall. It took an effort not to speed out to the street, but he couldn't because of the humps.

There was a slight ringing in his ears. It was nothing new—he'd had it for days, at least whenever he'd thought to listen. It was a little worse, though. But it should be—there was a steady drumming through his body.

He dreaded going home. Yet he had to be home. He had tried to leave fifteen minutes ago, but Old Man Cartwell had come in. That half-senile old fool. His brain was becoming mush, but his fingers were like talons; they gripped his forearm as he talked about doing this, building that, most of it gibberish.

Oh, how he'd wanted to grab him under those flesh-swinging jowls and shake him and cry out, "Face it with me! Wake up all the way and face it with me!"

Cartwell who'd been his mentor, just as he'd been Mark's.

But he mustn't think of Mark. He didn't most of the time; and whenever he did, there was the comfort that he'd had no direct hand in it. And that was true of the others, even of Sam Devereaux. He'd merely said to DeTurk—almost in passing—said something about his still being alert.

It was true. Never direct.

He kept driving through the bright afternoon sun.

But then why had he agreed—in fact, suggested—that Carla and the boy be brought to the farm?

He found Jeanne in the living room, reading a book, three others fanned out on the lamp table next to her, the drapes closed thickly against the sun. She looked at him standing in the archway, the only acknowledgment that he was home so early. She turned back to her book.

"Please talk to me. Please."

She looked up slowly. "I'm talking."

"They're—bringing her here."

She seemed momentarily startled, but said nothing.

"Jeannie, how did we get into this?" Tears were brimming in his eyes.

She flung her book aside. "Because we *wanted* it, goddam it! We talked it over and talked it over and that's what we *wanted! You* wanted—and whatever *you* wanted *I* wanted!"

"Then why aren't you with me now?"

"I am! Don't you see? We're both poisoned, poisoned! Only I'm poisoned in a different way!"

He went over and sank to one knee, his head on her skinny thigh. Her hand came from somewhere and rested on his head. He reached back and touched it. He hadn't felt her hand in so long! He found himself thinking of her the way he'd first seen her, through a hospital doorway, a little thing with auburn bangs that framed a thin pert face, the little lab technician who had every intern panting.

When had they first become poisoned? Five years ago? Three? Or hadn't he noticed all along?

"Why," she said, "are you letting them bring her here?"

He didn't know how to answer. But it had to be shared. "Just—till dark."

Mackey's? Bill Mackey's?

Carla, clutching Matt on her lap, her body pressed deep in the corner so not to touch the man sitting in back with them, stared around dazedly as they drove her car up the familiar, long, pebbled lane. They seemed to be heading to the house, but instead the driver turned into the cutoff to the barn. He stopped on the slight incline that led to it, got out and swung open the doors, then drove in. Climbing out again, he reached in and grabbed her by the wrist, half-dragging her out. She almost stumbled to the ground with Matt, then managed to straighten up. Matt was whimpering, trying to hold onto her legs. The man kept jerking her by the wrist, making them walk faster through the barn.

He opened a door and they entered a section of the barn that Mackey had converted years ago into a "house" for his children. It was like an old living room, with wicker furniture, some of it broken, and windows that looked out on the pasture.

He motioned her onto the sofa. She sank down on it, holding Matt to her. She huddled over him, as though trying to shield him from the sight of them.

There had actually been three men, but only two had brought them here. One was heavyset, with a crew cut; the other a powerfully built thin-faced man. The third man, the one with the blond hair, had either taken off in their car or was following them.

He came about twenty minutes later. She could hear the car approaching, then the crackle of tires on pebbles near the barn, and then silence. The thin-faced man went outside to motion him to the entrance.

The blond man came in with a large paper bag. He'd

stopped to buy sandwiches and drinks. He distributed them to the other two, and the three of them sat down in a semicircle to eat and chat.

Carla stared at them, her eyes darting from one to the other.

Her heart, her blood were thundering.

She and Matt were already dead to them!

Chapter 41

The men, sandwich wrappings and empty containers stuffed into the bag and set aside, chatted as if they were in their own living room, as if she and Matt were no more than a TV that they would take turns looking at indifferently. Pat, DeTurk, Al—they had names. Two of them liked the Phillies, one never went to ball games anymore. One, Al, had decided recently he hated summers, he hated the heat, and another— DeTurk—had noticed a boil on his right calf this morning, which Al looked at and said whatever you do don't squeeze it. Al, who apparently worked at Cartwell, agreed with DeTurk that some nuts acted more normal than some normal people. And about the ride here—Al, as though relishing it as an adventure he'd missed, said he was almost sorry they hadn't been stopped in her car so they could give the story that she'd called the institute to be picked up.

And as they sat and talked so casually, one with a leg over the arm of his chair, another leaning forward to make a point, her eyes kept going to the door, the windows, as though this time, *this* time she might see something, find a way. Crash through the glass? Desperately she kept coming back to that. But they were small, it was impossible . . .

Yet each time her eyes flashed over, it was as though with the hope they'd be bigger, that she'd dare.

She hunched quickly over Matt now.

"Don't darling." He'd begun whimpering again, his head still buried against her. "Everything will be all right. Please, darling, don't."

And this time when she looked up, the three of them were looking at her. But then they slowly turned away. Steak, Al said, would you believe he'd gotten tired of steak?

With these fingernails—their eyes!

With her teeth—their noses, their ears, their throats!

Hack at them, smash them, see them dead and gutted—

"No, darling, no more." She was rocking with him slightly, aware he could feel her own body's turbulence. "Everything will be all right. No more, no—"

This time when she looked up it was in response to a sound. The doorknob turning.

The door opened.

William Mackey walked in. He kept looking at his hand closing the door behind him, as though reluctant to meet her eyes, and then looked at the men. "I would like to be alone with her."

The man she'd heard called Pat seemed to be thinking it over. Then he stood up and went with Al to stand outside the front door while DeTurk went out the door at the rear. Mackey still had difficulty looking at her. When he did his eyes were mostly on Matt. "I— Can they have him just a few minutes? I don't want to talk in front of him."

She stared at him unbelievingly. "Why? Will it help

him?" Then her eyes filling: "If it will, here!" She tried to thrust Matt, suddenly screaming and thrashing, toward him. "Here! Here!"

He looked away. She drew Matt back to her, folded her arms across his back, pressed her lips against his head. Mackey turned slowly back to her, sank down on a chair. His chin was trembling as he said, "Why didn't you leave things alone? I begged you! I begged you! What have you accomplished? The blood? You have it? The police have it? It's not going to do anything anyway. Everything's covered. All you brought on was this!"

Tears filmed his eyes, then spilled over. He clamped his lips shut as the tears rolled down. Then he sank his forehead onto his hand.

"Help us, Bill."

"I—can't." He was shaking his head. "I can't."

He was breathing heavily, staring down. "I tried to save you. Mary—Mary Sundstrum—she tried to save you. Keep you busy with Matt. Didn't want to hurt Matt. Tried to save you."

"Then *save*— Please."

"I can't."

"Just Matt. Please—just Matt. You've got a phone, a car."

He was looking at her fiercely now. "I can't! Can't you understand I can't?"

She wanted to leap at him, beat at him. "Bill, wh-who are you? Who are you?"

"Don't judge me, Carla. Goddam you, don't judge me!"

"Don't *judge* you!"

"I tried to save you! God knows how I tried. . . . And what do you know about me? You don't know anything about me! Nothing!"

"What do I have to know about you? More than"—

she gestured wildly—"this. More than what you're doing."

He put his elbows on his thighs, clenched hands against his mouth. His eyes were closed. "He was my god."

She stared at him. He said nothing for a while, pressing his hands to his mouth, his eyes squeezed shut.

"He was my god. I was married—had little kids—a young guy from Indiana whose father wanted him to go into the drugstore, but who wanted to do great things, help people, help the world."

He was looking at her now. He was breathing through his mouth.

"Wanted to do great things. Wanted to do great things. And here was my god, one of my gods. The great and holy Dr. Cartwell. Would the great Dr. Cartwell do anything wrong? Would—"

The door opened and the man named Pat stepped in.

"What do you want?" Mackey demanded.

"Just checking to see how you are."

"Get out! Get out!"

"Hey," he said slowly. "Hey now. Don't talk to me that way, hear? You hear?"

"Just—leave us alone. Please."

The blond man kept staring at him. "Don't you ever talk to me that way." He waited a few more moments, staring, then withdrew, closing the door.

Mackey clamped his hands over his face. His body shuddered. It was a while before he let his hands drop. He held them clenched on his lap. "Like a god," he said. "Would the great Cartwell ever do anything wrong? 'Bill, I've had my eye on you and you're bright and there's a great opportunity here. We've a handful of beds for people who work for this certain corporation who, if they ever become mentally ill, might

273

reveal a lot of corporate secrets no one must know. You'll be able to do your own work, do whatever research you want, see your own patients, write papers, but you'll be one of the few of us who take care of these people.' "

He stood up, too agitated to sit. He faced the window.

"Okay?" he said, his back to her. "Anything wrong with that?"

"No." She didn't know, she didn't care, she would say anything to reach him.

"Oh, a person might be a little suspicious. But, really, it's like being an industrial psychiatrist in a way. And add to that all the extra money. The money! Oh, the money! And the travel. And the prestige of being known as Cartwell's protégé, of going up the ladder fast."

He stopped. She could see his shoulders begin to shake, could hear a short, quick sob. "Anything—wrong with that? That?"

"No . . . No."

He was crying quietly but convulsively.

"Bill."

"Anything wrong with that?"

"No, Bill. No."

She could see him fighting to calm down. "But then, then come the compromises. Don't ask me how they come, they come. Someone's just curious about what a patient said, and you know better but it seems harmless and you pass it along."

"We get drawn into things, Bill." Say anything, anything.

He turned to face her. "Oh, God, how it happens. Soon you're listening—you're listening to a suggestion that it might be better to put someone you were thinking of treating as an outpatient in the hospital. Then it starts getting heavier."

He sagged onto the chair again. He began picking at the tip of a finger as though it might have a splinter. "Gets heavier. Oh, just now and then, but heavier. Like now, you're in it so deep you're committing an executive they don't want going to another company, or a potential senator they don't want elected. Or"— he was rubbing his palms along his thighs now—"a John Delman who doesn't want to go along with the sale of his company and just happened to survive an accident."

She stared at him. He was still looking at his hands as they rubbed at his thighs. She said, "Tell me—about Mark."

He didn't seem to hear. "It gets heavier and you do it. It happens. You don't think it can happen to you, but it happens."

"Tell me about Mark."

"Mark?" He was looking at her now, hands still rubbing away. "You want to know what happened to Mark? I'll tell you what happened to Mark. You were on the right track. Devereaux? Sam Devereaux? He knew some relatives of Mark's, gave him a job at his firm, liked him, found out he loved medicine but couldn't get into medical school."

"And he got him in." The words just came out.

"Got him in. And paid. And there waiting for Mark was this great opportunity at Cartwell. With all the compromises. All the compromises," he said softly. "Only Delman's suicide finally was too much for him to take. And he thought he could just quit."

Matt was starting to squirm again, letting out little gasps. She clutched his head to her.

"But you just don't quit. It sounds like a bad movie,

but you don't, you can't. Not with all you know. And not when you've been making so much money that they even work out a way where you can own a Darby's to launder it."

"Oh, Bill." Her hand was trembling as she held onto Matt's head. "Help us."

He was standing there, chest heaving, spent. If he heard what she said, he didn't acknowledge it.

"You can believe this or not," he said, "but I loved Mark."

He turned and walked quickly to the door. He leaned his forehead against it.

"And I envy him."

He opened it quickly and walked out.

She was huddled over Matt as the others walked in. And only now, with all the hate in her, did she realize that he'd used her for some kind of comfort.

Chapter 42

A few minutes after four that afternoon Edwin Haywood's secretary came into his office with the day's letters for him to sign. She set them on his desk, each tucked under the flap of its envelope.

"Mr. Crew won't be going home with you. He had to go out and won't be back."

He nodded, started to read the top letter, then paused to reflect that it was probably Cartwell business. Patrick had been briefing him occasionally in his casual way. He was simply curious now, not anxious. He'd experienced too much to be anxious over something as simple as this—Christ, he'd helped finance coups, overthrown governments—and there were always walls of responsibility, of executives, between him and events. And Patrick, in his own specialty, was one of the best.

He'd had a hunch about him from the time they'd been thrown together for a game of racquet ball, and afterward in the steam room and on adjoining massage tables, sensed his desire to move on from the FBI, the hidden executive streak.

Like the hunches about so many things. Like the

institute. He'd met the Cartwells, the old father and son, when they were running a dry-out place and were looking for investors to turn it into a mental health center. The idea had come to him almost immediately—not only did it feel like a good investment, but it seemed a place where company secrets could stay secrets if any of his important people became mentally ill, as in the case of Samuel Devereaux: a place where he might eventually have a few psychiatrists in his pocket. So he had one of his subsidiaries buy into their corporation, then finally take it over by giving the Cartwells stock in several subsidiaries in exchange for their stock in the institute.

The phone. He waited to see if Mrs. Lake would buzz. She did, and it was Stu Bryand, president of his bank and executive vice-president of the chamber of commerce, wanting to know if he could possibly talk at their next luncheon instead of the one after. He agreed, and they chatted while he read another letter. The phone again, and another buzz—Stu again, this time, of all things, to tell him a joke.

"Mrs. Lake, hold all calls for about twenty minutes."

But when the phone rang, she buzzed. "I'm sorry, Mr. Haywood, but it's Mr. Tompkins. He said he's leaving his office and he'd like just a word with you if he can."

"I'll take it. Yes, Howard."

"Didn't mean to break in, Ed, but I wanted you to know that I've just heard from Delman and Sharples's lawyer, and Sharples has gone over the agreement of sale and everything's fine. There's one minor, very minor, change he might want to make, but it's no problem—it doesn't change a thing. We would have set up the meeting tomorrow for the signing, but Sharples can't make it, so the day after.

"Can you make it then?" Tompkins asked. "They suggested about ten, but any time you can make it."

Haywood flipped the pages of his desk calendar. "Ten o'clock will be fine."

"Good. I'll probably talk to you tomorrow."

Haywood didn't permit himself any great feeling of satisfaction as he turned now to the last of the letters; he never did until he had something signed. But still. How Howard had tried talking him out of it! And, from a practical point of view, he may have been right. Stuart Sharples, John Delman's cousin and co-majority stockholder, wanted to sell his interest in the firm, but John Delman didn't. And as Howard Tompkins had said, "Why waste your time when there are other pharmaceutical firms around?"

Well, it wasn't just because Stuart Sharples would have first option to purchase John Delman's stock in the event of his death. That was important, of course; but the big reason was that the company seemed just right. One of the so-called experts he consulted didn't agree: the company's patents were running out on the drugs it had developed; it was also coming up against stiffer competition on the generic drugs it manufactured; and it was pouring money—John Delman's idea, it turned out, which Stuart Sharples had disagreed with—into research that probably wouldn't pay off soon, if ever.

But that was the whole point; that was what made it right.

The price of the company, he felt, was depressed—and it was deeply involved in the new, mind-staggering biotechnologies, including receptor research and molecular genetics.

He'd never heard of receptors until a few years ago. Genetic engineering, of course, but never receptors. He'd learned about them at a party a few years ago, from an enthusiastic young biochemist who'd cornered him and then held him fascinated. Did you know that up until about 1900, scientists didn't really understand the basic way drugs worked? But then a couple of scientists, disputing the notion that a drug could have the effects it did by general absorption through the body, theorized that there had to be specific places, or receptors, in the body where specific chemicals were able to act. And though this theory came to be accepted, it wasn't until relatively recently, through advances in molecular biology, that scientists could begin to understand the chemical makeup of some receptor sites in cells, could begin to develop the first drugs that would act on certain ones. For example, there was the development of medication that could help cure and prevent the recurrence of ulcers by blocking off histamine, an acid-triggering substance within the body, at certain receptors.

Receptor research, the young man said, opened a new era of drugs, just as the first of the antibiotics did—an era in which drugs would be targeted more and more to do specific things with little or no effect on other organs or body functions. You could hardly guess at the future—what kinds of drugs receptor research and molecular manipulation and other biomedical technologies would produce to prevent or cure disease, extend life, change the human makeup.

And it stayed with Haywood.

Surely every pharmaceutical firm was involved in the new technologies, but he was going to be part of this wave; not only that, be in the forefront, be in the position of owning and controlling such drugs.

And perhaps even go far beyond the others.

So he'd set up the search committee to gather additional staff to bolster the Delman & Sharples team—scientists throughout the world on the furthest edges of the biotechnology revolution, a couple of them kooks, perhaps, but brilliant kooks: Dr. Montana, who'd triggered a scandal by publishing false data but who just might enable Haywood to own the patent on a compound that expands brain power; Dr. Schemenko and his assistant, from Russia, working on the body's immune system to hold off the aging process.

If the kooks worked out—well, that would be the icing.

What counted was that owning Delman & Sharples was just plain good business.

And this was another of his hunches.

He gave Mackey until about four, then called his office again. "This is Ross Robbins. I left a message a couple of hours ago for the doctor to call me back. Can you tell me when I'll be able to talk to him?"

"I'm sorry, Mr. Robbins, he had to leave for the day."

"Did you give him my message?"

"Yes, I did. But he had an appointment, he had to leave."

"Do you know if he'll be calling in?"

"I don't know."

No, she was sorry, she couldn't give out his home phone number. Was he a patient?

"No, but I want to talk to him about a patient—Dr. Keller?"

"I can call his home and leave a message there that you called again."

"Please. I just want to ask him something."

He knew there might not be anyone at Mackey's house to get the message. And the secretary would probably be leaving at five. How could he get the number when he didn't even know what county the

281

man lived in? And even if he did, there was a good chance he had an unlisted number.

He put through a call to Carla's office, spoke to her secretary. No, she couldn't go through Doctor's phone index and give out any numbers.

Who else?

And what was he even calling Mackey about?

His anxiety was wiping out the reason.

To find out if anything had happened before she tried to attack Mackey. If there'd been any warning, any sign.

But mostly just to talk about her. He had to talk about her, had to have hope. He just couldn't sit here. It was maddening to have to just sit here.

Carla's house. Yes. He dialed quickly. But Mrs. LeVine was a mess, it was hard to get through to her.

"I can't stay in this house anymore," she said weakly. Her voice sounded strained from crying. "I'm sick over it. My daughter says I shouldn't stay here. I'm going to leave. I wait, I wait, I run to pick up the phone—"

"Mrs. LeVine—"

"I'm no youngster. This isn't my family. After all. I'm going to make myself sick. My daughter's going to come for me. I don't want to leave, I don't know what to do. I can't make myself sick."

"Mrs. LeVine, listen to me. I'm looking for a phone number. Do you know where Doctor's phone directory is?"

"The phone book?"

"No, her address book. Where she keeps her numbers. Do you know where it is?"

"I don't know anything right now. I'm so confused. Her phone book?"

"Mrs. LeVine, can I come over? Can I look? I'm just ten minutes away. Please."

"I can't stay here. I don't know what to do."

"I'll be right over!"

He was at her house before he remembered that he'd forgotten to turn on his answering machine. Jesus, if Mackey called! Mrs. LeVine opened the door to a house from which every sound had been sucked out. It felt ghostly, frightening, as he walked up the stairs. He went, first, to the phone on the kitchen wall. A little telephone booklet hung by a chain. He went to the Ms. No Mackey. There were also several three-by-five cards and pieces of paper stuck into the backing of the phone. There were a few telephone numbers on them, most of them written in pencil, which she may have jotted down while on the phone. But no Mackey.

"Where are the other phones?"

"Upstairs. In her bedroom. The study."

She followed him upstairs. He went directly to the study. He spotted the Rolodex on her desk the instant he entered. He spun it to the Ms, went through the cards. Nothing. But maybe he'd missed it. He tried again, forcing himself to go slowly.

Christ, Mackey! And two numbers!

He knew the office, God did he know the office. He dialed the other one.

It rang for almost a minute. He'd heard they had a farm, maybe they were outside somewhere. He looked at his watch. Just about five. Maybe no one home.

He let it ring.

Then, as though someone were asleep in the room, a low voice. A woman's voice. "Yes."

"Is this Dr. Mackey's home?"

"Yes." A monotone.

"Is he home?"

"No, I'm sorry."

"Do you have any idea when he'll be in?"

"No, I don't."

"Would you take a message for him?"

"Yes."

He gave both his home phone number and this number, in case Mackey just happened to walk in within the next few minutes.

Now, sitting at Carla's desk, he looked at Mrs. LeVine. She was standing in the doorway. She'd apparently been hoping a sudden miracle would emerge from the call. He would call Carla's friend, Dr. Cassidy, next, but he knew he wouldn't learn anything from her, that she would have told the police and Mrs. LeVine anything important she might know. For the first time he found himself having real trouble holding himself together. He fought to think of the things she could have done—gone to another friend's, to an out-of-the-way motel. He pictured her afraid to come back, not knowing she could call him because she assumed he was still in California.

But he couldn't keep the images in his mind. And there was absolutely nothing more he could think of doing.

William Mackey walked with long strides from the barn to the house, went straight to the refrigerator. But you could never find anything you wanted in here, goddam it! He pushed aside milk, margarine, lettuce, a pot of something-or-other, bottles of salad dressing, every goddam thing but— Here, finally—the bottle of ice water.

He tried filling a glass but his hands were shaking and most of it spilled over. He lifted the bottle and gulped from it. He couldn't seem to get enough, drank more than enough. He finally set the bottle down on the cutting board next to the sink and stood, half sagged, over it, waiting for his strength to come back, his body to settle. Sweat ran down him, sucked his clothes to him.

He walked into the laundry room and sat on a tall wooden stool near the dryer. He didn't know why he'd come in here, or—he was only now aware of this— why he'd closed the door. But he felt a certain security here. Here in this room, one of the farthest from the barn.

They'd be gone with nightfall. How he wished the few hours would go!

Oh, how he'd tried for her, the boy! Only God, if there was a God, knew.

God knew him, knew his heart. Knew that he was incapable, absolutely incapable, of physically hurting anyone.

He was trying to rationalize all of this, he knew; he couldn't fool himself about that. He was an accomplice, even though he would never touch a finger to her or the boy. He couldn't! Never! He was a prisoner of those three creatures in the barn as much as she was, Matt was.

It went back as far as he could remember, this inability to hurt anyone. That time, for instance, when he was a class monitor in seventh grade and reported Jakie for something, and after school Jakie was waiting out in the schoolyard with half the school. Jakie, the orphan boy with the runny nose! He felt so sorry for him, regretted reporting him. But Jakie wanted to fight and kept swinging—and missing. And all the while he could have smashed Jakie good, could have been school hero, but he'd never once hit him in the face, only on the arms or shoulders. Or even that time when Eddie next door who was always shooting little birds, that time when Eddie handed him his BB gun, and there was a blackbird on the driveway—he had deliberately aimed to one side.

Even his kids, he couldn't remember ever spanking—maybe once or twice on the bottom—the kids.

He was rationalizing, yes he knew it, he knew it, but it was something. And he needed something.

She was sure the men were waiting for darkness. They looked bored with each other, sat sprawled in their chairs without saying a word. But every so often one would go to the window and look at the sky and perhaps at his watch.

Waiting for darkness so they could take her and Matt somewhere. And it would probably be an accident, or a suicide and murder—a crazed mother killing her child.

If she could only *go* crazy, not see, not think, not feel.

But to sit here with this beautiful little boy, every vein in her head pulsing with the effort to think of a scheme, a way— To feel him, to know— And these animals, this filth, this vomit. Vomit! Vomit!

And the dusk beginning to shade the fields.

"Mommy."

"Yes, sweetheart."

He was looking up at her. "I have to make. Pee pee."

She stared at them. "Can he at least go to the bathroom?"

The man called Pat stood up. He walked over to a small cubicle that held a toilet and sink. Matt went in, but looked up as he stood at the toilet, waiting for him to close the door.

"Would you close the door?" she demanded.

Patrick said nothing. But he made no move to close it.

"There's nothing he can do! There's no window! He doesn't have a bomb, a machine gun! He's seven!"

But he still said nothing, just hung onto the edge of the door. She waited, standing to one side and not looking in, for the sound of him urinating. But he apparently couldn't with the door open.

He came out, closing his fly.

"Sweetheart, Mommy won't look, let me do something." She went in and, with her back to him, turned on the faucet and let it run.

Could you believe this? Doing this now?

And being relieved that he was urinating?

And asking him, now, was he thirsty, like it was any ordinary day? He nodded. He reached over and cupped water in his hands, kept going back for more. She cupped some in hers and afterward put some on her face.

Patrick nodded toward the sofa. This time Matt didn't bury his face into her. He sat against her, staring at the men. She could see, her arm across his shoulders, his lips compressed in anger, a quivering under his eyes. She was afraid he was going to spring at them. Her hand tightened just a little on his arm.

She saw, almost in astonishment, that the dusk had deepened. It seemed to have happened in an instant.

And they were all coming alive as though they, too, had just noticed!

They stirred in their chairs, then two of them stood up. One of them, DeTurk, closed the shades all the way. Then he switched on a small lamp.

Were they going to do it here?

She whirled, caught by surprise, as someone reached over from behind and quickly coiled a rope around her wrists. She began to kick, tried to get up, but she was shoved down. Matt clung to her, screaming. But DeTurk pulled him away, shoved a rag in his mouth, and began wrapping rope around him.

"Let him go! Don't—" But her head was yanked

287

back by the hair, a wadded rag pushed her mouth open, touched the back of her throat. She gagged, tried to suck in air. Someone, Patrick, eased the rag out a little. She sat bent over her knees, forcing air through her nostrils. Kept forcing it.

She sat up slowly, wanting only to look at Matt. He lay on his side; little sounds came from his throat. She tried to scream; it was an animal sound. She felt herself suffocating again. She lay back wishing it were over, please let it be over.

But keep breathing. Slowly. In. Out. In. Out.

She heard words. From somewhere to her right. Honda. The trunk. Walk 'em. Then tie.

Breathe. In. Out.

Oh, Matt. Oh, Matt.

She began to move her wrists against the rope, at first only out of instinct. But all it did was hurt her. She stopped.

Then, eyeing the men, she began again, slowly at first, then faster, harder, biting her lips against the pain.

She saw the first spurts of blood. She kept twisting her wrists, sawing at the cord.

The men were looking at her now, smiling. They seemed to be thinking: have fun.

But then, all at once, Patrick ran to her, slapped her across the face, slapped her again, then began pulling at the knot.

"What the fuck's wrong?" DeTurk's big face loomed over them.

"Use your goddam, fucking head!" He had the cord off now, tossed it aside.

"What the fuck—"

And then it hit him suddenly—that, with those rope cuts and burns, anyone could tell she'd been tied before she died.

"Get the fucking doctor!" Patrick cried.

"All right, all right."

"Get him, will you!"

DeTurk ran to the door, pulled it open, started to close it behind him. But, before he could, she was there, then past him; had pushed through the opening.

Chapter 43

William Mackey whirled at the sudden pounding on the front door. He ran to it, flung it open. DeTurk. Tomato-faced, gasping. And pointing frantically over his shoulder.

"She ran out!"

Oh, no!

DeTurk started to dash off, looked back for an instant. "Come on! And flashlights!"

But he couldn't move. Not yet. He turned dazedly. Jeanne was looking at him from the entryway to the dining room.

Flashlights. He couldn't remember where the flashlights were.

In the shed. And the barn.

But all he wanted to do was sag into a chair.

Had to get flashlights.

He started for the shed, stopped. Then he burst into a run. Up the stairs to the second floor. He was almost to his bedroom when he stopped. No. Someone might hear far off.

Not his gun.

He ran down into the kitchen. He flung open drawers, grabbed hold of a carving knife. He looked at his hand clutching the handle.

Into the fucking bitch! Into her! Again, and again, and again!

He ran past Jeanne, into the night.

She raced into the blackness of the field. Stumbling over something—a branch—she jumped up frantically, but fell back, right knee blazing with pain. She pulled herself up, biting her lips against crying out, and began hopping forward, dragging her right leg. She flung herself, face down, on the short grass at the edge of the field; began wriggling and clawing her way through it, started hopping again, bent over, then plunged down, her face pressed into the damp, cool grass.

Lights had gone on behind her.

She turned slowly, saw two spotlights, one on a corner of the house, the other somewhere near the barn. Now, as though triggered by each other, two flashlight beams, and then a third. They slashed through the blackness, coming closer. She crawled away on her elbows and one knee.

She reached taller grass and stopped for a few seconds, gasping in fire.

It had happened in an instant, her running out. She hadn't thought of it, planned it; it was just there, that small opening.

Run!—and she ran.

But now, almost for the first time, she thought of Matt. Alone in there. Gagged. Tied. Maybe suffocating.

She should have stayed with him, no matter what! Shouldn't she have stayed with him?

But that was crazy. This was their only chance, their only hope of— But how could she get away from

291

them? Where was the lane to the road? Or any way out to the road?

She was completely disoriented.

She began crawling again, then almost cried out as her hand touched something hard and cold. She felt around it. It had to be their ice house. She crawled away from it quickly, from the temptation to go in there and hide; it was probably the first place they would search. Still taller grass now. She let herself rest for a few moments, face deep in the musty smells.

"Keller!"

She froze. Then, slowly, very slowly, raised her head.

Where did it come from? It had echoed across the field.

"Keller!"

Oh, God have mercy!

Near the barn. Someone was holding up Matt, a light on his anguished face. They'd taken off the gag.

"Keller!" Patrick's voice.

"Mommy! Mommy!" He was twisting, writhing.

"Keller!"

"Mommy!"

"Keller! Two minutes! One minute! You're not here, he's dead!"

"Mom-mee! Mom-mee!"

She started to crawl to him, stopped. She clamped her hands over her ears. She mustn't listen! They would kill him anyway! But she could still hear it: *"MOM-MEE! MOM-MEE!"* She squeezed her ears even harder.

"MOM-MEE!"

Crying now, she was looking around frantically.

A knife, a gun, a rock, something she could use as a club, even a pointed stick—if she only had something!

She would drag herself to them, stab them, hit them, claw at them—

She was suddenly aware of silence.

She couldn't see Matt. Just three flashlight beams, moving through the field. Where was Matt? Had they—killed him?

Maybe they'd locked him up in the barn again.

Oh, let it be that! That they'd just tried to use him to get her back!

The three beams were advancing, one near each side of the field, the other in the center—where she was.

A rock, a stick, something—

The only thing she could do was keep crawling through the fields until maybe she reached another farmhouse or the road. But she could end up in circles; she needed some sense of direction. The best thing was to try to get out to the road—better still, just near the road, so she could follow it to a neighboring farm or flag down a car. But where was the road? She was trying desperately to orient herself. There, the barn; there, the house. The lane—she had it now—the lane was somewhere to the right of the house.

She started crawling toward the right, dragging her leg; it kept pulsating, throbbing. Suddenly she stiffened, trying to squeeze her whole body into the grass. A flashlight beam was probing the grass ahead of her. She remained motionless, unaware her eyes were closed until she slowly opened them. The moving circle of light was gone. She inched forward, staying clear of the spotlight on the house. But the grass was also shorter here. And the pain from her knee was radiating up to her hip.

She had to stop. She lay exposed but had to stop.

One side of the house, only a few yards away, lay in darkness. If she could push through the pain and reach there, rest awhile. The beams were slicing through each other some distance away. She lifted herself slightly, began moving slowly on one knee—then faster. Her hand touched the wall of the house; she turned and lay back against it. Her hands closed over her knee to hold in the pain.

Matt, what had they done to Matt?

Slowly becoming aware of it, she found herself staring at a long storage bin attached to the side of the house. Several times during visits here, she'd seen Bill take tools from there—a hammer, a rake, something once to help start the car. She slid over to it. After a quick look around, she slowly eased up the hasp, then lifted the top until it rested against the wall. She raised herself onto one leg and felt around in the blackness. A rake. Okay, something. Now a very heavy thing—it felt like a chain saw. What else? Rags. Wires. What felt like batteries. Cardboard boxes of various kinds. A pitchfork? No, another rake. And this—what? A handle. No, two handles. She lifted it out. Hedge shears.

She hopped away with them, back to the wall. Now try to find the lane, the road. She felt her way around the house, on one leg, then tried to push away on two legs but had to sink to the ground. She sat, trying to wait out the pain, then began to crawl and hop on one leg to the field that fronted the house. She began to crawl through it, brushing away a sudden swarm of insects. She got through them. But then, slanting in from the sky, a circle of light dropped on the grass several feet in front of her. It began to slide closer.

She rolled away from it, lay frozen.

The beam passed her, a couple of feet to her left.

It began to move away from her, wavering, then stopped and started to come back.

She rolled away again, lay with her face pressed hard into the grass. The beam passed just inches from her head, went on to the right, stopped, went up and down. And then settled fully on her.

She turned, half lying back. She sat up quickly, then rose to one knee. She couldn't make out the face behind the flashlight. She held out the shears like a threatened crab its claws. Only trembling. She saw the knife first, then the hand clutching it—then Bill Mackey.

They stared at each other. He came closer. She tried to hop away, then stopped and turned again, holding the shears straight out. His foot shot out to kick the shears aside and, with a hoarse cry, he lunged forward, his knife coming down in an arc. But she'd brought a blade back, both hands on the single handle, and she rose with it, rose hard and pushing forward, and the blade hit something hard—bone—then sank in and up. Blood kept pumping onto her face, but she held onto the handle, wanted to sink it in deeper. But he was falling with a strained roar, thrashing on the ground, the thing sticking out of him. And only then did she scream, scream to herself, her hands over her face. And she tried to hobble away: falling, rising, falling, crawling, rising, hopping—

Hands grabbed her, threw her to the ground. She swung, kicked, but someone—Patrick—had hold of her now, his knee on her chest, yelling, "Rope! Get rope!" And now they were tying her wrists, hard, raising her up as they tied and then pushing her back.

She lay sucking in air, trying to rub at her eyes with her wrists. The blood on her face was dripping into them; she had to get it out, must get it out. And her mouth, it was trickling into her mouth. Someone grabbed her wrists, yanked them down.

"You bitch! You cock-sucking bitch!"

She began to gag, tried to spit out the blood. And her eyes burned, she couldn't open them.

Matt.

295

Oh, Matt. Where was Matt?

Voices, their voices. What do we do? Think! Someone, for Christ's sake, think! He's dead, how do we say it happened?

And then Patrick's voice. "Okay, listen. And listen carefully. We call the police. We tell them she called him for help—she wanted to give herself up, but she didn't want to go to the hospital. So he had you two pick her up and bring her here. And she ended up killing him."

Someone—DeTurk: "But she'll say what happened, the kid can say—"

Alive! He was alive!

"She's crazy and the kid's crazy!" Patrick shouted. "Can't you get that through your head? They're both crazy! So listen! They were sitting in there, you were outside, and you saw her run out and he ran after her. When you got to them he was dead. You got that? She's crazy, you understand? And the kid's crazy. All you got to do is give the story and stick to it. You got that?"

"We got it." DeTurk.

"Okay. But I can't be here. I was never here. So after I talk to the old lady, give me about five minutes and call the police."

Oh, Matt.

She was too drained to move, but she struggled to sit up. Someone pushed her back again but stopped when she twisted away and clung to her upraised knees. Then she sat hunched over, rubbing at her eyes with her forearms, blinking, trying to open them, to see.

Who was that? Jeanne? She could see Jeanne, now, hurrying toward them. "Jeanne!"

Jeanne had stopped, was staring at the body. Her lips were tight.

"Jeanne!"

Kept staring.

"Jeanne! Jeanne!"

Staring.

She could hear a siren now, then another. And now a squad car, lights flashing, was crunching over the pebbles toward them. It was followed by an emergency wagon and a car from the medical examiner's office. She struggled to her feet. Other cars were pulling up. A state trooper came over, untied her. She started to rub her wrists, but he took one and then the other and snapped on handcuffs.

"Officer!"

But he wasn't even looking at her. He had hold of her arm and was looking over to where several troopers were gathered around the two men and Jeanne.

She knew she mustn't scream—mad people screaming confirmed they were mad. But she screamed; it tore out. "They're lying! They brought us here, kept us prisoner, were going to kill us! My son, where's my son?"

One of the troopers looked over. "He's all right. He's fine."

"I want to see him! I want my son!"

"Later." He looked away.

"I want my son! They're lying! Lying!" She whirled toward Jeanne, who was still staring at the body. "Jeanne!"

This time she looked over slowly.

"Jeanne! You know. If you know, tell them! Jeanne! Don't do this, don't do this!"

"Come on, Doctor." Another trooper had come over, and the two of them were nudging at her elbows.

"Jeanne!"

They led her, hobbling, to the squad car. One of the

officers opened the rear door. She struggled against going in, though she knew she mustn't, because that, too, would mean she was mad, would—

"Poisoned!"

The scream froze them, whipped them around.

Jeanne was standing back there like a wraith, hands to her temples, clawing at herself.

She kept shaking her head with each word she screamed.

"Poisoned! Poisoned! Poisoned!"

Chapter 44

Detective Harris put on his bright lights to make the oncoming driver lower his. But he didn't.

He wished he could turn around and go after the bastard.

Sometimes it was so easy to understand how guys got in fights over some stupid incident.

He was, he guessed, still burned up at Marie. He knew that the call he'd just gotten from Division had wakened her just as it had him—it *had* to—but she'd lain there, pretending to be still asleep, not even saying good night or good luck as he'd left. They'd had an argument earlier in the evening, and this was probably her way of making him feel bad, of letting him know she was still hurt.

Maybe he had said some things he shouldn't, but he just didn't want to hear any more about going to a marriage counselor. Sure they had their quarrels—everyone did—but there was nothing they couldn't work out between them.

He tried to concentrate on his driving.

Didn't she know what a goddam, ball-breaking job his was?

He'd thought he had become hardened to everything, but the call from Division that Mackey had been found dead at his farm and that Carla Keller had killed him really blew his mind. Everyone knew the broad was crazy—but to do that? *That?*

It was almost one-thirty as he pulled up to the state police barracks. The street and parking lot were jammed with cars; he saw at least three television news vans as he strode from his car to the building.

Inside, he made his way through reporters and cameramen to the front desk. He showed his identification. "Detective Harris. Philly."

The trooper led him to an office in back, introduced him to a state police detective lieutenant named Olson. With him were two Philadelphia homicide detectives Harris had known for years; they'd arrived only a few moments before him.

"I don't know what you people were told," Olson said, "but this could be as big a case as you can get. And it's going to call for a lot of cooperation between us if we're going to break it completely. Now, at twelve minutes after nine"—he consulted some notes for a moment—"we got a call to go to a farm near here that belongs to a Dr. William Mackey. Did any of you know him?"

"I did," Harris said.

The troopers, Olson continued, found his body in a field. There, too, were Dr. Keller, her young son, Dr. Mackey's wife, and two men who worked as security guards at Mackey's hospital in Philadelphia.

"Dr. Keller admitted she killed him but claimed that Dr. Mackey and the men—actually there was supposed to be a third man we haven't located as yet—anyway, that they held her prisoner and were going to kill her and her son. She claims she got away and killed Mackey when he tried to attack her with a knife. Now,

300

I think the best way to start filling you in on all of this is to let you hear this statement."

He turned on a tape recorder.

The first voice was Olson's, making a statement that the person had the right to remain silent, to have a lawyer . . .

And then:

"I want to tell everything I know," Jeanne Mackey said, sobbing.

Ross, snapped awake by the ringing of the phone on his night table, grabbed the receiver.

"Mr. Robbins, Mrs. LeVine. I'm sorry to call you so early"—it was about twenty to five—"but I knew you'd want to hear. The police just called. They have the doctor and Matt."

"Where are they?"

"They have them."

"I mean"—could you believe this?—"where?"

"Some state police barracks. Let me see, I marked it down. It's—somewhere here, I can't find— Here it is."

A few minutes later he was talking to an officer at the barracks.

No, the officer said, after asking if he was related to Dr. Keller, he wasn't able to give out any information on her.

"Is she charged with something?"

"I'm afraid I can't say."

"But can't you at least say where she is? Is she in jail? Why can't you tell me? Why?"

"Hold on, I'll refer you to someone else."

Ross sat with his hand clenching the phone to his ear, the other hand in his hair. Could you believe this? Could you believe this?

* * *

Harris tapped lightly on the door to the hospital room, even though it was open.

"Come in."

He walked in slowly. Carla was lying in bed, her son, in a little robe, pressed next to her. A very tall, lean man, in jeans and a V-neck sweater, was in the chair next to the bed.

"I just came from the barracks to see how you are."

Her voice was almost a whisper: "I appreciate that."

"A silly question, but how do you feel?"

She nodded, her eyelids heavy. "Just twisted my knee."

"The boy all right?"

She nodded. She pointed weakly, then: "This is Mr. Robbins. Detective Harris."

Ross rose and, towering over him, shook his hand.

"Well, as I say, I just stopped in to see how you are," Harris said. "I also want to say—I'm sorry."

She shook her head. "No reason. It was a crazy story."

"I—just feel very sorry. You went through hell."

She swallowed. He could see the movement in her throat. She rubbed the boy's shoulder. He clung to her. His eyes seemed about to close; occasionally he shuddered.

"I'll see you," Harris said quietly.

"I do appreciate your stopping in."

He walked down the corridor. What a brave, brave lady.

And what a terrific person. It was hard to believe, but she didn't seem to have an ounce of anger at him.

He stood by the elevators.

She was—it was funny, him thinking this way—the kind of person he could see himself really talking to some day.

Chapter 45

Wasn't Mark dead? What was he doing out there?

Carla stared at him in panic from the dining room. She had been setting the table for dinner for Ross and Matt when she'd looked up to see him standing in the garden, near the stone bird bath. Now he was walking toward the sliding glass door, was standing with his face almost pressed against it. He was crying softly.

He began tapping at the glass, his lips forming words she couldn't make out.

Now he was trying to open the door. But it was locked. He kept tugging at it, then began tapping again.

"Carla."

She couldn't run to him or away from him.

"Carla!"

She was crying now, still unable to move.

"Carla!"

She opened her eyes and Ross, lying next to her on the bed, was leaning over her in the dark.

"Carla darling."

She was still crying; her pajamas were soaked with

sweat, she was icy. She wrapped her arms around him. "Just hold me."

"Yes, sweetheart. Yes."

She was shivering violently. He held her tightly. Her body kept jumping. Gradually it eased. "I'm—all right."

"You're soaked through and through. Let me get you some other pajamas."

"No, just hold me." His hands were stroking her back. She pressed her cheek against his bare shoulder. "I—had a nightmare. About Mark. He was in the garden, trying to get into the house. He was crying."

He kept stroking her back.

"I had a dream about him a couple of nights ago, but I don't remember what it was. This one was so frightening, so sad." She paused. "I feel so sorry for him, Ross."

"He was someone to feel sorry for."

She nodded against him. She would always feel a kind of aching pity for Mark. She would never know what demons had been in him that he couldn't reveal to her. Or what had given him the courage to try to break free at the end.

She felt Ross's hands stroking her shoulders, her hair, now and then squeezing her a little harder to him. She looked up at him, pushed his hair back from his forehead. "I love you, Ross."

"Christ, how I love you!"

He kissed her softly on the lips, then harder, then softly again. They lay back on the same pillow now, looking at each other, holding each other.

"Sometimes," he said, "I still can't believe you're alive. Sometimes I still wake up in a panic. You're still missing and I've got to find you, I can't lose you. But

304

then I remember and I—just go sort of weak with relief."

"Sometimes I wonder if I'll ever get over it."

"I think you're doing just great. Carla, it's been only three weeks."

He was right, of course—she was doing so much better. She no longer found herself suddenly trembling in the middle of the day, or constantly reliving those hours in the barn, or even thinking as often—or with the same sharp edge of horror—of the blade sinking into Bill Mackey, of all the blood. And as for Matt, he still had occasional nightmares, still didn't like to be away from her too long, but he was showing improvement in just two and a half weeks with Dr. Clemmon. In fact, he was doing so well that she'd been reluctant to take him away for this two-week vacation at the beach.

No, go away with him, Dr. Clemmon said.

And, oh, how they needed it!

Ross said, "How do you feel?"

"Good. Good now." She felt so secure lying in his arms. He'd come here yesterday for the weekend— maybe for a few more days, she hoped, if he could postpone some appointments.

She could feel her body gradually release its tension. Soon his hand began to loosen a little on her shoulder as though he were starting to fall back to sleep.

"I had fun with Matt today." His voice was beginning to trail off.

"He enjoyed you."

"He's a good guy, a real—good—guy . . ."

His breathing was becoming even. She watched him as he slept. The house, on the beach front, was maybe a hundred yards from the ocean. She hadn't quite shaken off the nightmare, but the sound of the surf was

305

never more soothing than now, with his body so close, his arm across her.

She woke to a dazzle of sunlight, and the smell of coffee. She slipped out of bed, instinctively standing up slowly though her knee was no longer tender, and put on her robe. Ross was drinking coffee in the dining area adjoining the living room, in shorts and striped crew-neck shirt, his feet bare. He stood up and they kissed.

She said, "What time is it?"

"Ten of eleven."

"Eleven! Where's Matt?"

He cocked a finger toward the large picture windows, which she assumed meant he was on the beach. She looked out and saw him playing near the dunes with the owner's son, who lived in the first-floor apartment. No one who hadn't been through this, she thought, could possibly appreciate what that simple scene meant. The first days here, Matt had shied away from the boy, who'd wanted to play with him. But gradually . . .

"Do you know if he ate?"

"Yes, Mother."

She laughed and kissed him again.

He said, "Coffee?"

"Let me shower first."

She came out in a bathing suit, with shorts over it, and a kerchief around her hair. They went out on the porch overlooking the beach. They sat in cushioned, slanted-back chairs, he with his tanned legs up on the railing. She sipped at her coffee. The sky was a bright, cloudless blue, the ocean remarkably calm, with only a small rolling-over near the very edge. Only three or four people sat scattered on the beach.

"Ross!" Matt was standing up, waving him over.

Ross said, "Will you excuse me while we gentle-men—"

She squeezed his hand. She watched him walk to the path through the dunes. Now he held up something the boys had found; it looked like a tortoise shell.

She leaned her head back, her eyes closed behind her sunglasses. Only a few weeks ago she'd worried about how Matt would take to him. Now, whenever Matt saw him, he just about clung to him, looking for excuses to show him things, to be with him.

She thought of how beautifully Ross was handling it, this little boy's need.

She turned her head slightly to face the sun squarely.

Fragments of the nightmare began drifting in. They were so real they quickened her heart. She tried to push them from her mind.

How slowly they were going. But they were going.

She felt her body gradually easing again.

The sun, it felt so good to feel the sun.

And to breathe quietly, it felt so good—just to breathe.

And not to worry. Not to worry.

She hadn't even glanced at a newspaper in the five days she had been here. Not just Philly papers, none of the local papers—the case was being followed throughout the country. But the police knew where she was if they needed her.

She found herself thinking of Jeanne Mackey. Was glad for her.

The last she'd heard, the state was considering dropping or reducing several of the charges against her since she was such an important witness. She had implicated a raft of people—Edwin Haywood, Howard Tompkins, seven psychiatrists—including the two

Sundstrums—three nurses and three security guards. But no one else confessed until the laboratory report came through—they'd found no Haldol or any other antipsychotic medication in Helene Tysdal's blood. Then the Sundstrums broke down, hoping, Harris said, for a deal.

But those were the only confessions so far. Edwin Haywood, calling the charges "outrageous," was even threatening to sue Stuart Sharples for backing out of the sale of his stock in Delman & Sharples.

Harris, though, was confident they would tighten their case even more, would tie up all the murders: Mark, Nora—

"Mommy." Matt had come out of the water and was waving to her from the path between the dunes.

"Yes, Matt."

"Want to come in the water?"

"Soon."

Would tie up all the murders: Mark, Nora, Stephen Cohen, Samuel Devereaux, Wayne Delman, the male prostitute, the poor little nurse's aide, and the "accident" that killed John Delman's wife. The key, he said, was Patrick—and the two guards she'd identified as the ones who'd abducted her and Matt. They had them on that and related charges, of course, and were trying to play one against the other on the murders. They were also trying to convince Patrick that Haywood would be out to put all of the blame on him.

"Mommy."

"I'm coming."

Just go and have yourself a good time with that boy, Harris had said; we're going to put all of them away.

She stood up and went to the railing and took several deep breaths of the ocean air. Now she walked down the wooden porch steps to the pebbly ground, then over to the opening between the dunes. There she took off her beach sandals and carried them. The sand was hot but she loved it.

Just past the dunes, on a slight hill, she stopped and looked around. She smiled. Then she walked to where Ross was playing with Matt in the water.